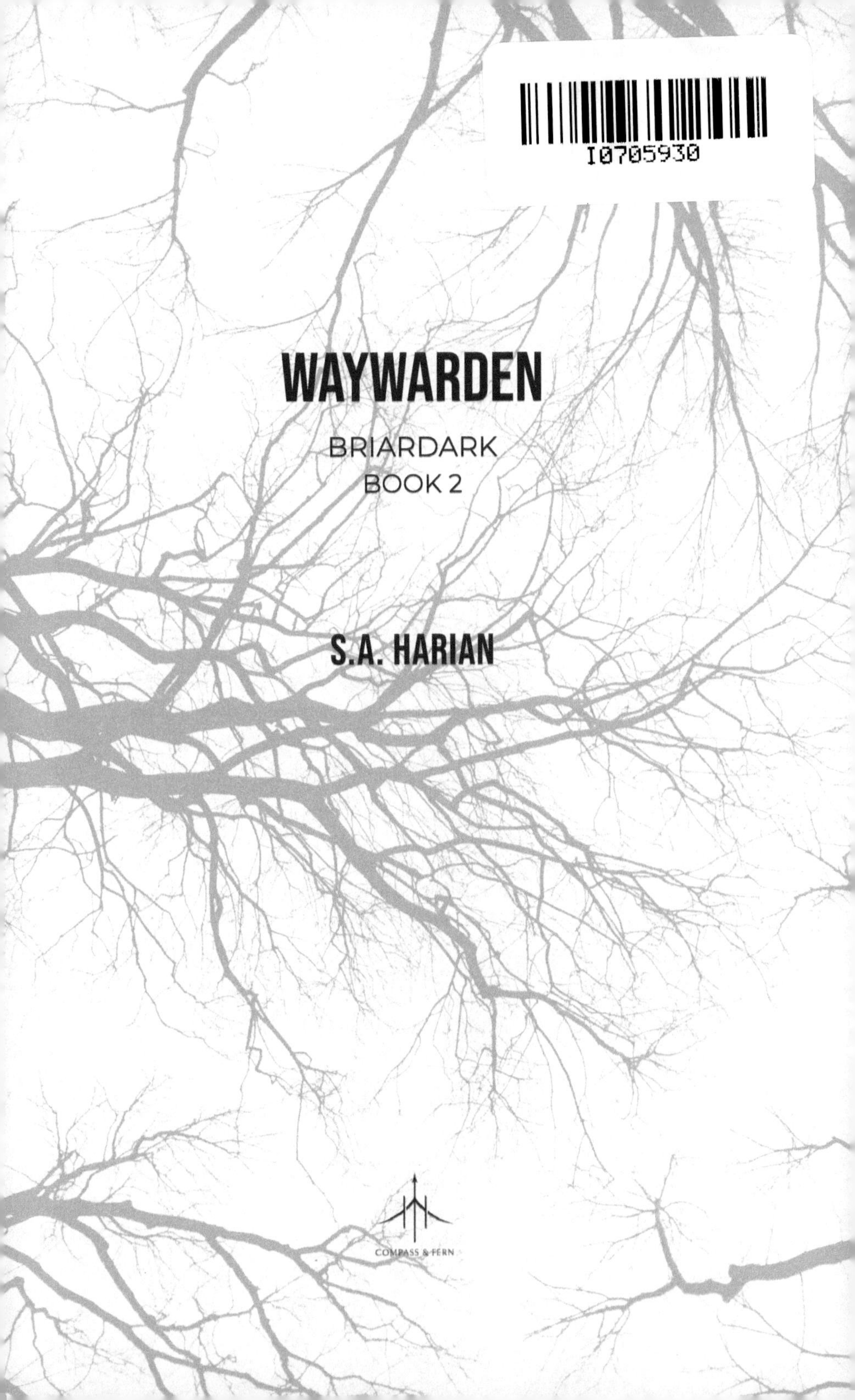



# WAYWARDEN

BRIARDARK
BOOK 2

S.A. HARIAN

COMPASS & FERN

Waywarden - Briardark Book Two

Copyright © 2024 by S.A. Harian
Library of Congress Control Number: 2024914094
Paperback ISBN: 978-1-959500-05-6
Ebook ISBN: 978-1-959500-04-9
Audiobook ISBN: 978-1-959500-07-0



Published by Compass and Fern
compassandfern.com

Cover Design by Ivan Cakic

Copy Editing by Nia Quinn
editor.niaquinn.com

2 3 4 5 6 7 8 9 10

*For anyone who has ever returned from the dark.*

# SEVEN YEARS AGO

Alpine air burned Avery's throat.

She slowed to a stop and leaned against a scruffy pine tree to catch her breath. Silhouettes filled this pocket of the forest; the sun was still approaching the horizon. She squinted until a structure formed where the trees parted up ahead.

Avery released a whimper in relief and jogged toward the building—a cabin she'd never seen before. Maybe a ranger outpost. If someone lived here, they could help her. And if the cabin was empty, she could take shelter and come up with a plan to get out of here.

She jogged to the door and tried the handle. Locked. Her hand left a smear of blood from the injury she sustained in her earlier fall, when she'd failed to save Naomi.

Avery knocked on the door and winced at the sound. Did the thing chasing her hear it, or did it track her in a different way?

Did it track her at all?

"Hello?" she whispered after knocking again, the wood beneath her knuckles flimsy.

The back of her neck prickled. Behind her, maybe twenty or thirty feet, something waited between the trees. She couldn't hear or see it, only sense it, like an intrusive thought.

She took a step back and then lunged forward, kicking the door. It predictably held, but the frame near the handle cracked. She kicked the door again, then repeatedly rammed her shoulder against it until the knob's latch busted through the frame.

She stumbled inside and rebalanced. Musty darkness surrounded her. Avery pressed her back against the door until it swung shut, her ragged breath filling the room.

Now the door was broken. She could have just looked for a window instead of ruining the lock.

A laugh built in her chest, but bubbled from her mouth as a sob. Avery slumped against the wall and jammed her fingers into her eyes.

No one was dead for certain. Simply gone. First, Paige, haunted by a watcher from beyond the perimeter of their camp. She'd claimed they whispered to her at night. Janet had wanted to return to the trailhead, but Avery fought back. Paige was only nervous about the hike.

Then Paige's posture changed. She cowered when she walked. Stopped eating breakfast and lunch and merely picked at her dinner. One morning, she was gone, sleeping bag rolled up inside her tent and stacked next to her bag.

And Avery still wanted to wait. They couldn't leave Paige alone in the wilderness, wherever she was. Tasha, Paige's sister, agreed. So did Naomi. But not Janet. Janet, who'd claimed she heard a recording of one of her own songs on their two-way. Avery had called her a narcissist. What a terrible thing to say.

Janet had disappeared this morning, same way as Paige. Then Naomi, stolen from right in front of Avery. Dragged downward through granite and into the depths of hell by an entity neither tangible nor ethereal. Tasha was the only one left. Or maybe not. She, Avery, and Naomi had scattered from camp when the thin, dark evil showed up.

If they were all dead, it was her fault. She should have canceled the trip; things had felt wrong for months. First, her online career, cracking quicker than she could glue together the broken pieces. Then, the game. That *game*.

Blinking away tears, she reached up and touched the plastic device on her forehead. Light burst forth as she clicked on her headlamp. The beam shone on a vintage couch and a small kitchen cozied up to the living room. Two wooden benches surrounded the table. She had to find a chair and angle it beneath the knob, or else push the couch in front of the door.

Avery crept down a short hall. Bunk beds crammed the room on the left, so she stepped into the one on the right.

A large window covered the adjacent wall. As she stared through it, terror hijacked her body. She stumbled backward and grasped onto the door frame for balance.

Dawn seeped into the outside world and brightened the forest with color. Behind the window, an amorphous smear of nothingness floated, the void sucking the new light straight from the atmosphere.

It spoke to her. No . . . *he* spoke to her. And she recognized him.

*You're here. Let us play.*

I saw myself in the woods
A newborn wandering through
Skin broken, yellow, dying too
I saw myself in the woods
Staggered steps across autumn feast
No thought thrown to ferns and fruit
Rot and roots
I saw myself in the woods
Myself found me watching, and broke in two
—*The Church of Bounty*

# THE WARDEN

# SIENA

Grief was a fickle bitch.

It didn't grace her in linear stages like her high school psychology class had taught her, nor was it cyclical. Instead, she wallowed in the trenches of depression until rage rudely assaulted her out of nowhere.

She'd buried Isaac only a couple of hours ago, and since beginning her descent off the mountain had already punched a few trees. She was not the type of woman who went around punching trees out of anger. And so the bargaining began.

*If I get out of here, I'll never punch a tree again.*

Although dust-flecked beams of light broke through the canopy, she couldn't spot the sun behind the dense expanse of lichen-drenched evergreens. A bird tittered somewhere above, its song enigmatic and unfamiliar. The air smelled warm, like morning. She followed the trail through the forest, the straps of her ill-fitted backpack already chafing her shoulders.

The Briardark.

That was the name of this place, wasn't it? She'd heard it first in the research cabin when she tuned into the strange frequency.

*Meet me in the Briardark, beneath the moon we will embark . . .*

Eventually she'd have to come to terms with the theatricality of the name. A name conjured by the mind of someone haunted, lost, and unpragmatic.

She may be lost and scared, but this forest could pry her pragmatism out of her cold, dead hands. It was all she had left to keep herself sane, so she recited every recent event, teasing apart truth from speculation.

Isaac had died the day before yesterday. That was a fact. Cam had left Agnes Cabin shortly after without saying goodbye, also a fact.

Cam was dead set on tracking down Avery Mathis, the famous gaming influencer who'd gone missing seven years prior. Avery mattered more to Cam than her own survival—and Siena's.

*Hypothesis*. Not fact. Siena thought she knew Cam's intentions with the whole of her heart, but hearts couldn't know anything.

Emmett borderline loathed Cam, and he'd taken off to bring her back. Fact. But then he never returned to the cabin, leaving Siena alone with two sets of instructions:

One from Dr. Wilder Feyrer, her dead mentor, admitting in a letter that he'd been studying the Briardark all these years. He wanted Siena to find The Mother, whatever that was.

And another from Isaac, her dead mentee, who'd disappeared and mysteriously returned three decades older. He wanted Siena to hike out of the wilderness immediately, or else a god, The Shadow, would kill her.

Cancer had killed Feyrer. Isaac had died from a parasitic shadow bursting from his body, and subsequently a shot to the chest. Both facts.

Ultimately she'd listened to Isaac because she couldn't forgive Feyrer's secrets, and left Agnes Cabin to find an exit from this "Briardark."

She'd also gone without Emmett, who'd wanted her to stay and wait for help. But she'd never been the type of person to just sit around and wait, and she didn't trust Emmett's instincts.

Stopping, she took a deep breath. The path continued to steadily decline. Her knees ached, her pack now chafing the center of her back. Sweat and mist clung to her clothing. Staying dry on the journey was already proving a challenge.

Before her, the thin trail faded into a carpet of moss. The ferns and flora beyond formed a verdant wall she'd have to plunge through.

The first time she and her team tried escaping Mount Agnes, the path had ended in a wall of foliage, confusing all of them. But Siena wouldn't be tricked again. She needed to hike south, regardless of what south *looked* like, and follow Isaac's dubious map. If everything went according to plan, she could clear fifteen miles a day, spending only three nights on the trail.

Only problem was, she was already off track. She should have reached the mountain's granite face by now.

Her eyes flicked between the thick growth ahead. Once she kicked through the dew-covered ferns, she took a water break on a rotting stump and studied her boots, the right sole peeling away from the toe. She could fill the gap with superglue and stitch it closed if needed, but hopefully the shoe in its current state would last another forty miles or so.

She took stock of her surroundings, including the grove of giant evergreens she wandered through, trees too large to survive this high elevation. Trees identical to the one Emmett had found near Agnes Cabin. A tunnel had led from a hollow in the tree to the cellar of another cabin.

Fact: Siena had crawled through the tunnel and felt the tree's heartbeat. (No, *theory*. Trees shouldn't have heartbeats. More evidence needed.)

Fact: a mule-murdering man in a gas mask had awaited her at the tunnel's end, and told Siena she needed to leave, his reasons unknown.

Fact: according to her tape recorder, she had not hallucinated any of this.

Hypothesis: maybe she didn't have delusional disorder after all.

Siena tugged her pill bottle free from the small pocket in her bag's belt. She'd picked up a three-month refill a few weeks before the trip, which meant no matter how long it took to get out of this place, she'd have enough meds. Even if she could prove her hypothesis that she'd been misdiagnosed, she couldn't stop the meds cold turkey—not these antipsychotics. The last thing she wanted was to lose control of her motor skills in the middle of an unknown, possibly metaphysical wilderness.

She tucked the pills back in her pocket and zipped it up, stood from the stump with a groan, and kept moving.

Farther along the trail, she carefully climbed over a nurse log and around a tangle of roots. The ground hardened and leveled, which made no sense. She couldn't have hiked to the bottom of the mountain already; the air was too thin. So why did it look and feel and smell like she was at the center of a lush valley?

All the knowledge she'd accumulated over the years—everything she knew about geology and ecosystems—was useless here. Why did *this* place have different rules down to its very atoms?

Had the government known about this *Briardark* before Feyrer discovered it? Did they call it *Briardark*? No, it probably had some name like Area T or Zone 75 or Third Sovereign Interrealm Discovery. But if the government knew of this place, maybe they'd help track down Emmett and Cam once she made it out.

Or maybe they'd permanently shut her up.

Even though she expected it, panic didn't smoke out the quiet resolve in her chest. *Ah, yes.* The acceptance stage of grief had returned once again to say *hello.* And that was just fine. She was tired of panicking, of replaying Isaac's death in her head, of fretting about Emmett and Cam. And The Shadow.

*I am everywhere.*

If The Shadow were actually everywhere, then he would have already found her and sought her out. Made her do—what had Isaac said? *Things more horrible than you could dream.*

And then after, The Shadow would kill her.

The Shadow had shown her the beating heart of this Briar-dark, deep within the mountain. The Shadow once had her in his grasp, after he slaughtered Isaac.

And yet she was here. Alive. Hiking away and focusing on the path in front of her, because worry burned energy, and she had none to spare.

Eventually the foliage thinned, the gargantuan evergreens growing farther apart. Siena shielded her eyes upon meeting the forest's edge, stepping beyond the last of the ferns onto granite.

Wind cooled the sweat prickling the back of her neck. She tugged on the collar of her shirt as she tried making sense of this unfamiliar landscape. An Ansel Adams photograph, but if a nightmare had gotten hold of it and made it big, bigger, too big.

She kicked a pebble, which bounced down the mountain slope toward the gaping maw of a valley wider and deeper than the Great Rift in Ethiopia. The jagged teeth of the range beyond gnashed at the horizon, peaks taller than the one she descended, and more dramatic than the Himalayas. Bigger, too.

*Too big.*

Siena fought a wave of dizziness and looked west, following a ridge that enclosed the other side of the valley. Even when she squinted, she couldn't see the southern lakes. They were too far away.

She scuffed the ground with her boot, the geological composition different from the Sierras. Squatting, she traced her fingers over the coarse dirt, methodically ruling out felsic minerals and carbonates. Mineral composition wasn't the reason these mountains were so damn huge. Neither was gravity.

The colossal scale of this place could be from tectonic or volcanic activity. She could almost hear Cam bantering and bickering over the possibilities.

*Cam.*

She shut her eyes to think around the anger. What was the size difference between the Sierras and the Himalayas? The average peaks in the Sierras were around 3,300 meters, the Himalayas—she tried to remember—6,500 or so. Which meant this place was twice as big as Deadswitch Wilderness.

*Hypothesis.* Mountain height didn't correlate to wilderness size. But from the gigantic peak on which she stood, the Briardark felt twice as big as Deadswitch.

No, *bigger.*

Siena freed herself from her bag to dig into it, and pulled out her phone and map of Deadswitch Wilderness. She unfolded the map and laid it flat on the ground.

Hidden behind wallpaper in the research cabin was a map of the Briardark Isaac had drawn in his decades away from them. She'd copied the important things from that map onto her own, and while she hadn't gotten everything, she'd noted the landscape and topography between the two maps were relatively the same.

Siena had studied a U.S. Geological Survey map of Deadswitch before the research trip had even begun. She was supposed to know these mountains, this forest. After following the drawn line of the trail she'd traced from Isaac's map, she stood and studied the valley once more, lifting her hand to shield her eyes from the sun.

She could picture the path skirting the marsh below and continuing southeast through the valley. As far as she could tell, the trail from Isaac's map was sound.

A flash of red drew her attention to her raised hand and the blood beneath the crescent of her thumbnail.

*Isaac.* The blood pouring from his eyes, The Shadow crawling from his mouth. The shotgun. If something like that happened to her, there would be no one around to blow a hole through her. She'd have to endure the torture.

Maybe she should stop standing around on the open face of a mountain.

She soaked in the depths of the valley and the far mountain range—this terrifying geological wonder she'd never see again—one last time. Nothing like this existed on the Earth she knew.

The landscape spoke to her.

*Discover me. Stay with me.*

All the things she could learn in those tall peaks. All the theories she could conjure on their formation.

But no. Isaac had said she would die if she stayed, and the risk was too high if she ignored him. She didn't want to die. She didn't want some Shadow tearing her apart from the inside.

*Isaac . . .*

Siena shook the thought away. There were three or so hours of daylight left. She needed to get moving.

She snapped a few photos of the divide, then wrestled her bag back onto her shoulders and resumed her descent. Not a single cairn dotted the mountain face, her only safe option to focus on her feet and follow the most gradual route. No one would help her if she slipped and fell.

When she stopped to rest, the sinking sun cast gaunt shadows over the rocky facade and lit the belly of the clouds. She followed the clouds eastward until they billowed into the stratosphere, almost black.

*I am everywhere.*

No, not The Shadow. A storm. A brutal one, one she hadn't seen back at the top of the mountain. It crawled closer before her eyes, and she was only a third of the way down the granite.

Tall fast clouds. Colliding particles. Lightning.

Siena lunged forward and scrambled down the side of the peak, staying low. It had taken her an hour to get this far from the top, and now she had twenty, maybe thirty minutes to reach the bottom. Impossible at a cautious pace. Maybe impossible, period.

Her foot slipped, and she caught herself, loose pebbles bouncing down the smooth terrain. She would fall and break something if she kept moving this fast.

Better than getting fried to death.

She picked up her pace, but one wrong step was all it took. The world tilted, her knee buckling to a sharp bite of pain. She cried out as rock tore up her palms.

This was her own damn fault for being so careless, and now she had to cope with the pain. Stopping wasn't an option.

Gritting her teeth, she bore a jolt of agony and stood. The sun kissed the western horizon. She should have waited and begun the descent tomorrow.

But she hadn't seen the storm. She couldn't have known, and now she was wasting energy beating herself up for it.

*Move.*

The darkness above slid ever closer, thunder rolling over the jagged landscape and wind threatening to knock her over. The storm was too damn quick.

She continued her descent, crawling over rock, biting back pain until the crack of thunder rattled every bone in her body. She looked up into the pitch-black promise of a deluge.

*I am everywhere.*

The clouds ripped open and pummeled her with rain.

# HOLDEN

In the dark room at the top of the Fort, Holden's fingers grazed the paper edge of the lampshade. He felt around for the chain and yanked. Dull light flooded the A-frame attic, the floor's faded planks. Francis lay on top of the bunched yellow quilt at the bottom of Holden's bed. The German shepherd raised one sleepy eyelid to give Holden a *look*.

He exhaled, the residue of despair pervading his chest. Tonight's fleeting dream had featured his ex, Becca, and an unfamiliar bed in an unfamiliar room. They had lain facing each other, her eyes tired and bloodshot, face warm and damp against his palm.

And that was it. The entire dream. So why did apocalyptic dread linger in his gut?

A short whine escaped Francis, who shimmied up toward Holden to lick the sweat from his face. Holden wrapped his arms around the dog and buried his face in soft, stinky fur.

"You need a bath," he muttered.

Francis wriggled out of his grip and gently bit him on the nose, as if to say *fuck off*.

He scratched Francis's ears while compulsively prodding the memory of the dream like a toothache. He didn't use to believe dreams held meaning, not until he was compelled like some New Age freak to drive from Oregon to Deadswitch because he couldn't stop dreaming of Dr. Siena Dupont.

This dream shook him just as deeply. He would not drive back to Oregon for Becca, but he could at least check in on her before joining search and rescue efforts later this morning.

Two days ago, Holden had seen a flash of Dr. Dupont's face in the noise-filled feed when Zaid sent his drone to investigate the cabin on Mount Agnes. No one else in the room—not Zaid, Angel, Maidei, or Frank—could corroborate. He was Siena's only witness. She needed him, and even though they'd never met and she didn't know who he was, not continuing the search for her himself felt like betrayal. He'd been trying to find her for months, after all, ever since he stumbled upon her dire audio recording from the future.

*Cam ran off yesterday without saying goodbye. Emmett's off looking for her . . . never came back last night. Which means I have to bury Isaac all by myself.*

So he would keep looking, even if he didn't know the first thing about organized search and rescue.

Worry kept him up, and he tossed and turned until dawn broke. He got out of bed, showered, and told Francis goodbye before sneaking down to the first floor of the Fort. He grabbed his backpack near the door and slipped outside to where Frank waited for him in the Jeep.

Crowded around the map-covered desk in the ranger station, two new search and rescue teams listened to Frank's summary of the mission.

"I got word the research team was in trouble. We tried radioing two rangers, one at Triplet Lakes and one south of Mount Charlotte. Couldn't contact either ranger, and that's when we sent in the first search team. They found nothing. No rangers at their posts, and no researchers at their cabin. That's our current status."

Holden would join them in a couple of hours but didn't need to be briefed. What he needed was some damn privacy.

He inconspicuously stole the rotary phone from the desk, yanked on the line for slack, and took the phone in its entirety into the station's tiny bathroom, shutting himself off from the noise. He sat on the toilet and called Becca, predictably getting her voicemail. She didn't recognize this number.

"It's Holden. If you get this in the next hour, call me back at this number. Just . . . want to talk."

He hung up the receiver and stared down at boots that weren't his. They weren't Zaid's, either, but a SAR member's. Even if Zaid had the same shoe size as Holden, the researcher could only find three mismatched boots, all from fifteen years ago, one missing shoelaces, another a sole.

The phone rang. Holden jumped and fumbled with the receiver before pressing it to his ear.

"Deadswitch Ranger Station," he said.

"Holden?"

It was Becca. He hadn't expected her to call him back.

"Hey. Sorry. Umm . . ." He struggled to find the right words. "Are you okay?"

"What do you mean?" she asked hesitantly.

This was a mistake. "I just wanted to check . . . It's nothing. I'm being stupid. Sorry I bothered you. I shouldn't hold up the line here—"

"No, wait. Holden, are *you* okay? Where are you? Did you say Deadswitch Ranger Station?"

He sighed. "I'm in California. Long story."

"You moved to California?"

"What? No. I'm here for a couple more weeks . . . I think."

"But you moved out of your apartment."

Holden frowned at the dingy bathroom sink. "No I didn't."

"I stopped by your place a couple of days ago. I didn't like the way we left things when I came to get my stuff. I was just hoping we could talk, but the door was open and they were replacing the carpet. The place was empty. Looked like they were moving someone else in."

"I didn't move out. I *haven't* moved out. You were probably looking in the wrong apartment."

"I wasn't."

"23C?"

"Holden, I lived there for years."

He opened his mouth to retort, but couldn't conjure up any reason she'd be wrong, unless she was flat out lying to him. But that wasn't like Becca, and she had no reason to do such a thing.

"Holden." She spoke his name slowly. "Are you sure you're not in trouble?"

*I am now.* "I'm . . . fine. I need to go. I'll call you later."

She called his name again right before he jammed his thumb against the hookswitch. He called Lauren, his roommate in Corvallis, nearly ripping the dial off the rotary phone.

*"We're sorry, you have reached a number that has been discon-nected or is no longer in service . . ."*

Just like the last time he tried calling her.

Holden slammed the receiver back down, thankful he was in a bathroom because his stomach clenched as if he would throw up.

He needed to call the apartment manager, but he'd only emailed her in the past, and her number wasn't in his phone. Connecting to the internet was his only hope of figuring out what the hell was going on. Zaid had gotten the satellite internet up and running at the Fort yesterday, but the signal was so bad that Holden had yet to connect.

A deep breath settled his stomach. Lauren didn't seem the type to pull off a con to steal his belongings, and if she was, the joke was on her because he owned nothing of value.

Someone knocked on the door. "You alright in there? Getting cold feet?" Frank asked.

"I'll be out in a second."

Holden stood, set the phone on the toilet seat, and leaned over the sink. In the mirror, his dark hair hung over his face. He reached up and parted it like a curtain, cautiously peeking through as though to shield himself from his own image. The California sun had darkened his naturally tan skin, yet something about his appearance seemed pallid. Exhausted. Maybe it was the scraggly facial hair. He hadn't shaved since he and Angel left Oregon.

Or maybe it was fear.

He *should* be getting cold feet. Heading into a forest infamous for disappearing people would scare the daylights out of the most equipped wilderness junkie, let alone him. And now he had a reason to stay behind: drive toward town until he got cell service, and figure out why Lauren had emptied his apartment without his consent.

At least he'd taken Francis with him.

So what would it be? The missing researchers, or his stuff?

Finding Siena, or Lauren?

He already knew his decision. He also knew it was the less logical one.

The station was still crowded from the briefing when Holden left the bathroom, so he snuck the rotary phone back onto the desk, grabbed his backpack, and headed out to his car, which had been parked at the back of the station lot since he and Angel arrived in Deadswitch weeks ago.

Holden held his bag open on the hood, squashing it full of equipment as he mentally calculated the right amount of under-wear to take. The bag itself was from Zaid and about twenty years old, sturdy but frayed around the edges. He'd also borrowed a mess kit from Frank that was little more than a tin cup and a fork. Other SAR members had donated a sleeping bag and other bits and bobs to him, likely out of pity more than anything.

Francis's collar jangled, and the dog pressed his wet nose to the back of Holden's calf.

"Hey, how did you get here?" He glanced up. Angel walked toward him with a frown, a leash folded in her hands.

Holden dropped his gaze. He'd left early this morning to avoid this very confrontation. Partner in crime from the beginning, Angel had convinced him to drive down to Deadswitch Wilderness in the first place. She was as dedicated to the mystery of Dr. Dupont as he was, but drew a line when it came to actually entering the wilderness area where almost a dozen people had disappeared.

He cleared his throat. "Thanks for taking care of Francis. Don't worry about walking him, not unless Maidei or Zaid or someone goes with you. Though I don't think either of them like hiking around here anymore. Anyway, you should also take my room. It's a lot nicer than yours, and the bed is—"

"Don't do this."

Holden pressed his lips together. It was one thing for her to ask this of him. It was another for her to ask every waking hour for the past two days.

Holden yanked the zipper of his bag shut and wiped the beading sweat from his forehead. It wasn't even nine, and the day was already hot. *Sunscreen.* Someone had to have an extra bottle.

"You have my car keys, right?" he asked. "In case you need them?"

"Stop trying to change the subject. You're being so . . ."

Holden threw his pack over his shoulder, his patience tenuous. "What, stupid?"

Angel's expression morphed from anger to injury. Her curly hair was frizzier, and dark bags cradled her big brown eyes. She must have slept as well as he had.

She fiddled with the leash. "I was going to say selfish."

He stepped back, as if putting more space between him and Angel would also give room for her logic to make sense. "Risking my safety to go search for someone I don't even know is the opposite of selfish."

"Depends on why you're doing it," Angel shot back.

"Because I'm the only one who—"

"Saw her ghost in the static, yes," she finished for him. They had a version of this conversation yesterday. And the day before. "That won't matter if you get lost or hurt. I'm not sure why you *seeing* her matters, anyway. It doesn't mean you have some special power to make her appear at will." Her words carried a condescending lilt, the way she used to talk to him back on campus, before they tolerated each other.

"Look," he began. "You really should go back to Corvallis. I'm sure Maidei can watch Francis. Take my car and—"

She scoffed. "And what? Live in it? You're so caught up in this that you don't even remember I have nowhere to go."

He winced. Days ago, he and Angel sat on his bed in the Fort's attic, Angel confiding in him about the outcome of her messy divorce. Her husband had left her with nothing. Holden still didn't really understand how that was possible, or what could have made Angel's ex so vindictive. Now definitely wasn't the time to ask.

"Then stay here," he said. His back was already aching from the weight of his bag. "I shouldn't be gone over two weeks. We'll try to get to Agnes in four nights and then search the off-trail area north of the mountain."

She crossed her arms and glanced at Francis, who sat by her feet.

"You won't be alone," he added.

Angel's jaw clenched. She swiped her eyes with the back of her hand. "You really don't value yourself at all, do you?"

Anger flared in his chest. She knew *nothing* about him. "Until a month ago, you didn't miss an opportunity to tell me how pathetic I am. You clearly don't value me either, so why does it matter what I do?"

She winced. "Is it really that hard to believe the past couple of weeks changed things, and I actually care what happens to you now?"

*Yes.* Why *would* she care? He'd done nothing to deserve her caring. They'd simply existed in the same space. It wasn't enough.

When she looked at him again, her eyes were glassy and puppy-wide. She straightened as though steeling herself, like he'd slapped her across the face and she was taking the high road.

Holden could do that, too. "Thank you for taking care of Francis. I'm coming back, just like the SAR teams before us. Two are on their way back now, and two more teams are entering from the west, by the lower lakes—"

"Frank told me," Angel interrupted. She whistled to Francis. "Come on, boy. Let's go annoy Zaid."

Francis looked up at Holden, his tongue sticking out. Holden scratched the back of his ears. He'd considered taking Francis, but if something happened to him, Holden would never forgive himself.

Maybe joining Search and Rescue was a stupid and dangerous decision. And maybe he valued his dog's life over his own. It was still *his* choice.

"I'll miss you," he told Francis. "Now, go on. Be good."

Francis took off after Angel, who turned her back on Holden without saying goodbye.

He needed to prove her wrong by coming back in one piece.

Holden adjusted his bag and joined the rest of the SAR team as they circled up near the ranger station. He double-checked that his water bottle was still clipped to the side of his pack and touched the sunglasses hanging from the neck of his shirt. The older man who had loaned him the boots—Clyde—nodded as he approached and tossed a bottle of sunblock, which Holden caught clumsily.

"Thanks. And thanks again for the boots."

"Don't thank me." Clyde pointed to the woman next to him. "She won't let me go anywhere without backups of my backups. I swear, she's the only reason I'm alive."

The woman smacked his arm. She wore tight jeans and a white blouse, a designer bag thrown over her shoulder. She rubbed at the smudged mascara beneath one of her red-rimmed eyes.

Teresa and Clyde Yarrow—Dr. Cameron Yarrow's parents. They lived a few hours away and had driven up the mountain as soon as Frank relayed the news about their daughter's disappearance. Country folk, but affluent, Clyde their hometown's only pediatrician. Teresa looked like she drank her chardonnay on ice and had a rustic sign in her kitchen that said, *The best things in life aren't things*. She was *not* joining the search.

Clyde's gear was old, but designer. The kind of man who prided himself on not being wasteful, but also didn't realize how lucky he was.

They were nice enough and clearly cared about Dr. Yarrow. Both of them were easily in their midsixties. Hopefully Clyde was in shape enough for this venture. Then again, here Holden was in borrowed gear, completely out of his element and about to mosey into a forest that had swallowed at least nine people whole.

"Deadswitch Wilderness isn't easy. You ready for this?" Clyde asked, like he was reading Holden's mind.

Holden smiled nervously. "Hell no."

Clyde's somber expression lightened. "Same."

# CAMERON

Avery's map lay unfolded on the log in front of Cam, doing a piss-poor job of resisting the rain.

*Waterproof coating, my ass.*

She sat on a stump, the hood of her rain shell up as she sipped an insulated mug of cowboy coffee. She liked this mug. Liked it enough to remember to grab it as she'd bolted out the door of the research cabin before Siena could stop her.

"You're a real shit person," she muttered to herself. Shit for not responding to Avery's texts seven years ago before the Deadswitch Five vanished, and now shit for leaving Siena behind. Cam had to accept she was shit in order to get over being shit in her quintessential spiritual journey of acceptance.

She squinted at Avery's revised legend in the map's corner. Cam had found the map at the top of Mount Agnes, along with Avery's decomposing bag and the knit hat she now wore. She'd given the hat to Avery years and years ago.

*Full circle.*

Avery's revised legend also contained an updated scale. If Cam read the water-stained Sharpie correctly, the Briardark—Deadswitch Wilderness's alter ego—was twelve times larger than Deadswitch.

She dragged her finger from her location—a few days' hike north of the sisters—toward the isolated peak. On the map, the peak took the form of an upside-down V that Avery had drawn in with a marker. Avery had also circled it and written, *Find the Butcher's Daughter.*

According to the legend, it would take Cam roughly twenty-five days to reach the peak. She'd seen this mountain twice from the top of Agnes, but now she was too deep in the forested valley to have a good view of anything beyond the understory.

She would keep walking north, because she'd made her bed back at the research cabin. Isaac had told Siena she would die if she didn't hike out of the Briardark, adding that Cam would only hold her back. He'd given Cam the perfect excuse to leave Siena to fend for herself.

But that was exactly what Siena was supposed to do, according to Isaac, assuming he knew what the fuck he was talking about. If Cam would only impede Siena's escape, then Cam wasn't a shit person at all.

This didn't change the fact she felt like one.

It also didn't change the fact that, if Avery's legend was correct, it could take Siena months to get home . . . if she could get home at all.

But Siena could handle it. She'd often ventured into the wilderness alone when she needed solace or to grieve. In that way, Siena differed from Cam, who went to the woods every time she wanted to avoid grief. Every time she wanted joy. Every time she wanted to pretend she wasn't lazy or irresponsible or distracted or bad with relationships.

Cam lived in the woods. Breathed its air, drank its water. Climbed its mountains, the rigor further sculpting her lean, hardened body. And that was the actual difference between her and Siena. Siena knew how to survive in the woods for long enough. Cam was a resident.

She finished her coffee, then pulled off her hood and pushed her hair back. The ends of her ash-brown locks reached the nape of her neck, and she tugged on them while scrutinizing the drawn landmarks one last time. After shaking the water off the damp paper, she folded the map and tucked it into her rain shell pocket —Siena's pocket. She'd meant to grab her own jacket, but had left the cabin in a hurry. By the time she'd realized the mistake, she was miles away.

The jacket somehow still smelled of Siena's apartment. And CLIF Bars. It was cleaner than the sodden pants sticking to her skin.

Around her, flat-leaf ferns cradled pools of rainwater. She'd traveled through forests all over the world, the bulk of her time in the Sierras, where snow was more of a problem than rain. The rain was a pleasant change for now, but she would hate it the second she began chafing.

A trail appeared as daylight brightened, a rutted, muddy pathway snaking through the spruce. Surprised, Cam consulted the map again, finding no trail here. Avery had charted mountains, rivers, and bizarre landmarks, but nothing here. Then again, it wasn't like Avery'd had the chance to chart the whole damn wilderness.

Cam's boots sank into the waterlogged path, the wet seeping into her socks. Her eyes roved, scanning for anything unusual. She couldn't let the tree canopy trick her into feeling protected, especially not after what happened to Isaac.

And her.

She tried to keep her mind off her descent into this place. The irresistible compulsion to swim in the tarn, the fluctuation of gravity that had dragged her straight to hell. She'd been trapped in disembodied agony for what felt like months. Thinking about it was just as bad as living it.

An unexpected scent prickled her nose, and she inhaled. Woodsmoke clung to the air.

Cam whirled, boots squelching. Trees. Nothing but fucking trees, and an intuitive warning that clung to her like a second skin.

Red flashed through the trees up ahead. *Careful.*

She crept from the trail and into the woods, approaching the cherry-red color. A tent. Listening, she heard nothing from the glade where the tent was erected. But if anyone was nearby, she didn't want to alarm them.

"Hello?" The word was swallowed by the woods. Cam slipped into the clearing.

A pair of new branded bags lay haphazardly tossed. The tent was also designer, and another lay flat on the ground, half-assembled. Despite the day's dampness, a dry fire pit smoldered.

She approached the fire pit, and her boot nudged the smoldering embers. The embers didn't spark, nor send up a lick of smoke. If it weren't for the smell, she'd have thought they were fake, stolen from someone's gas fireplace.

She turned to the erect tent—both unzipped and completely empty. Whoever's site this was, all their gear was still packed away in those shiny new bags.

A sound unfurled and suddenly quieted. Cam whipped her head around, disoriented before taking a moment to process the noise: a blip of conversation between a man and woman like they sat right here, around this plastic fire. Had the woman been laughing? Crying? The man had said, *I can't believe*—before the sound bite abruptly ended. Like someone had flipped the channel.

In place of the voices, a ringing grew.

"Hello?" she called again. Vertigo washed over her, and the memory of her descent into the Briardark arose—unforgiving agony, the deep loss as two worlds tore at her.

Cam stumbled from the clearing and back into the forest, jogging toward the path. She reached the muddy trail and stopped to brace her hands against her knees. Her mind raced from the tarn to Naomi Vo dead and dangling from a branch. On their way up to the research cabin, they'd found her frozen in time, seven years after the Deadswitch Five disappeared.

Cam couldn't follow the rhythm of this forest, but she knew one thing: time didn't play by rules she understood. She'd gotten lost on Mount Agnes in the blink of an eye and found Avery's bag in a place that had already been searched. Now, this smokeless fire pit smoldered.

Everything preserved by some fucked-up interdimensional pause button.

Cam ducked beneath a fern leaf and continued along the trail twisting northeast. With a swift tug, she pulled her hood up, then stepped over a log sheathed in a grotesque fungus.

Fucked-up pause button or not, she couldn't dick around at a frozen campsite until she figured out what was going on. And those campers—wherever they actually were—were lucky she didn't rifle through their things and steal shit.

The scent of woodsmoke still clung to the air and grew stronger the farther she walked from the campsite. She scanned the lichen-dressed evergreens and spotted a pillar of smoke up ahead.

Now *that* was where the smell was coming from.

A sound broke through the rain—a man singing an unfamiliar tune in a voice like full grain leather.

Her hand slipped into her pocket, and her fingers curled around her knife. Its reassuring weight reminded her of what she lacked: the guns left behind in the cabin. Then again, guns were loud, and if she drew attention, she wanted it on her terms.

Tucked away off the path, a shelter made of fir branches materialized. A man sat on a stump beneath its open front and poked at a wet, smoldering fire. Cam dipped behind a tree to watch. The man sang and prodded at the ashes, oblivious to her presence. He was a mess, too, unkempt and disheveled. Like old Isaac, but frailer. Sickly.

She could overpower him if she needed to. She could also pass unnoticed, but if she wanted answers, hiding wasn't an option.

Cam's grip tightened on her knife as she stepped away from the tree, approaching the man enough to study him. He was maybe in his forties, garb variously torn, patched, and resewn. Some of his clothes were modern while other pieces reminded her of dated military or park ranger gear.

He either grimaced or smiled at her—Cam couldn't tell the difference—and extended his leg to reveal torn trousers and an oozing gash covering his shin. The wound was infected.

Her observation sliced through smoke-filled air. "How'd that happen?"

His features were unreadable, his eyes gleaming with an inscrutable spark. "Fell. Need to get to The Tooth." A gruff urgency tinged his voice.

She had no idea what the fuck The Tooth was, but this man's leg needed attention, and quickly. "I can help. I've got medical training. Should be able to clean and dress it here."

He laughed, a harsh, grating echo through the forest, punctuated by a single word. "Newborn."

Cam prickled at his casual dismissal. Before she could respond, he shot a question her way. "You out here alone?"

She knew better than to admit she was, but he nodded anyway, as though sensing the truth. "There are folk at The Tooth."

Did he know she was searching for someone? No . . . he couldn't. She'd mentioned nothing of Avery. She'd hardly said anything at all.

"Can't survive out here alone," he continued. "Help me, and I'll help you."

# SIENA

The storm arrived with hostile darkness. If even one lightning bolt hit the wet granite, she would be dead before she knew what was happening.

Better than being torn apart by The Shadow. Better than a shot to the chest.

Siena's headlamp beam sliced through the deluge as she searched for secure footing somewhere along the slick granite. She moved too quickly to be safe.

Her headlamp cast light on a patch of earth beneath a cluster of trees, and she cried out in relief. The saddest little haven she'd ever seen. Dropping onto the dirt, she threw her backpack aside and curled into a tight ball beneath the smallest tree in the cluster. She was supposed to crouch on the balls of her feet to stay off the ground, but her knee screamed in pain as she tried.

She unzipped her bag and yanked out Cam's rain shell, the only waterproof jacket she could find in the research cabin.

Cam. If she were here, she'd laugh at their shit luck. She probably would have told Siena to wait until tomorrow to descend. Cam was so much better at wilderness survival than she was, and she'd left Siena to fend for herself. Like she wanted her to die.

Thick rain pummeled her, less disorienting than her recollection of every betrayal that had shaped her adult life, starting with her father, who left a year after her mother's funeral. Because Siena had gotten over the death, right? Conquered her grief like a tricky summit. And she was a legal adult headed off to college, so it was safe for her dad to move to the Yukon, to tend to his own emotional wounds in isolation.

Then Emmett, smashing everything they'd built together, like glass beneath his boot. Wilder Feyrer, whom she so naively trusted.

And finally, Cam.

Siena was either unlucky, or these betrayals were a part of a larger pattern. She was obsessive, distracted, a workaholic. Trusted the ones she cared about to never hurt her. Now she had no one left.

When she escaped this place, she would find new people and learn to love them. But trust—trust was another thing entirely.

As dark and deceptive and unpredictable as it was, this Briardark was more trustworthy than any person. It promised to challenge her and test her resolve, offering secrets and discovery in return. Knowledge was all she had left to love.

Why even try to leave?

She didn't struggle against the urge to cry; there was no reason to pretend she had her shit together. Emmett used to tell her that she looked pretty when she cried, and she did. Her eyes shone neon blue, her lips red and full. The pale, freckled skin covering her cheeks glowed. When she cried, it was like some vulnerable, beautiful creature—her Mr. Hyde—fought to emerge from within and take control of the situation that hurt her.

Perhaps this creature was emerging now. Perhaps it was how she would make it home, even if she wanted to believe there was no reason to try.

The rain washed away her tears. Lightning slashed across the sky, but she didn't sense an electric charge. Still, she dared not risk moving and tried staying warm by just imagining she was.

Siena ducked her head when the deluge grew too heavy to breathe.

*I am everywhere.*

If the Shadow was everywhere, then why wasn't he taking advantage of her vulnerability at this moment? She was about to get barbecued, for chrissakes, and if that happened, then he couldn't use her for his evil plans because she would be literal toast.

Five, maybe ten minutes crawled by before thunder rumbled to the west. The worst was over, but the rain refused to let up. She waited, drenched and battered. When her legs were too tired to support her weight, she fell back against the tree trunk and rested her head on her knees. She must have fallen asleep, because when she lifted her head, dawn bled through the inky sky to the east. It was over.

She'd forgotten about her knee until she stood, clamping her jaw around a gasp. One of those sprains that would hardly be noticeable if she were sitting in a lab.

Or sitting back up at the research cabin with all her and Feyrer's data, trying to make sense of this world.

*So much depends on you,* he told her in the letter he'd left for her. *Find The Mother, Siena.*

His legacy had died the moment she left, and although her mentor had tricked her from the grave, leading her into the Briardark without her knowledge, leaving all that research back at the cabin made her sick.

She pushed the thought from her mind and rifled through her first aid kit in the middle of her pack. At least the ACE bandage was dry. She shimmied her soaking pants down to wrap the bandage around her knee and got dressed again, popped a couple of aspirin with her antipsychotic, and hoisted her pack onto her shoulder.

Reaching the marsh would take her the whole day, but the lightning storm hadn't cooked her, and while the clouds were thick and marbled overhead, the threat of rain was gone. She began her scramble downward, her cold, soaked clothing more uncomfortable than her twisted knee.

Upon reaching the midway point between the summit and the swamp, she smashed a Snickers bar, and drained most of her water.

The mountain was slowly leveling off, but fewer footholds scattered the granite than yesterday. She would need to move carefully. The last time she and Cam had trailblazed down a peak like this, her nose had been buried in the map the whole time as she read the topography lines to find the safest descent. Cam had just read the rock in front of her, singing Third Eye Blind's "Semi-Charmed Life" badly and making up lyrics when she forgot them, her version somehow more offensive than the original. She'd left Siena in the dust that day to teach her a lesson: you can't book-smart your way to a trailhead.

The topography on her current map was wrong anyway, because this wasn't Deadswitch.

"You got what you wanted, bitch," Siena muttered.

She spent her remaining time on the mountain mostly crab walking, sliding downward on her butt and sweating bullets. Eventually the incline eased as sunset approached. She rested for a minute to massage her knee and then hurried into the grove of cypress-like trees to find a place to camp.

Her boots sank into the mucky ground as soon as she stepped beneath the canopy. The surrounding air thickened with the stench of plant rot. With hardly an ecotone, the environment had changed from arid mountainside to boggy swamp.

Up ahead, a skeletal relic of a wooden footbridge provided enough of a surface to set down her bag. She searched through her things, dug out her sample kit, and scooped a bit of muck into a clean tube before sliding the vial next to the one with Isaac's blood, and then closed the case.

She could still study this place after she escaped, as long as she took enough of it with her.

Before she embarked again, the silhouette of a hut caught her eye. It stood on stilts beyond the bridge, surrounded by algae-infested water. Abandoned, most likely, and if there was anywhere she could take cover and spread out her things to dry, it would be here.

Siena found some footing on solid ground and crept toward the structure. The murky water stank of sulfur, and the hut, neglected and decaying, stood silent.

*Who built you?*

There had to be others, like the masked man she'd met at the other end of the tunnel. Like the person who had written the song she'd heard on the radio.

*And then I'll follow you way down, the moment we're about to drown.*

Hopefully, they hadn't meant this swamp.

A meter of water separated her from the shack's ladder. She leapt, and caught a rung with her right hand while bashing her bad knee. Biting back her pain, she climbed to the edge of the platform. Rotten wood groaned beneath her as she stood, before her a sagging door that clung stubbornly to a primitive metal hinge. Where would someone find hinges out here to build such a shack unless they'd brought them from somewhere else?

Her pack made it difficult to stay balanced. She took it off and set it against the outer wall of the shack, then edged toward the door. She pushed against it, the hinge protesting with a squeal.

Out of the darkness, a hand shot toward her and grabbed her arm, yanking her inside. Alarm sparked in her chest as her assailant threw her against the wall. She screamed, lashing out to claw at them, but recognition struck them both at once.

"Emmett?"

His dark eyes widened. "Holy shit," he whispered, dragging her toward his broad chest and wrapping his arms around her. "I . . . can't believe you're here. I can't believe I found you."

She'd technically found *him*, but this wasn't the time to argue semantics. She clung to him in shock.

Emmett's lips pressed against her temple before his hold on her relaxed. She stepped back to study him in the shadows.

She'd been with him for years and had seen him scared. But he didn't look scared—he looked shaken. Rattled to his core, like he'd come straight from the losing side of a battlefield.

What the hell had happened to him?

Her gaze dropped to his hand, which gripped his hunting knife.

"I didn't know who you were," he blurted, lifting the knife like he suddenly didn't know what it was, either, and then slid it into the sheath on his belt. He clenched and unclenched his hand, his fingers trembling, and then touched her shoulder.

"I looked for Cam, and then backtracked when I couldn't find her," he said. "But you weren't at the cabin."

His tone wasn't accusatory, but her defenses went up instinctively. "You didn't come back! Isaac . . ." She shuddered at the memory. "Isaac was in pieces all over the porch. I couldn't wait any longer to bury him, and then I just felt sick and scared. I needed to get out of there."

"Yeah." He scratched the back of his neck. "I don't blame you for taking off."

"You . . . *don't*?" It made little sense. He'd specifically told her to wait until he got back. He should be angry she hadn't listened, especially because he'd done everything he could to keep her at that cabin until rescue came.

"How did you get here before me?" she asked. "I would have seen you pass me."

"I hiked down the western side of the peak. I took that way because I thought you would do the same. It's a longer route, but easier."

It was like him to think she'd take the less strenuous way, especially alone. She was relieved he was safe, and that she was no longer alone, but he was definitely hiding something.

His fingers glided over her collar and down the front of her jacket. "Did you get caught in the storm?"

Emmett was clearly comfortable touching her. He'd kissed her before he had left to find Cam. When they were trapped in the microverse and couldn't breach the perimeter of the cabin, they'd done more than kiss. She didn't regret it, but she'd have to set the record straight with him—again—when they got out of here.

She nodded. "Last night was brutal. My things are outside . . . not really sure how to dry them out."

"We can try."

As he went to retrieve her bag, she shook off her unease, her attention wandering over the hut's interior. Half the roof was caved in, and much of the floor bore the telltale signs of rot. Against the only sturdy wall, right next to where Emmett had pushed her, a menagerie of dirty jars stocked a set of shelves.

Curiosity edged her forward. The jars were of varying sizes, but none bigger than her palm. Cloudy liquids and decomposing substances filled most of them. She slid her phone from her pocket, wiped water from the screen with her palm, and took a picture of the shelf.

"What are you?" she whispered. *Herbs, food, medicine?* "Who put you here?"

"What?" Emmett entered the hut and set her bag on one of the safer floorboards, kneeling next to it.

"Just trying to figure out who lived here, and what they were doing."

Emmett's fingers hesitated on Isaac's bow strapped to the outside of the pack. She thought he would question why she'd taken it, especially because she wasn't a good enough shot to use it for defense. But he said nothing, unzipping her bag and rifling through her things, then pulling out her sleeping bag and wet clothing.

"Hey," she said.

He stopped and looked at her, deadpan.

"Did something happen?"

He frowned as though he genuinely didn't know what she

was talking about. "A lot of things have happened, I don't know—"

"To you. Did something happen to you? You're not acting like yourself."

"You mean after I blew apart our research assistant with a shotgun, or before?"

She flushed. "Right. Sorry." She'd been so caught up with everything that had happened since Emmett left, she kept forgetting he'd put one of their team out of his misery only a few days ago. That moment—his sacrifice—would live with him for the rest of his life. "Do you want to talk about it?"

He hesitated, scratching his scalp. He usually kept his dark hair very short, but it was growing out, flecks of gray cropping up around his temples.

"You were right," he said. "We should have left Deadswitch when Isaac said to."

His admission threw her off-balance. He'd spent so much energy arguing they wait for rescue. "Why?"

He shrugged noncommittally. "I had time to think."

"About what?"

His face grew somber. "Isaac said this *Shadow* was after you, and then died proving it. I'm not putting you out of your misery like I did him, Sen. I'm getting you out of here."

A knot tightened in her throat. *But you would if you had to, right?* She thought better of asking. He was processing a lot right now, and she wanted to remain optimistic about their chances.

He patted down one of her t-shirts and tossed it to her. Dry enough. She unzipped her rain shell, shrugged out of it, and hung it from a protruding nail.

"Did you run into anything out there?" She tugged her damp shirt over her head. "When you were searching for Cam?"

"Nothing. Noises, mostly. But everything's different—soil, vegetation—like we're in the Olympic Peninsula or something. What about you?"

She slid into the mostly dry shirt. "Other than getting caught on the mountain in a storm?" Emmett knew little of what she'd uncovered since she found Feyrer's letter. Isaac and The Shadow had distracted them both.

So she told Emmett everything, starting with Dr. Feyrer's letter. How his research wasn't about the glacier but the Briardark, all his findings hid in the cellar. How she'd been tasked by her dead mentor to read through it all and then find The Mother. She told Emmett about the bloodstain on the map, and the strange symbols Isaac believed marked the way back home.

He kept his mouth shut and listened to it all without interrupting her once, and it was so strange that a part of her wondered if he had died standing up.

Once she finished, Emmett said nothing for a long time. His glazed eyes fell to the jars. He worried his lip until he broke skin and licked away the burst of blood. Outside, some wriggling swamp creature flopped around in the water.

He finally asked, "Is there any part of you that wants to do what Feyrer asked you to do?"

The question was bizarre coming from his mouth. It had been years since he cared about her wants. He was fishing for something.

"Yes," she said hesitantly. "Of course I'm curious. But I took pictures of many of his research documents . . . the stuff that looked important, at least. I don't need to stay in this place to learn more."

It wasn't a lie, but it wasn't the full truth, either. The farther she hiked from that cabin, the more she wondered what she was giving up, and how much she could discover about this place, using Feyrer's research as a jumping-off point.

But given how Emmett's shoulders relaxed, she didn't want him to think that she'd changed her mind.

"Good," he said. "We need to get the hell away from here."

She smiled patronizingly. "I'm aware."

"Sorry," he muttered. "And I'm sorry I didn't listen to you before."

"Thank . . . you . . ." she said cautiously, then nodded toward her sleeping bag, which he'd unrolled. "How wet is it?"

Kneeling, he patted the synthetic fabric. "Not too bad."

"I'll fall over if I don't rest soon."

"Alright." His eyes shot to the shack's broken shutter. "But we should start moving again at dawn."

She agreed, and they fell silent as they got ready to sleep in the light of Emmett's camp lantern. She didn't want to waste any of her little water on cleaning up, instead pulling off her filthy, damp pants and changing into her second pair. Her boots were soaked and muddy, and she set them in the corner to dry while wincing at her tender, waterlogged feet.

She peed while hanging off the edge of the platform outside, one of her greatest feats. When she was back in the hut and settled in, Emmett rolled his bag out next to hers on the unrotted section of the floor and turned the lantern off.

He rested his hand atop her sleeping bag, and her thigh inside. "I'm glad you're here."

Her throat constricted. She'd left the cabin without him when he was only looking for Cam. Panic had gotten the best of her; she should have waited.

"Same. Good night, Emmett."

He shifted in his sleeping bag, and before long, his quiet snores rose and fell beneath the drone of the crickets.

Siena wanted to sleep. *Needed* to sleep. But adrenaline still ran hot in her blood.

Something splashed at the water's edge, and a bug or crustacean scuttled over the hut's platform. A rustle of leaves, the scramble of tiny feet up a tree. Rodent or reptile?

The background hum of the swamp was harder to decipher. She strained her ears to pick out individual sounds, patterns that might hint at an approaching predator.

She jumped when Emmett snorted in his sleep, then dug her

phone from her fleece pocket and turned it on, tapping into her photo app.

Siena's fingers swiped mechanically over taxonomy sketches, her eyes tracing each illustration. Bugs with antenna configurations she didn't recognize, birds with elongated beaks and odd feather patterns sketched in monochrome. Unnaturally curved spines of reptiles, mammals with tusks or fangs and never without—all meticulously arranged under respective families and genuses.

Her thumb paused, the screen illuminating with an illustration of a deer. It was ordinary at first glance, save for a pair of tusks curving upward from its muzzle. Sharp and menacing, almost surreal. Were the tusks for gathering food, or for defense? And against what?

A hollow unease gnawed at her. Would a deer with tusks look as surreal in a photo as it did in the sketch? She wanted certainty, to spot them in their natural habitats and know they were truly creatures from the Briardark.

She kept scrolling, taxonomy drawings transitioning into a jumble of mathematical notations and sketches. Advanced calculus and synthetic geometry equations filled the browned pages of Feyrer's field journals.

The equations were nonsense, the calculus far beyond anything she'd ever tackled. Symbols and formulae—cryptic proof of *something*?

*Theories. Not proof.*

Frustration simmered within her. Every swipe brought additional equations, each more baffling than the last. It would be easier to decipher an alien language. All science involved math, but these journals looked more like the workbooks of a physicist, not of a geomorphologist, even a seasoned one.

The promise of Dr. Feyrer's letter seemed far-fetched now. Answers in his research? All she found was more confusion, more questions. Siena's thumb moved almost involuntarily, swiping to the next image. This time, sketches of cells and bacteria filled the screen.

She zoomed in to the one in the center. A prokaryote—bacteria, most likely. The parts were labeled like a biology test: capsule, envelope, flagella, nucleoid. The gelatinous innards were shaded darkly and labeled *mycelplasm* instead of *cytoplasm*.

What the hell was mycelplasm?

She zoomed out, and a rectangular drawing in the page's corner caught her attention. Her breath hitched as she expanded the detailed sketch of a hog standing upright. Its bulbous eyes glared at her, gnarled human hand clutching a bloody cleaver.

**The Butcher** was scrawled in messy print above the pig's head, just like the cards in the deck from the research cabin. No matter how many times she'd shuffled the deck, she always pulled the same two, while the others were blank.

**The Butcher's Daughter**, and **The Verdantry**.

The Butcher's Daughter hadn't been an abomination like The Butcher, just a woman wounded by an arrow. If The Butcher's Daughter was supposed to be the actual daughter of the pig—well—that was one messed-up genetic mutation.

Someone from Feyrer's team had known about the cards. Did they also understand how they worked? Would they have known what her cards meant? Maybe the answer was still in the cabin's cellar.

*He betrayed you.*

Yes, but there was nothing she could do about that now. Feyrer was dead.

Siena furiously swiped across a few more pages, the unlabeled equations returning. She couldn't tell if any of them were related to the card.

Turning off her phone, she tucked herself back into her sleeping bag, the image of The Butcher stubbornly persistent in her mind.

A distant splash yanked her from her sleep, and her heart leapt into her throat. She opened her eyes to an oppressive darkness. Something stirred in the swamp water.

She stretched her arm out until she found Emmett's sleeping

bag, reassured by the steady rise and fall of his chest. A consistent, low rumble infiltrated the night. She listened, unable to pinpoint where the noise was coming from. Maybe her own head.

Siena dipped back into sleep, but jolted awake when the rumble rattled her bones, her adrenaline screeching to life.

*Run.*

# HOLDEN

On a scale of "quiet nap" to "worst decision of his life," this one was up there.

Holden tailed the group as he trudged up the mountain, sweat drenching his t-shirt. The sun beat down on the back of his neck and seared the top layer of his skin. Five miles back at the trailhead, the thirty-five-pound weight of his pack was uncomfortable but manageable. Now, his extra underwear crushed him alive.

But the worst of the pain wasn't in his shoulders. Instead, the belt of the pack distributed the weight to his hips. When the hell did he ever work out his hips? *How* was he even supposed to work out his hips? Squats?

When was the last time he did squats?

Never. He'd never done a squat in his life. Cardio? Yes. Push-ups? Sure. But squats? Kyle had invited him to the gym on so many occasions, and Holden had turned him down every time. He'd never thought he'd ever regret *not* hanging out with Kyle, but now he replayed all those would-be texts in his head with pensive longing.

*Wanna lift weights, bro?*

*Yeah, actually. I'm planning on rescuing a bunch of strangers in a few months, and I gotta be jacked so I can carry my underwear up the side of the mountain. Good looking out, Kyle.*

Every breath he took needed to be accompanied by two more. How did anyone trail run above five thousand feet without an oxygen tank strapped to their back?

He was staring down at his feet when someone clapped his shoulder. Startled, his eyes darted up to the tanned and lined face of Clyde. Not a bead of sweat dotted his forehead.

"You hanging in there?"

Holden grimaced, thankful Clyde didn't tack on *"son,"* which would have made Holden feel extra incompetent. "Fine. Out of shape," he admitted with a huff. "But fine."

Clyde walked by Holden's side. "A couple more switchbacks and we'll be out of this gorge before you know it. Saddle Lake's only a few miles after that."

Too out of breath for words, Holden merely nodded. Clyde stepped in front of him when the trail narrowed, and Holden stopped for a few seconds to rest. Out of the ten hikers in the SAR group, the only one behind Holden was a woman in her midforties. She was in much better shape than Holden, but kept stopping to peruse their surroundings, as though she'd never seen a forest before. Holden had already forgotten her name.

The plan was to camp for the night once they reached Saddle Lake. In the morning, the more experienced half of the group would trailblaze east through the valley toward Mount Lucille. They'd then make their way north along the ridge toward Mount Charlotte.

The other half of the team, including Holden, would continue up to Mount Agnes. Since the first Search and Rescue team had found no evidence that the research team had even made it to the cabin, their job was to search for signs they'd veered from the trail.

Clyde had already caught back up with Diego, a SAR veteran and leader of the part of the team that would continue along Wolf Ridge to Agnes. The two chatted away like they were strolling through a sea-level park. Holden returned his attention to his feet and the pair of boots that didn't fit quite right, wielding his borrowed trekking poles to keep himself from eating shit. Blisters had already torn his heels to shreds, and he was too ashamed to make the group stop for him to bandage them.

He needed to get it together; the last thing he wanted was to become a burden and detract from the mission. Lives were on the line.

As he struggled around the bend and up the next switchback, he caught bits of Clyde and Diego's conversation.

"Cameron changes her mind more than she changes clothes. We had her enrolled in college at eighteen . . . Nice school, too. A UC. She started attending, and Teresa and I never heard from her —figured she was busy with friends and studying. A couple months later, she called us from a pay phone. She had dropped out and joined up with some strangers she met online to hike the PCT. They ditched her in Humboldt, and she needed help to get home. I'd never seen Teresa so furious in my life."

"I have two in high school," Diego said. "If they ever pulled that kind of stunt with me, I'd book a three-month all-inclusive trip to Buenos Aires with the rest of their college savings."

"She still owes us money from the deposit on her dorm. I even bug her about it. Uses the excuse of being a poor academic." Clyde sighed loudly. "She's out there, safe. I know she is. Cameron's just being Cameron."

"Are the others like her?" Diego asked. "Dr. Dupont?"

"I'm not sure," Clyde said. "Met Siena twice. Lovely woman. But you don't really get to know your kids' friends once they're adults. Not like when they're little."

Diego was asking the wrong question. It didn't matter whether Siena Dupont was as impulsive as Cameron Yarrow. The real question was, why? Why deviate from the plan when they'd finally secured funding and permission to use the cabin?

They wouldn't have diverted unless they were forced to, but Holden didn't believe that had happened, either. Siena had been at the cabin. He'd seen her on the drone footage, staring right at him. Which meant the first team had missed something crucial.

He'd need to convince both Diego and Clyde to do another sweep of the cabin. Maybe tonight, he'd have the chance.

Saddle Lake swarmed with mosquitos.

As the team set up camp, Holden chose a flat space at the edge of the site. He fumbled with his tent poles, dropping one to smack a bug off his neck. He'd been in high school the last time he'd set up a tent, on some science field trip. Miserable then, too.

He fished a bent tent pole out of the nylon bag, threw it to the side, and tugged free several more poles, all mismatched. He glanced around at the other tents. Everyone but him had finished and moved on to the communal spaces.

This was what he deserved. He wasn't meant for the woods. He wasn't even meant to exist outside for more than ten minutes at a time.

He shouldn't have left Angel on bad terms. She was just looking out for him, and he'd been a tool. He was terrible with friends. That was what she was now—a friend. He hadn't had a good friend in a very long time, and the concept of someone just caring about him for the sake of caring was so foreign. If he could only apologize to her right now. But neither of them had cell service.

If anything happened to him up here . . .

He laughed out loud. *You did this to yourself, idiot.*

The Deadswitch Five had vanished into thin air, and now Siena and her team were also missing. He imagined the probability of something terrible happening to him, given all the current circumstances.

*Today's Danger: Extreme. Remember, kids, only you can prevent poor decisions.*

"You making progress?"

Holden looked up. Clyde approached, his hands shoved in the pockets of his water-resistant nylon shorts, which he probably paid full price for at REI.

Holden stood straight, pressing a hand to his aching lower back. "I think some poles are for a different tent, and a few are bent."

Clyde frowned. "I asked Teresa to see if all the parts were here. I guess she didn't know what she was looking for. Here." Clyde bent down and flipped the nylon bag so the rest of the poles tumbled out. He arranged them, grumbling to himself, and smashed two together until they fit.

Now that he knew violence was the only answer, Holden took heed, and eventually they made two long poles out of the little poles. Clyde gestured to the rolled-out tent, and Holden helped feed both poles through the top.

A few painful minutes later, they pitched the tent. The others had already established the kitchen, and even though fires weren't allowed, the scent of bacon wafted through the campground.

Holden expected his stomach to rumble in anticipation, but he wasn't hungry, even though he'd hiked all day, sweating his guts out and burning half his body weight in calories.

He grabbed his water bottle and followed Clyde to the kitchen. As Diego passed out heaping bowls of bacon mac and cheese, Holden sat on a flaking log, out of the way. The woman who'd hiked behind him all day sat on the other end of the log and offered a brief smile. Crow's feet defined the corners of her eyes, an ash blonde ponytail cascading from the back of her ball cap. She took off her hat and slid the elastic from her hair, shaking it out. Gray streaked the crown of her head.

"Quite the feast," she said.

Clyde passed Holden a bowl and spork, and he took them hesitantly, before prodding the noodles with his utensil. Normally, he'd inhale a cholesterol-drenched meal like this.

Clyde sat across from Holden. "Not hungry?"

Holden smacked another mosquito off his arm, almost spilling his noodles. "Not sure why."

"You're not used to this kind of intense exercise, are you? That's your body telling you it's in shock."

"That's . . ." Holden searched for the right word. "Pathetic."

"You're doing great," Clyde added cheerfully. "But you still need to eat. If you don't get enough calories, you'll really be miserable."

Holden took a bite of the mac and forced himself to chew, even though it tasted like chalk. He gulped down water and shoveled another bite into his mouth.

Diego sauntered over. He was salt-and-peppered and stocky, skin pockmarked from teenage acne. He sat, grinning. "Hello, team!"

"So it's the four of us, then?" Clyde asked.

"Yep, us four headed up to Agnes." Diego glanced at Holden, and then the woman. "We all know each other, right?"

It was a weird question, especially because Diego had never said a word to Holden.

The woman piped up. "I don't know anyone."

"Okay." Diego plopped on the ground, somehow not spilling a single noodle. "Let's start with you, then."

The woman straightened. "I'm Tiffany. I—uhh—used to live here, I guess. During the summers, down in the foothills. Now I live in El Paso."

"SAR background?" Diego asked.

Tiffany stabbed at some of her noodles with her fork. "A bit in my twenties because of my dad. Nothing formal recently." She took a bite. "He was Dr. Dupont's mentor. That's why I'm here."

This surprised Holden. "You're Dr. Feyrer's daughter?"

"You know him?" Tiffany asked.

Holden shook his head, hyperaware of everyone's eyes shifting to him. "Just from what I read in Dr. Dupont's files. He was supposed to be on this trip with them, right?"

Tiffany nodded.

"I . . . uhh . . . I'm sorry for your loss."

"Thanks," she mumbled before pressing her lips together and looking away, and Holden wished he'd said nothing. "I'm here because he would have wanted me here. He cared about Siena—and the others—a lot. He's probably rolling over in his grave as we speak." Her tone was flippant, but Holden appreciated the levity.

Clyde drew a shaky breath. "Well, we're happy you're here. I'm happy. It's good to know there are people willing to help my daughter's team."

"Cameron's brilliant," Tiffany acknowledged. "Dad talked about her all the time."

Clyde swallowed and looked away. A solemn pause lingered before Diego spoke. "How about you?" He nodded at Holden. "The untrained kid. Probably shouldn't have let you come, but Frank said he'd claim responsibility if you did something dumb."

The way Diego called him *kid* irked Holden more than the insult. He also wished he'd known Frank had taken responsibility for him. He didn't want *anyone* to take responsibility for him. It wasn't fair to them.

Holden batted the thought away. This was his chance to explain what he'd seen in the drone feed.

"My name's Holden. I, uhh, work with Maidei Chari and Zaid Handal." Not necessarily a lie. "When Zaid sent the drone over Agnes, I saw someone right before the feed died."

"Someone?" Clyde leaned forward. "What did they look like?"

Holden carefully chose his next words. "It was a brief flash, but she looked like Dr. Dupont."

"Really?" Tiffany said.

Diego frowned and crossed his arms, leaning back on his log. "Frank didn't tell me this."

"There was a lot of commotion when it happened. I was the only one who saw her," Holden admitted.

Diego raised an eyebrow, clearly skeptical. "I see. Well, the cabin isn't on our agenda, since another team already searched it."

"So let's search it again." Clyde clapped Holden on the shoulder. The man sure enjoyed doing that. "You heard Holden. If someone has been up there recently, it's worth investigating." Clyde smiled hopefully. Fingers crossed it wasn't false hope Holden had given him.

"Let's just focus on making it up the mountain first." Diego's jab was directed at Holden, but he didn't care. Something told him Clyde wouldn't leave this forest until the cabin had been searched again, and that was enough for Holden to feel like he'd made a difference.

"What about you?" Clyde asked Diego, seamlessly shifting the topic back to introductions.

"I'm Diego, army vet and Search and Rescue for twenty years. I grew up in these parts—well, a backwoods community on the other side of the wilderness area. Maybe six or seven houses in a small cluster. Town called Walnut. Not even a town, really. There were four of us kids back when I was growing up. Had to take a bus two hours just to get to the nearest high school."

Holden wasn't sure of the point to this history, other than Diego trying to prove he absolutely, definitely belonged on this team, which absolutely, definitely was overkill.

"I bet you were bored." Tiffany scraped the side of her bowl.

"We were bored all summer long. Spent too much time on the outskirts of the wilderness, meddling in stories that shouldn't have been meddled with. Folklore."

"Ah, yes." Tiffany smirked. "The cult. I know about them, too."

Diego glanced at Clyde and Holden as if expecting a prompt to continue, but he continued regardless. "The story goes that a bunch of pioneers packed up their covered wagons and their children and traveled west from Missouri. No one really knows why they inhabited these hills. Back in the day, the snowpack was deadly. I'm sure you've heard about the Donner Party. But the snow didn't scare these folks. Doesn't make a lot of sense until you wonder if something other than fertile land and prosperity drew them to these hills."

Holden couldn't imagine hauling a wagon up any of these mountains. He could hardly haul his underwear. And he wasn't a geology expert, but land was supposed to be fertile in the valley. He hadn't heard of anyone climbing a mountain to start a farm.

Diego continued. "The first settlers built their log cabins in the heart of Deadswitch, far away from common trails. Soon, another party arrived. Left their covered wagons at the trail and carried all their supplies on their back, certain they'd found their promised land. More settlers came, the same story. Abandoned their wagons to hike into the mountains."

Clyde took the bait. "Why would they do that?"

Diego shrugged. "There were documents—spiritual ones—found in these woods. Those pioneers worshipped an entity called The Mother. Sacrificed to her. Animals, humans."

"The Mother?" Holden repeated, scrambling to catch the bowl that had slipped from his hands.

"A goddess with antlers," said Diego. "No, not the Deer Lady. Not a Native American spirit. The Mother is different. Not a warning, but a ruler—ruler over these lands, over her people. As kids, we loved to make up stories about her. Scare each other, dare each other to run into the woods and call for her. The Mother was our Bloody Mary. Scared ourselves silly. Our fear made us see things in the woods. Shadows, antlers, the like. Of course, we were just having fun, but I still can't get over the fact that those documents are real. Someone made them, once upon a time. A Bible of sorts."

*The Mother.* That card the goth girl had pulled for Holden at that stupid party. Was The Mother the same entity? How was that possible?

Avery Mathis—Avablade—one of the Deadswitch Five. The last game she'd been playing . . . was Holden remembering wrong? No, he'd looked it up. The Mother had appeared in that game too, and after Avery had disappeared in Deadswitch Wilderness, The Mother had appeared for Holden on the card.

And now he was here. Just like Avery. And not only that, he'd already fallen into some weird-ass trance at the ranger station, where he'd hungered for a buck made of shadow. If that wasn't culty, he didn't know what was.

This connection with The Mother and Deadswitch was so specific it had to be kismet and not coincidence. Holden had no reason to *not* believe in fate. Hell, he was here because of audio files from the future.

Plus, to conjure a rational explanation was way out of his poor brain's league, but there was something to Diego's story—to The Mother—that he would pocket and save for later.

Holden choked down his entire dinner, something he was very proud of, before kitchen cleanup. When the teams turned in for the night and he entered his secondhand tent, he lingered on the lack of urgency in the camp's atmosphere, slowly rolling it over like a hard, bitter candy on his tongue.

As far as he knew, this was still a rescue—and not a recovery—mission. Diego and the team breaking off to hike toward Lucille all seemed like experts, but it felt like they could do more—at least, those who were trained and acclimated. Weren't lives at stake? Wasn't time of the essence?

He was supposed to trust the experts. Then again, if he'd listened to Maidei back in Oregon, who had told both Holden and Angel to leave this well alone, no one would know Dupont's research team was in trouble.

The recordings, Siena in the static—his reason for being here was to get the team back up to the cabin, regardless of Diego's skepticism.

He wouldn't leave these woods until he searched that cabin himself.

The night dragged on, Holden's eyes snapping open with every rustle of the trees. Muscles mocking him, he tossed and turned until morning broke and he tried sitting up. His head would feel better if it was *literally* filled with hot cement.

Sourness hit the back of his tongue, like remnants of a cocktail made of battery acid. He blinked up at the nylon of the secondhand tent, the morning light filtering in sickly yellow.

Beyond his tent, the rest of the SAR team was already bustling about. He changed and rolled up his sleeping bag, his movements laborious. As he emerged from his tent, Diego ambled over with a bowl of grits and Spam. Holden's stomach revolted, and he shook his head.

Diego pushed the bowl toward him. "You need to eat."

"I'm fine," Holden snapped. Diego's brows knitted in surprise, and then he shrugged and returned to the kitchen to pass off the grits to anyone wanting seconds, and Holden was left alone to pack up his tent.

The Lucille team took off from camp first, and soon after, Holden, Clyde, and Tiffany followed Diego up the trail leading to Wolf Ridge, leaving Saddle Lake behind.

Holden lagged and eventually fell behind the others as his pseudo hangover intensified. He resisted the urge to shout out and ask for a break; he'd let himself get out of shape after breaking up with Becca. He *deserved* this, and wished he'd funneled his grief into something physically productive.

Tiffany fell back to walk beside him and offered a small pack of gummy bears. "Sugar can help."

He accepted with a mumbled thanks. The gummy bear was sweet but took too much energy to chew, so he let it dissolve in his mouth. A quiet dread bloomed inside him as the day crept toward noon. He felt worse than when he woke up.

The group hiked out of the confined gulch, and the sun blazed down, unrelenting as they embarked on the trail's steepest set of switchbacks yet. Holden could do little but focus on his blistered feet in the worn leather of his boots, each step taken with gritted teeth and tunnel vision. The thin mountain air couldn't fill his lungs no matter how quickly he gasped.

Pain pulsed behind his eyes. He dared to glance up, only for his stomach to lurch as he spotted the distant specks of his team. Tiffany lagged behind Clyde and Diego. Was it genuine admiration for the wilderness that kept her back, or was she merely accommodating his pathetic pace?

Holden stumbled. He unclipped his bag and shrugged out of it, and it hit the ground and rolled. Hopefully not all the way back down the mountain, though when he swiveled to check, he fell ass-first onto granite. Ears ringing, he cradled his head in his hands, his tongue swollen and throat too dry to call out for help.

Gravel crunched behind him as someone descended the granite switchbacks. "Hey!" Tiffany called out. "You okay?"

"Out of shape," he choked as she squatted next to him.

"Does your head hurt? Are you dizzy?"

"Yes . . . and yes." He raised his chin as she reached toward the water bottle clipped to his bag.

"Drink. Now." She pushed the bottle toward him, and Holden complied, the water providing little relief. Yet, as Tiffany flew up the switchbacks to summon the others, his heart sank.

Diego's jabs last night made more sense. The SAR lead probably planned to camp at Saddle Lake for Holden's sake, knowing he couldn't move faster. If Holden weren't here, the rest of the team would be halfway to Agnes by now.

As Tiffany disappeared, he lowered his gaze toward the trail they had ascended, and a dark shape coalesced at the forest's edge. A shadow rendered in three dimensions, half-concealed, both part of the landscape and apart from it. A majestic rack of antlers atop a sleek, muscular four-legged body, absorbing sunlight and destroying it.

The buck. It had found Holden again.

He sank into an unsettling abyss, the creature whispering to the primal parts of his mind. His mouth filled with the copper tang of blood, just like before. The veins in his hands and arms hummed, the vibration infecting every nerve in his body.

Diego's rapid-fire questions bombarded him.

Tiffany, Clyde, and Diego stood around Holden. When had they arrived? No matter—he nodded absently at their queries and took another gulp from the bottle in his hands.

Clyde touched Holden's shoulder. "Altitude sickness."

"We need to get you down the mountain," Diego said, his usual gruff expression a little softer.

Holden responded only with a shake of his head, and Diego continued, "Altitude sickness is not something you can walk off or tough out. It will get worse if you push yourself. Your brain is swelling inside your skull. Headaches, dizziness, hallucinations . . ."

*Hallucinations.*

Holden looked back down the mountain. The buck was gone.

"Have you heard of high-altitude cerebral edema? That's when things get grim," Diego said.

Holden couldn't even muster the effort to argue.

"I'll go back down with him," Tiffany said.

"What if he gets worse? You won't be able to hike him out yourself," Clyde said, as if Holden wasn't sitting right there. He lowered his face to his hands again.

"I went to med school for two years. I know wilderness first aid. You and Diego need to continue on. Better me than anyone else."

"Fine," Diego said. "Just . . . be careful."

"You okay with that plan, Holden?" Clyde asked.

Holden finally lifted his head to the concern etched on Clyde's face. With a weak nod, he surrendered.

# TWELVE YEARS AGO

Winter break was a blink away at San José State, anticipation permeating every corner of the university. Cam sat on her dorm bed, pecking at the last paper she needed to turn in before she could bounce and head to her parents' place in Clovis.

Avery lounged beside her beneath the window, having finished everything she needed to get done for break a couple of days ago. Typical. She had a penchant for focus and making straight freakin' As look effortless. Avery could have gone back home to Clear Lake, but stayed until the end of the week—for what reason, Cam didn't know. She'd been spending a bunch of time in Cam's room, today busying herself with a girlie whipped frapp-a-something from the campus coffee shop.

Avery had mastered focus as well as she'd mastered destroying Cam's, digging out whipped cream with the end of her red straw and licking it clean. Her holiday sparkle-painted toes reflexively curled every single time before she dredged more from her cup. Cam had to have died and gone to hell. This was torture.

She scowled at her paper as though it would help her magically create a topic sentence for her next paragraph on why climate change was destroying porpoise communities. God, Bio 20 *sucked*.

"What's your take on games?" Avery asked out of the blue.

Cam blinked and lifted her eyes, her brain scrambling to place the question within the context of the last twenty minutes. The only things she could think of were *whipped cream* and *licking*.

Avery's lips twitched, her chestnut eyes gleaming coyly, like Cam's thoughts were written all over her face. Cam willed her body not to flush.

"Video games," Avery clarified.

*Oh.*

Playing it cool, Cam glanced down at her laptop and shrugged. "Distractions for boys who hate touching grass."

Avery barked a laugh, then tossed her mane of sun kissed hair over her shoulder. "Okay, sure." She sounded mildly irritated, but Cam kept her eyes on her screen. "Aren't you being a little sexist?" Not waiting for a retort, Avery plowed on, "You don't think they're just as valid of stories as books? Fantasy or sci-fi or—"

"I don't read fiction," Cam said.

"Oh, sorry. How silly of me. I guess I didn't realize I was trying to hold a conversation with a joyless potato sack."

Cam repressed a smile. It was fun getting Avery worked up about something so meaningless. Too much fun. "You also didn't realize I am trying to finish a paper. Clearly."

Avery scoffed. "Climate change affects porpoises because it kills off their food supply. They don't die of starvation right away. They use their blubber for energy and eventually die of hypothermia. There you go. Write it down."

Cam leaned back against the wall and watched Avery with a smirk. Avery stared right back, unblinking and adorably invoking a challenge. Cam gave in. "I like reading about adventure, just real ones. Like Krakauer or Jamie Zeppa."

A spark of interest ignited in Avery's eyes. "You hike?"

The door burst open, and Brittani waltzed in. Avery's roommate, Lyndsey, followed, carrying a box labeled *Bitch Crap*.

Brittani clapped her hands. "Both of you listen up, we got a change on our hands. Ben Shavers has a class next semester at eight a.m., and he'll be walking through the campus village every Monday, Wednesday, and Friday. Lyndsey's trying to hook up with the guy." She twirled her fingers. "So we're going to do a little room switcheroo."

"So you can watch him?" Cam asked slowly. "Cross the CV?" Was this some straight girl shit that she didn't understand?

Lyndsey scrunched her nose. "Umm... yes?" she said in Cam's intonation, making fun of her.

"Does this mean Cam and I are rooming together?" Avery asked, before her tongue darted out to lick the end of her straw.

Lightning bolts of euphoria and unbridled terror struck Cam at once, and Avery grinned slyly. She smiled only because she tolerated Cam more than Lyndsey. Yeah, that was it. That *had* to be it. Nothing more, right? Unless sitting here for the past half hour as she made out with a straw was how Avery flirted. *No.* Cam was misreading her—

Brittani scoffed. "Ugh, no. You think Lyndsey and I can room together? We'd murder each other."

"True," Lyndsey sang, dropping her box of bitch crap onto Brittani's bed.

With a frown, Avery gave a delicate shrug. Her eyes lingered on Cam, like she was waiting for her to say something. Argue. Demand that Brittani and Lyndsey room together if they really wanted to disrupt everyone's living situation.

And Cam *wanted* to. But her fear of rejection won out.

"Whatever, just don't touch my stuff." Cam turned her attention to her paper, shielding herself from Avery's disappointment.

# CAMERON

This guy's leg was a mess, and nothing Cam carried in her pack could help.

Black ooze seeped from the gash on his shin, which was the length of a kitchen knife. The more she cleaned it, the more discharge bubbled from beneath the skin. The smell was something between a shit-covered gas station bathroom and a rotting corpse.

It was hard to even assess the damage without getting sick.

But now that she was crouched next to the man in his makeshift shelter, he didn't look as old as she'd first thought. He might be younger than her, his patchy hair and leather skin a token of the elements more than a sign of his age, just like Isaac. He kind of looked like Isaac, actually, but a few features on his face were more distinct.

"Isn't worth it," he grunted. "Appreciate you trying, though."

Cam hated giving up a clean shirt from her bag, but only a monster wouldn't at least try to keep the wound clean. From her pack she chose a t-shirt included in the mule shipment and never worn, nicked the edge of the hem with her knife, and tore the shirt into strips. She then wrapped his wound, though the black discharge seeped through in seconds. It would have to do until he got to a doctor . . . or a medic . . . or whatever the hell was out here. Cam didn't want to think about that yet.

She stood and threw her pack on. The man drained his canteen, and she helped him up. His belongings comprised a school backpack patched and sewn in so many places, the only things left of its original form were the busted zippers and fraying nylon straps.

The man wobbled on his beat-up leg, but despite the damage, he didn't wince. He pointed down the path. "This way."

He walked slowly, and when he began to limp, Cam offered to take his bag and carried it in her hand.

"So, what's this *Tooth* place?" she asked.

"Commune," said the man. "Only one for miles. Maybe only one, period. Dunno. Ruby says there's more."

"Is Ruby someone at the commune?"

The man shook his head. "Ruby's at the other backpack."

"Backpack? You mean *commune*?"

"There's only one commune around here."

The man clearly wasn't all there, and she wouldn't push him just to figure out what he was saying. In fact, the slower he walked, the quieter she became. This didn't feel right; it felt stupid. The path was muddy, but wide and straight, murky water filling imprints of dozens of boots and animal tracks. *Well trodden.* She hardly wanted to be somewhere *well trodden* and out in the open. Anything could be watching them from beyond the fringe of the forest.

A trap.

It had all the makings of one, though why would she be led into a trap unless this Tooth commune was full of hostiles? She carried nothing of value other than her rain shell, knife, and the bit of dehydrated food at the bottom of her bag, but maybe that was enough.

A tall unmoving shape on the road ahead gave Cam pause. "What's that?"

The man stopped. His breath rattled, circles beneath his eyes so dark they looked like bruises. He motioned a limp hand toward the shape, and when he'd caught his breath, they approached together.

The statue of a cloaked man stood on a pedestal, the stone dark from age and covered in moss and lichen. Limestone, most likely. The workmanship was good—no, excellent. Despite the wear of the stone, Cam could tell the man's bearded face was once finely detailed.

"The Ranger," said the man. "Bastion of The Mother."

*The Mother.* The photos on Emmett's phone—the statue of the antlered woman. *The Mother Reigns*, the message Siena claimed was written in blood on the wall of the cabin she'd found through the tunnel.

"Who is she?" Cam asked. "The Mother."

Cam swore the man's upper lip twitched in a sneer before his expression flattened.

"Is she a saint? A goddess?" Cam pried.

"The Mother," the man repeated, "must be protected at all costs." He meandered past the statue and down the road.

That wasn't much of an answer.

Cam followed him. "Why?"

"Because she will save us all from The Shadow."

The Shadow—was this the darkness that had killed Isaac? The black shapes that had shot through the air like missiles? She'd write the whole thing off as a fairy tale if she hadn't witnessed it herself.

Cam played along. "How is The Mother supposed to save us all from The Shadow?"

"It doesn't matter how. You too will have the same blind faith if you stay here long enough."

*Blind faith.* Seven years ago, when Cam and the rest of the rescue team searched for the Deadswitch Five, the ranger had provided a lore refresher of the local pioneer cult just in case some freaks had kidnapped the women. Could it be that the pioneer cult from Deadswitch history was alive and well in this place?

The man didn't seem like he really believed in this Mother or Shadow, which made Cam like him more. "I'm Cam, by the way."

Giving away her name felt like giving away a limb. Impulsive —maybe even stupid.

"Lee," he gasped.

They both fell silent and continued to walk. The forest darkened as dusk fell.

"How far away is The Tooth?" Cam finally asked.

"We'll reach it tomorrow," Lee said.

*Well shit.* "We should probably find a place—"

"Fork." A few more paces and Lee limped off the road and into the brush.

"What are you—" Cam cut herself off when she spotted the narrow overgrown path Lee followed. Despite his slowness, she fell behind to keep her distance from whatever waited ahead. The wet evergreens before them reflected a soft pink light. Between the trees and the hollow of a cliff, a shack rested on a mossy platform, the light coming from the window.

Cam gaped at the light. "Does that say *Coors Light*?"

Lee emitted a rusty chuckle. "Not anymore, but I reckon it once did."

He was right. Mostly burnt out, the neon sign now read *C-o —-Li—t*. This building had enough power for a kitschy decorative sign.

Something flashed from the treetops. She pulled her light from her pocket, clicking it on. Copper squares strung together by wire or string littered the branches of the nearby firs. Garland? Ornaments?

Wood screeched beneath Lee's feet as he stepped onto the platform. "You coming?"

Cam pointed up. "What's that in the trees?"

Lee shrugged. "Gotta ask Ruby."

*Ruby.* Cam's eyes darted to a handmade sign above the door. *The Other Backpack* was burned into the smooth wood.

Not a commune. A tavern.

"Unreal," Cam whispered.

The door screeched louder than the porch when Lee shoved it open, his grunt more from pain than effort. A deep but feminine voice greeted him. *Ruby*, Cam assumed. She followed Lee through the door and was met with a rifle pointed at her face.

Cam lifted both her hands in surrender. *Yeah, good going, walking face-first into that trap.*

"She's good, Rubes." Lee sounded almost bored. "Look at her skin. She don't know who The Mother is either. How about we don't scare off the newborn, yeah?"

*Newborn.* Why did he keep calling her that?

The woman holding the gun was both big-boned and bone-thin. Her left eye looked weird, but Cam was too distracted by the rifle to get a better glance.

Ruby lowered the gun, distrust lingering on her pockmarked face. "Can't be too careful."

Cam dared to pull her attention away from the woman and study the room. A bar split a makeshift kitchen from a common area with two large tree rounds for tables. Photos, handwritten notes, and newspaper clippings covered the back wall. Crap filled the shelves—beat-up paperbacks, cassettes, VHS tapes, DVDs, CDs, and vinyls. An old radio softly played static on a bar top lined with unlabeled bottles of various shades of ocher liquid. The smell of cooked meat wafted from a pot in the kitchen area.

The filaments in the room's hanging bulb buzzed more loudly than the radio, and Cam suppressed the urge to reach up and flick it. "You have electricity."

Ruby grunted. "Sometimes." Her eyes still drank Cam in. *Eye.* Her left eye socket bulged with a rainbow-swirled shooter marble.

"How'd you lose it?" Cam asked.

Ruby's lips pulled back in a tight smile. "Infection. Plucked it out myself."

Cam swallowed. The thought of scooping out her own eyeball, especially in a place like this . . .

Her travel partner had already sunk onto a stool. He looked about as bad as he had on the trail, the shirt Cam had wrapped around his leg now entirely black with mud and ooze.

"Tell me you're not hurt." Ruby tucked the gun behind the bar, scowling at Cam the entire time. She hurried to Lee's side, but backpedaled when she saw Lee's leg. "Fishin' fuck, Lee!"

"Ain't even a good reason." Lee's shoulders wilted, and he leaned against the wall. "Scaling a ridge to get back up to the road. Fell and got snagged by a rock. Should have known better."

Ruby knelt and unwrapped Lee's leg. The gash somehow looked so much worse than it had a few hours ago.

"You got that from a *rock?*" Cam asked.

Ruby heaved an enormous sigh, and again, Cam got the feeling she'd asked a stupid question. But how the hell was she supposed to figure things out if she wasn't asking stupid questions?

"When did this happen?" Cam took off her pack.

"Nah-ah." Ruby pointed to the first door down the very short shotgun hallway. "Bags go in the mudroom. Shoes, too. I just cleaned these floors. Did you touch this?" Ruby gestured to Lee's leg, and Cam just stared at her, unsure where the question was directed. "His leg," she clarified exasperatedly. "*Did you touch his leg?*"

Irritation pinched inside Cam's chest. "I wrapped it. Is that what you mean?"

"Stay right there. Keep your bag on. Don't *touch anything!*" Ruby stood and scuttled behind the bar, sweeping up bottles from the shelves as she moved to a basin in the kitchen's corner.

"Two days ago," Lee said, answering the question Cam had asked about his injury.

"You fell *two days ago?*" The wound looked like it had been festering for months. "Why does it look so bad?"

"Infection," Ruby said.

"No shit, I've just never seen—"

"Anything like it?" Ruby returned with a bowl of milky

water, a brush, a damp rag, and a dry rag. "Take off your shoes right there. Pick 'em up, and bring 'em into the mud closet. Shoes on the rack, bag on a hook. Wipe the door handles when you're done and then come wash up. Scrub beneath your nails good, but don't break your skin. We'll worry about bathing the rest of you later." Ruby cried out of her good eye as she fussed about, then scowled at Cam and sniffed. "Don't tell me you're dumb, too."

Cam removed her boots, and did as Ruby asked, crossing the front of the tavern in her wet hiking socks. Despite Ruby's first impression, she wasn't dumb. Two mentions of infection plus a cleaning ritual likely wasn't coincidence. But really—a rock? What bacteria or virus was malignant enough to turn Lee's leg into a rotted ham hock in two days?

She placed her things in the mudroom, a tiny closet covered in backpacking tent tarps. As she hung up her bag, she caught a whiff of sulfur either from cleaning reagents or bad bacteria. Clearly this forest was swimming in bad bacteria.

Ruby had stopped crying when she returned to the table. Cam focused on carefully scrubbing her hands and scraping away the gunk from beneath her fingernails.

"Just don't die *here*, alright? I've got no room out back for another body," Ruby whispered.

Cam froze in her scrubbing.

"I need to make it back to The Tooth, Rubes," Lee said. "I wanna be the one to let him know."

"Of all The Mother-loving places to keel over, The Tooth? You sure it's worth it? Even knowing what they'll do to you?"

Cam *had* to butt in. "Are you serious? You're making funeral plans?"

Ruby shot Cam another scowl.

"Listen." Cam shook her hands off and dried them with the rag. "I know you think I'm an idiot, but I'm actually a doctor. Not a medical doctor, but I have a PhD and know a lot of wilderness survival bullshit. Plus my dad is a pediatrician. An infection like this doesn't happen, but clearly it does here because you're both acting like he's already dead. *Why?*"

Cam expected Ruby to respond just as combatively, but she got up from kneeling and went to the bar to change the washbowl liquid. She returned with a bucket and the washbowl, placing both next to Lee.

"Rags in the bucket. I'll burn 'em later."

Lee tossed the remnants of Cam's shirt into the bucket and then washed his hands in the bowl. He stretched out his injured leg, the wound glistening black in the light of the dull bulb above.

Ruby returned to the bar and picked out a bottle and a set of scratched glasses from the shelves. She pointed to the empty table, and Cam sat as Ruby popped the cork and poured two fingers of the ocher liquid into each glass.

"What's that?" Cam asked.

"Single barrel reserve bourbon shat from the ass of Colonel Sanders himself." Ruby slid Cam a glass. "The fuck you think it is?"

Cam picked up the drink. The liquid smelled like piss and tasted like bathtub hooch, but at least it burned all the way down. Something sharp to wake her up from this fever dream.

"You a researcher?" Ruby asked.

Cam's insides jolted with alarm until she remembered she'd told Ruby about her PhD. "Yeah."

To her surprise, Ruby smiled. "Me too. Or I used to be. I don't know how many years have passed since . . . well, you know."

No, Cam didn't know. But instead of interrupting for the millionth time, she sipped at her piss juice.

"I don't mean to be so gruff. You don't know any better, and sometimes I feel too jaded to even think straight. But I'll tell you one thing, C— What's your name?"

"Cam." She took another sip. Maybe she should have used a pseudonym. Then again, no one here knew her, so why did it matter?

"I'll tell you one thing, Cam. You're lucky you found Lee, and you're lucky he took you here. There may not be many people in these parts, but there are stories. Unless newborns like you are whip-sharp with their survival skills or someone teaches 'em real quick, they tend to not make it very long." Ruby knocked back the rest of her glass and set it on the table with a wince. "Wherever you came from, those rules that run your little world don't apply here. And if you don't accept that, and you don't accept what this forest can do to you in a matter of hours, you might as well waltz outside and stuff your face with the first mushrooms you see, because you ain't gonna last."

Cam leaned back on the stool until her shoulders hit the wall. "You assume I have some fucking idea where *here* is."

Ruby laughed. "Not at all, little baby. I think *you* assume *I* do."

# SIENA

*Run.*

Siena woke on the floor of the abandoned shelter as the frogs choked on their own croaks. The skittering in the trees, the splashing of scavengers in the muck, the entire swamp fell silent like the land itself feared the approaching rumble.

It was the same noise she'd heard before, first on Wolf Ridge when they found the body, and again on Mount Agnes. It sounded like hunger—like the forest itself was starving. Never had it sucked the sound out of the atmosphere before.

It was stronger now.

She shook Emmett, and he shot up in his sleeping bag.

*Something's wrong,* she tried to say, except the words didn't leave her mouth. She couldn't speak, just like the frogs.

Siena kicked away her sleeping bag. Emmett was quicker to act, grabbing her wrist and dragging her to her feet. They fumbled around each other in the dark and shoved their stuff into the bags. She held her breath like it would prevent her from accidentally stepping on a rotten plank and quietly crashing into the water beneath.

The rumble strengthened, the vibration drowning her pounding pulse. Her trembling fingers slipped on the wet bootlaces as she tied them, and she hissed a muted swear, panic revving in her chest.

Emmett helped her into her backpack and stayed close as she opened the silent door, the wood of the platform not even creaking beneath their feet. She maneuvered down the ladder, clinging to the rungs. How deep was the water? Half a meter? Dawn revealed only a murky surface. She'd hurt herself further if she jumped right, toward solid ground.

The rumble muddled her thoughts. She could feel Emmett's impatience wordlessly simmering behind her.

Siena let go of the ladder and jumped.

Her boots slammed into mud, and she gasped as pain punched through her knee.

The ground shifted as Emmett landed to her right. The moment he grabbed her hand to run, the rumble evaporated, and the swamp crashed back.

The crickets, the frogs. Every reptilian splash. The creaks, groans, and rustles of the cypress trees. The water. Everything thundered so loudly, Siena clapped her free hand over her ear.

"Siena!" Emmett roared, and touched his fingers to his own throat in surprise.

Releasing a strangled cry, she dropped Emmett's hand and whipped her head to scan the cypresses beyond the water's calm surface.

He spoke to her through the trees voicelessly, in a language meant only for her.

*You've imagined nothing.*

Dawn was still young, but strung across the branches, a silken web caught the first glimmer of light.

Beetle webs. Not a threat, but a sign. Everything she saw was real. Everything *happening* was real.

"What the hell was that?" Emmett said.

She brushed beneath her eyes, fingers wet when she pulled her hand away. *He* couldn't know, could he? Every delusion, every moment she'd second-guessed her own beliefs. If everything was real, then nothing made sense.

If she had imagined nothing, then she'd been right all along.

"Siena—"

She cleared her throat. "The Shadow. The thing that killed Isaac. He's here, or was."

"What? How do you—" He cut himself off. "We need to leave, *now*!"

But The Shadow didn't want to hurt them . . . not right now, at least. Siena couldn't explain this to Emmett. She couldn't even explain it to herself. A gut feeling wasn't a conclusion. It wasn't even a hypothesis.

He spoke to her again. *You imagine nothing.*

He was still here, watching them, and capturing nothing but her attention. He only wanted to deliver a message so she could have faith in herself.

She swiped her hand over the belt of her bag and the outline of her pill bottle in the pocket. *Why do you want to soothe me?* she thought. *Why aren't you attacking?*

Even though he hadn't attacked yet, Siena standing here granted The Shadow an invitation. She gritted her teeth to keep them from chattering, turning back to Emmett. "Help me get out of here."

He complied, threading his arm between her waist and her pack to help keep the weight off her bad knee. They hurried south.

"How do you know that was The Shadow?" he asked, out of breath from their pace.

"It's just a hunch," she admitted. "That rumble—remember when I woke you up on Wolf Ridge because I heard something?"

"That was what you heard?" he asked, the question deeply skeptical.

"Other times, too."

Emmett released her and swept in front, and Siena followed as they maneuvered across a hardwood hammock, the only natural areas of the swamp that were dry, keeping clear of the water.

"I thought it wanted to kill you," he said. "That's why we're running, isn't it?"

She mimicked his footing as he stepped over a rotten log in their path. "Yes." Except The Shadow hadn't wanted to kill her this morning. He'd only wanted to talk to her, to tell her she had imagined nothing, something she'd desperately wanted to hear for years from anyone who'd agree. The Shadow had somehow known, which meant it could infiltrate her thoughts.

No, she wouldn't dare believe he could read her mind, not without evidence. A cold sweat broke across the back of her neck regardless. "I can't explain what happened back there, not with experiencing that silence only once."

"I'd rather us avoid that ever happening again, if we can help it," Emmett said. "Scared the shit out of me."

"Yeah." She fell quiet, focusing on the path and the easiest way to wind south around the water. She and Emmett worked together by pointing out crossable hammocks. With the help of her adrenaline, the pain in her knee dulled to a manageable ache.

The swamp atmosphere remained both cold and humid. Every time Siena stole a glance at the sky, she was met with cloud cover.

"It's strange," she said. "Plant life here is thriving. It's so humid that the rate of evapotranspiration must be high, but it's cold. It shouldn't be cold, not with all this summer growth." She slid her phone from her jacket pocket to take a few pictures.

"Maybe it's a cold spell," Emmett offered, but that conclusion didn't satisfy her. Other processes were taking place in this swamp. She doubted Emmett would let her set up a picnic right now to further study the biome.

She needed to understand the Briardark better to learn how to escape it. All Isaac's map had offered was a symbol for the exit, but not how to get out.

Emmett kept casting glances at her. His behavior was another little awry thing. A man who'd do everything to keep her at the research cabin was suddenly the man leading her forward. She couldn't chalk it up to just a change of heart. Whatever else had happened to Emmett was a missing puzzle piece she needed.

Eventually, she'd have to pry it from him.

The swamp habitat finally subsided, and the land grew drier and firmer beneath their feet.

"You need a break?" he asked.

She nodded, slipped out of her pack, and massaged her knee. Bending over, she grabbed her bottle from the side pocket of her bag and greedily drank the inch of fresh water left.

Emmett held his bottle out to her, but he only had a couple of inches left in the bottom of his.

Siena shook her head. "Save it. I'm fine."

He gave her one of his dad looks as he screwed the lid back on, still skilled at sensing her anxiety. "We'll fill up as soon as we find a creek, okay?"

"Sure." She cast a glance over Emmett's shoulder and the route south.

Siena envisioned her map and matched it to the surrounding environment. They were in the valley. On her Deadswitch map, the valley swept below the U-shaped range of the sister peaks: Agnes, Charlotte, and Lucille.

Thick overgrowth covered the valley in Deadswitch Wilderness, the terrain usually difficult to traverse. Siena wasn't the kind of wilderness survivalist who traveled with a machete. Hacking through brush triggered her allergies, and there was no peaceful way to relieve your bowels when everything poked you in the ass.

But instead of overgrowth, a trail wide enough to be a road led south, foliage and trees growing wildly everywhere else. The vegetation off trail basked in a sheen of light from the partial sun, but darkness covered the path. None of it made sense until she looked up.

"You see that?" Her voice trembled. "Or am I seeing something that isn't actually there?"

*You imagine nothing.*

Emmett's expression shifted to horrified. "No, you're not seeing things. Unless I am too."

Above, a black gash split the sky in half, like the darkest part of the universe had bled through the atmosphere and created a river south.

"Is this The Shadow, too?" Emmett took hold of Siena's wrist again, readying them to run. Except according to their map, south was the only way out of the valley.

"I don't know," Siena said. "But it's covering the path perfectly, which is why nothing grows on it. How is the streak in the sky blocking the light from hitting the ground at all times of the day?"

"Something is unzipping the sky, and you're thinking about plants?"

Her lips perked in a smile, but when she dropped her gaze, unease lingered on Emmett's face.

This felt like a trap, except Siena didn't understand how, or why, or what. Every question she had could only be thrown atop the pile that crushed her, and the fever dream of anomalies without data or evidence made it impossible to be cautious.

*I am everywhere.*

If The Shadow wanted to capture her, he wouldn't hand over an easy path out of here.

Siena drew a breath, crawling from a brewing cesspool of her primal fear. She couldn't forget to collect data in her panic, so she snapped pictures of the sky and the shadowed path before them.

She refocused her attention on Emmett as he wiped his hand on his shirt. It left a rusty trail. "You're bleeding."

Emmett lifted his hand to inspect it. "Yeah. Caught a splinter on the way down that ladder. Not as bad as a paper cut." He quickly changed the subject, nodding toward the clear path before them. "Looks like the only way to go."

She stepped forward and winced as her knee twinged. "Looks like."

"Shit," he muttered, and followed her south.

Despite the sun, thunderheads rolled toward the gash in the sky. Light crept through the clouds' cracks and shot through the forest in rays, and Siena could almost hear the sighs of delight from the ferns and tender saplings.

She fell behind Emmett to scan the woods. Everything rustled and shook, not as though the thickets hid deer or predators, but like a great wind was caught within the foliage and trying to escape. Before her eyes, a hemlock bent beneath an unseen force and into a beam of light.

No—not an unseen force. The trees were heliotropic, flexibly stretching toward the light in a matter of seconds. Sunflowers could do such a thing, but not trees.

Awestruck, Siena opened her mouth to tell Emmett, but he was far in front now, and her knee prevented her from running to catch up. He slowed at a brook.

Perfect timing. She was no longer thirsty, which meant that dehydration was setting in.

Once at the water, she helped Emmett filter and fill four bottles between the two of them, then chewed up an energy bar, her initial excitement over the trees deflating. There was no point in telling Emmett. He didn't care about reasons or consequences, only whether the short-term result gave him more control.

She'd keep this discovery to herself, for now. Save it for when she could tell someone who cared.

They kept moving. The trail offered little variance, like they were stuck on a treadmill. Only her level of anxiety fluctuated.

*You imagine nothing.* How could she believe such a thing when nothing behaved like it was supposed to?

Siena glanced up to gauge the time of day, but the black streak through the sky still covered the sun. It had shifted west, too. Earlier, the gash had split the sky in half.

"Wait a second." She ventured off the trail and into the brush. The sun peeked out from behind the gash.

It moved with the sun. That was why light never touched the path.

Siena returned to Emmett. "We have two hours of daylight left."

He caught his breath. "How much ground do you think we can cover with your knee?"

Siena stretched out her leg, massaging it again. "A few more miles."

Thankfully, they didn't need to travel so far. Fifteen minutes later, the path fanned into a clearing, and a humble cabin stood before them, its logs cracked and faded, the roof covered in debris. Vines twisted across the ground and up the cabin's sides.

"Sen." Emmett pointed up.

The onyx river through the sky abruptly ended above the cabin. Beyond the clearing, the thicket thrived, vegetation no longer forced to cower away from shadow.

*A trap,* her brain screamed again, even though they'd covered miles more with the trail than they would have otherwise.

"What if someone's in there?" Emmett asked.

She studied the cabin's perimeter. "There aren't any tracks. The place looks overgrown, but we should still be careful."

Sick dread filled her gut. A possible inhabitant mattered little compared to the danger of having been led here.

Emmett crept toward the cabin, and she followed at a distance. The closest window shutter hung ajar, nothing inside but darkness. Still, her pulse raced with a warning. Both of them were weaponless except for their knives. They weren't equipped to face someone hostile.

Once he reached the cabin's back wall, Emmett hooked a finger beneath the shutter and gently pulled it back. The hinge shrieked, and Siena winced.

He turned toward her. "Empty."

She gingerly climbed over vines toward the front of the cabin. Above, clouds poured across the sky from the east, a storm imminent. They'd made it just in time.

She rounded the cabin. A sign hung above the front door, letters burned into the wood.

**Outpost 2**

Emmett approached from the other side, battling the brush. Siena stepped forward and pushed open the unlocked door.

The air smelled of dust and pine, the only furniture inside a table and two chairs tucked against the wall. Floorboards creaked beneath her as she crossed the room to the back shutter and propped it open with a stake.

"Look at this." Emmett nodded to the top of the table. Approaching, Siena made out the symbols and shapes of a map painted on the table's surface, the design similar to the one on the wall in the research cabin.

"Isaac," she said reverentially, brushing her fingers over a circle with two slashes atop Mount Agnes. She traced a line down a weaving path to the same symbol at the bottom of the map: their destination. Isaac had called them passages. He was here once. This map was his. She knew it. She also knew the same Shadow that had poured from Isaac's eyes and mouth had led them here.

*Unproven.*

"Look at this." Emmett pointed to a pattern of waves and cattails, *Outpost 1* written above a hut symbol. They'd stayed there last night.

Siena's finger landed on a hut farther south. "Outpost 2. We are here." She counted the huts along the trail—seven in all. "This trail winds through the valley. Why was ours straight?" She drew a straight line with her finger from Outpost 1 to Outpost 2.

"Probably has something to do with that thing in the sky, but other than that . . ." Emmett trailed off. "Maybe it will still be there tomorrow. Clear our route again."

"Maybe." She turned toward the open window.

The trail they'd taken here had vanished, an impossibly dense thicket in its place.

The gash in the sky was gone.

There is no hope in the darkest part of the forest unless we are children.
As children we are timid, hiding behind the skirt of our Mother when our wonder dares to flourish into curiosity.
When there is shadow in curiosity, the shadow festers.
When there is shadow in curiosity, our Mother can no longer protect us, and we grow up only to die.
—*Second Sermon, The Church of Bounty*

# HOLDEN

The landscape shifted around Holden as he ventured deeper into the night, his eyes already adjusted to the dark. The once-descending ground now leveled out amongst pines perfectly spaced apart. Moonbeams dashed across his face like Morse code. *Too* bright. He'd never seen the moon illuminate the sky like this.

Why had he gotten up? To pee? No, his bladder didn't feel heavy. Unless he'd already done so and was on his way back to camp. He couldn't remember.

The forest smelled different. An entire world of vegetative rot, festering and nutrient dense, waiting to grow something beautiful. Up ahead, a curtain of mist glistened. The trees parted for him in a path.

He dredged up a memory from deep within the folds of his brain. This place was a sanctuary, the land, the trees meticulously maintained by those who serve . . .

Panic throttled Holden's heart. He could still escape. Turn around and run.

No . . . a despicable option driven by fear. Change was coming, and it was time to embrace it. Not hide.

The towering pines fanned outward and circled an enclave,

the center glowing like a hearth. Torches, each one held by a moss-eaten statue. Spindly mushrooms covered the statue of him, a crack splitting the stony version of his face. He wouldn't look but instinctively knew it was there, just beyond the grasp of his vision.

Before him, a woman in a plain linen dress sat atop a rotting stump. She stood when she saw him, graceful but frail. Mortal. Her ashen hair should be dull, but it shone like silk, undulating waves brushing the bottom of her rib cage. She held something dark and glistening in her stained hands.

Holden hated towering over her, so he knelt, the damp ground soaking the knee of his pants.

"Look at me." The woman's voice was quiet and carried no hint of authority. Holden looked up just as she knelt in front of him.

Once beautiful, still was. Painfully so. Her face was a familiar warmth that coiled around his belly. She did this often, demanding reverence without asking for it simply by falling to his level. By reminding him that despite her power, they were the same.

Her eyes glistened. She offered her hands, and Holden glanced down at a heart made of shadow, expanding and contracting as it beat.

"You may have come into the fold on your own," she began. "But I chose you from the moment you entered. Trust me, and I will protect you."

*Trust.* The heart resting in her soft hands could kill him, but he needed to show as much loyalty to her as she had with him.

"Thank you," Holden whispered. And then he lowered his head to the offering, and bit.

Sharp rays of sunlight pierced the jelly of his eyeballs and cooked his brain.

He came to on top of his deflated tent, sitting upright in a sleeping bag soaked in sweat. Hopefully sweat. God, had he pissed himself? No, he couldn't have . . . Where the hell was he?

A pounding rhythm struck every nerve in his head with the persistence of a tolling bell. His attention drifted to a plum-red tent. Tiffany's.

He rolled to the side, an automatic, desperate response to the sudden revolt in his stomach, and vomited into the dirt. His nostrils stung with the harshness of it, a punishing welcome back to reality.

Memories of yesterday intruded: the towering mountain with its relentless switchbacks, his own defeat at the hands of altitude sickness. Tiffany, guiding him down with unwavering patience, her presence both a comfort and a reminder of his own fucking incompetence.

They had set up camp as best they could at Glass Lake. His failed attempt at erecting his tent without Clyde's help had left him sleeping on top of the limp nylon, too sick and exhausted to do anything else, even when Tiffany tried helping him into her tent so she could fix up his.

And then what? He'd woken in the middle of the night to take a leak, illness magically vacant, and walked down the hill into a sanctuary.

No. That was a dream. An extremely screwed-up dream, a symptom of the sickness, a reminder of his vulnerability, a figment of his imagination, a remnant of his fear, a dream, a dream, a dream . . .

Dust speckled the collapsed tent, evidence of a tumultuous sleep. Uncomfortable itching spread across his arms and neck and distracted him from the throbbing in his head. Mosquito bites. He cringed at the swollen, angry marks, and a fresh wave of humiliation washed over him.

It was almost as if the universe was mocking him, piling up one inconvenience after another. He scratched at the bites before dragging his body from the damp sleeping bag, and studied the blood caked beneath his dirty, broken toenails. He'd hiked over twenty miles the past couple of days, having never hiked before. His feet had taken a beating.

Holden blinked against the sunlight, lifting his hand to shield his eyes. Cheerful laughter and the splash of water drifted on the breeze from Glass Lake a couple hundred feet away. God, what time was it? *Noon?*

Residual bile stung the back of his throat, and the pounding in his head had ramped up to a full-blown construction project.

"Tiffany," he croaked. Her tent was gone, but her pack was still here. Before Holden could panic, she entered the clearing, a collapsible bucket of lake water in one hand and a filter pump tucked under her other arm.

Her brows knitted as she took him in, a sympathetic grimace pulling at the corners of her lips. "You look like hell."

He winced. "Thanks."

"I really tried getting you in my tent last night. Don't think I gave up easily." Tiffany set the bucket on the ground, blanched at Holden's vomit puddle, and then moved the bucket to his other side. She unraveled the filter. "Where's your bottle? I'll fill it."

He pointed to his bag propped against a nearby tree. Tiffany fussing over him was unexpected and not necessarily unwelcome, though he couldn't get over the guilt of pulling her away from the mission. "I'm sorry—"

"Please, not again." She handed him his bottle, a flicker of humor in her eyes. "If I figure out a way for you to pay me back, will you stop apologizing for something you couldn't control?"

Holden swallowed a gulp of the cold, clear water. "Only *if.*" It was kind of her to remind him the altitude sickness wasn't his fault, except it was. He'd spent most of his life a few hundred feet above sea level. He'd never backpacked a day in his life. He'd voluntarily joined the search team. Altitude sickness or not, Holden had set himself up to fail.

"I hope they search the cabin on Mount Agnes again."

"They will." Tiffany pumped the filter as she filled her own bottle. "I don't think Clyde would have it any other way. I know what it's like, being a parent. You feel you know your kids better than anyone, even if that isn't true. Clyde probably thinks he can find evidence of Cameron better than the last team. He told me he wanted to see the cabin for himself, anyway."

Holden breathed a sigh of relief. "That's good."

She stole Holden's bottle to top it off. "So, you really saw someone on the drone feed?"

"Dr. Dupont," Holden said. "I don't know for sure, but I think it was her. It *felt* like her."

"Felt . . ."

"*Felt* as in intuition. Not *felt* her spirit pass through me, or some shit."

Tiffany's eyes crinkled as she smiled. "Thanks for the clari-fication."

She was easy to talk to. Holden really hoped he *could* pay her back for helping him get back down to the ranger station, and not superficially, either. Everyone liked food, right? Maybe he could cook something. He was much better at cooking than climbing mountains.

Tiffany handed his bottle back. "We've got only three more miles until we hit the ranger station, but I was hoping . . ." She hesitated, winding the tube around her hand and walking to her bag, stuffing the filter inside. "Well, last night I was hoping we could reach a certain spot on the other side of the lake, but you were in terrible shape. But maybe we can stop by today. It may have a thing or two to make you feel better."

She was being vague on purpose. "A certain spot?" he asked.

"A cabin." She returned to Holden's deflated tent, picked up the bucket, and dumped the rest of the water at the edge of their campground. "*My* cabin."

Holden raised his eyebrows. "Yours?"

"Yeah," she said lightly. "Let's pack up, and I'll show you."

Despite how horrendous Holden felt, he was too intrigued by this mysterious cabin Tiffany owned to say no to the visit. So they took the trail around the lake, the shore busy with midday hikers and families breaking for lunch. Glass Lake was beautiful. He wished his head weren't screaming so he could actually appreciate it.

On the western edge of the lake, Tiffany led him off the main trail to a branching path, which slithered into thick brush. "I don't think anyone's been back here in a couple of years," she grunted, shoving her way through the thicket.

The brush soon parted, and a cabin stood in the center of the clearing. The word *cute* came to mind, tiny evergreen cutouts carved into shutters above empty window boxes once painted white. Two hundred square feet at most, hardly bigger than some rich kid's playhouse. Needed some serious TLC, too. A solar panel covered one side of the A-frame roof, but it looked dated as hell. Holden would be shocked if it was still working.

"Looks sadder than I remember it." Tiffany pulled a key from the belt pocket of her pack, walked to the door, and wiggled it into the deadbolt. The door groaned loudly when she pushed it open, like the wood had expanded beyond the frame. She stomped her feet before entering, and Holden followed her.

The cabin's innards were small and stale. A twin bed, covered in a limp comforter, took up a corner of the room. A narrow counter with a pump sink lined the opposite side, beneath it an antique upright cooler and a military ammo box. Dust motes plumed in the air as Tiffany shoved a window open. "Filthy," she stated, clapping her hands clean.

"This is . . . *yours*?" Holden peered through the back window at the collapsed outhouse. He took off his pack and sat on the bed, groaning louder than the mattress springs.

"My dad's," she elaborated. "One of the few private pieces of property left in Deadswitch. State wouldn't let him sell it, only give it away. He was going to give it to Siena before he rewrote his will last year, when the cancer came back."

Based on her audio files, Siena and Dr. Feyrer had been close, but to pass up his daughter seemed callous, especially if . . .

"You wanted it?" he asked.

"No. This place is a craphole." With her hands on her hips, Tiffany scanned the emptiness of the small room. "But it's *my* craphole."

In other words, this dinky cabin in the middle of nowhere had history. Holden sensed that was why Tiffany had brought him here. Her eyes flitted about, searching.

Maybe she'd wanted to come here in the first place, and that was why she'd volunteered to escort Holden back.

"What are you looking for?"

Her eyes met his, and she flushed, as if caught in the act. "I don't know." She knelt near the cooler and opened it. Bottles clinked as she rummaged around. "Here." She popped off the bottle cap on a Mexican Coke with the carabiner on her keys and held the drink out. "The good kind. None of that high-fructose garbage."

Holden took the Coke and spun it, the expiration date stamped on the bottle neck. "Expired last year. Your dad used this place recently?"

Tiffany shrugged, flipping the latches on the ammo container lid. She pulled from the container a wad of gauze bandages and blister pads and continued to dig, finding an orange prescription bottle and shaking it. "Here." She tossed the bottle to Holden, who missed. He picked it off the floor and read the label. *Dexamethasone.*

"Take two. Anti-inflammatory for your altitude sickness," Tiffany explained. "Surprised Diego wasn't carrying any on him, being SAR and all. Seemed a little full of himself, didn't he?"

Holden smiled as he twisted the lid off, happy he wasn't the only one who felt that way. He took two pills and swallowed them with a swig of warm Coke.

Tiffany shoved the ammo container back beneath the counter. She seemed disappointed. Maybe her mood had something to do with the state of the cabin. A *craphole*, she'd called it.

Holden took a large gulp of Coke and set it on the floor, lying on his side on the bed. It was too early to feel the effects of the dexamethasone or the sugar, but the placebo effect was almost as good. "So, what will you do with this place?"

"Probably give it to Siena like Dad wanted, if we can find her. Just wanted to see it one last time while it was mine. Felt like I had to."

"Did you spend a lot of time here?"

Tiffany's gaze swept the low ceiling as though she were staring up at the inside of a gothic cathedral. "You could say that. Summers, mostly. When Dad worked. But that was a long time ago."

Holden rolled onto his back and stared at the ceiling. The only thing he noticed was a water stain.

His ears started ringing again, and he sat up with a grunt, jamming a finger into one. Altitude sickness? Diego hadn't included ear ringing in his laundry list of symptoms.

"You hear that too?" Tiffany winced.

Holden dropped his hand. "Yeah. I thought it was inside my head. Some inner ear thing."

"What is it?" She stood to peer out a window. "Is it coming from the lake?"

Holden shook his head. The ringing sounded like it was literally originating inside his skull. "This isn't the first time I've heard it since driving up here a few weeks ago. I thought it was a part of the altitude change."

Tiffany glared at the window. "I don't think this is the first time I've heard it, either." She took a step back, as if expecting the window to shatter, and then stuck her fingers in her ears. "It's terrible. Drink up so we can get out of here."

He didn't need to be asked twice, swiping his Coke from the ground as Tiffany hoisted her bag onto her shoulders.

Holden slumped against the wall of the ranger station, an ice pack chilling his sunburnt neck. As the EMT—a wiry, stoic woman who'd introduced herself as Liz—rummaged for something in her bag, Holden drank occasional gulps of ice water to wash away the residual taste of Coke-flavored vomit.

The AC on the wall opposite kicked on with a *whir*, the cold blasting him in the face. The filtered air made his body odor smell even worse. How anyone could live in the wild for weeks at a time was beyond him. He couldn't handle two days.

Frank sat in his chair with the phone's receiver, relaying information to whoever was on the other end. Liz squatted in front of Holden and gripped his wrist, her fingers pressing into his pulse point.

After checking the rest of his vitals, Liz said, "You're probably fine. You need fluids and rest."

All that vomiting and he was *probably fine*? "What's my diagnosis? Weak constitution?"

Liz blinked at him, either not getting the joke or not finding his self-deprecation amusing. Tiffany was a better medic. She'd already taken off to the Fort to shower, but he needed to thank her again the second he had the chance. She'd given up helping with the search to coddle his *probably fine*, pathetic ass. The research team needed Tiffany's efforts out in the wilderness, and Holden had impeded that.

He needed to not just thank Tiffany again, but make up for what he'd done. Figure out some other way to uncover where the research team was and why they were in danger, even if he had to do it from the Fort.

Frank hung up the phone and turned to Holden, his weathered face breaking into a friendly grin. "Don't be so hard on yourself. Even seasoned hikers get altitude sickness."

Holden scratched the cluster of mosquito bites on his neck. Seasoned hikers got altitude sickness, but they also had boots that fit right and could set up their own tent and applied sunblock correctly and knew the limitations of their own bodies. He wasn't being hard on himself for getting altitude sickness, but for burdening the rest of the team.

Holden wanted to say something like this, hoping at least Frank would forgive him, but he was interrupted by the door to the station flying open. Francis barreled in, jumping on Holden to lick his face. The dog's whimpers and squeaks of joy sounded more like a Pomeranian than a seventy-pound German shepherd.

Holden scratched the dog's scruff, a much better option than scratching at his bites. "Sorry to worry you for no reason, boy."

Frank stood. "I've got a supply run to make. Liz, you need a ride back to town?"

Liz nodded and packed up her supplies, and they filed out as Angel entered. Her hair was pulled back in a tight bun that could rival a librarian's, though she was dressed in an old t-shirt and jean shorts. She avoided Holden's eyes and sat across the room, pulling a lip balm from her pocket and applying it. She crossed her legs, then uncrossed them, then sighed, standing, and walked to the mini fridge behind Frank's desk.

She could make an Olympic sport out of ignoring the only other person in the room. He didn't blame her—he'd left things on a shitty note, and had regretted it the entire time he was on the trail.

When the fridge opened, Francis immediately forgot Holden's existence and wandered over to Angel, sniffing around.

Angel stood with the door open, though it didn't seem like she was staring at anything in particular. Either she didn't know what to say, or didn't want to say anything.

Or was waiting for him to say something. So he did.

"I'm sorry."

"For what?" she asked without looking at him, bending over

to select a cheap beer from Frank's meager stash. After pushing Francis out of the way, she shut the fridge door.

She would make this hard for him, and he deserved it. "I'm sorry I didn't consider your feelings. I'm not used to people caring about what happens to me."

Angel scoffed like he'd said something dumb, and he immediately *felt* dumb, but couldn't think of anything to add. He was telling the truth, after all, not because he wanted her to feel sorry for him, but because it had been a while since he took up someone else's emotional bandwidth, and he'd forgotten how complicated friendships—hell, all relationships—were. He couldn't reconcile both Angel being Angel, and Angel being someone who didn't want Holden to get hurt.

"Yeah," she finally said when she sat again. "And I'm not used to people considering my feelings, so I guess I should have expected you not to listen."

"That . . ." He scrambled for a way to refute her belief, but doing so would only prove her right. "That sucks."

Angel blinked, her guarded expression softening. "I gotta say, Holden, I'm also not used to men owning up to their mistakes. Thank you. But I also don't buy the pathetic loner act. Just because you're too big of a knucklehead to notice people caring about you doesn't mean they don't exist." She paused before a marked shift in her tone broke the quiet. "I'm glad you're okay."

"Same." Could he name anyone other than Angel who actually cared about him? Even the woman he'd been living with had moved all his shit from their apartment and disconnected her phone so he couldn't call her. That didn't seem very caring.

"You ready to head up to the Fort?" Angel asked.

He picked up the rotary phone's receiver. "I need to call my apartment manager first."

Even with the help of 411, it took a bit for Holden to get connected to the right person. When he finally reached his apartment manager, she gave him the same news as Becca.

"Lauren said she spoke for the both of you, and according to our lease terms . . ."

Holden interrupted her. "But how could she end the lease without my agreement? We cosigned. Isn't that why there are two names on the contract?"

"Normally, yes, but she claimed you'd already moved out. Given those circumstances, it was her decision. She was very convincing."

Holden gripped the phone tighter, mentally detangling every potential consequence that stemmed from this woman believing a *very convincing* Lauren.

"What about my things? All my stuff is gone."

"Lauren must have packed it up and taken it. I know there was a van, but I can't tell you much else."

"So that's it, then?" he asked.

"I . . . I'm truly sorry," she whispered, her voice lost between the cracks of their conversation and the static of the landline.

Holden numbly hung up.

He'd already tried calling Lauren. Fourteen times, to be exact, the unfriendly, mechanical voice greeting him each time: *We're sorry, the number you have reached has been disconnected.* A mantra of betrayal, mocking him.

Angel monitored him from the top of Frank's desk as Francis lay sprawled at her feet, his alert ears twitching at the tension in the room. Holden leaned against the desk as he relayed to Angel what the apartment manager had told him.

"A couple months after I broke up with Becca, Lauren responded to my post on a local message board about the room. I didn't know her, but she had seemed desperate, so I only charged her half the listed rate. And she pays me back by screwing me over."

Angel sighed. "Oh, Holden." She cracked her can open. "Sorry, sickie. I know this moment calls for a beer, but you can't have one until you've recovered." She jerked her head toward the battered screen door.

Holden grabbed his ice water, pushed off from the desk, and followed Angel outside, where she sat on the porch's worn steps. He sat next to her, the sun's heat prickling his skin. Francis wiggled his way between them and nudged his snout against Angel's can, licking the condensation with long swipes of his tongue.

"I should go back to Corvallis," Holden said more to himself than to Angel. "Find a place to crash and figure out what the hell happened." He ran his fingers through Francis's soft fur, the rhythmic motion calming.

"You think Lauren stole and sold your stuff?" Angel asked.

"The total value of my belongings is probably less than three grand. More effort to sell than it's worth." His gaze drifted to the shadows stretching across the parking lot. "Lauren was a bioengineer here in California. She left all that to work the front desk at the Marriott in Corvallis. Made no sense."

"Maybe she's running from something. People don't just leave a career like that for a front desk job." Angel took a sip of her beer, her gaze drifting toward the sun. "People rarely abandon a life without good reason."

Holden followed her gaze. The sky carried the hue of an orange sunset, even though it was only afternoon.

"If her past caught up to her, she would have just left, right? Why take the time to pack up all my stuff?" He tightened his grip on his water as his head throbbed, far too exhausted to piece together any sound reason Lauren would clean out their apartment and disconnect her phone.

Angel noticed. "You okay?"

"I got my ass handed to me in the woods."

"Sure did," she drawled.

"I was just trying to help. I feel useless."

Angel laughed, and Holden regretted opening up until she said, "You know, we're not here for a Boy Scout merit badge. We're not the A-Team of wilderness rescue. We're here for the evidence protocol misses." She paused, dramatically swirling her beer can before finishing, "All those IT skills and sleuthing that got us here. We can still help out around the Fort. I'm even getting comfortable walking to and from the station. Not alone, don't worry. I made Zaid go with me. That dummy needs some exercise."

Holden whistled. "A walk in the woods. That's a big deal for you."

"Yeah, yeah. Don't be too impressed. Anyway, your stuff. You can file a police report from here. Let them sort this mess out. How much is your crap actually worth to you?"

Holden thought. "Well, I liked my bed."

"Which I'm sure reminded you of Becca. Perfect opportunity to get rid of it."

"And my desktop?"

She threw him a side-eye. "How old?"

Holden shrugged. "Ten, twelve years. Fine, I see your point." Plus, he wanted to stay in Deadswitch. Find a way to not be worthless with Search and Rescue efforts to pay back Tiffany and the others.

Angel raised her beer can in a mock toast. "Here's to getting all your crap carted away for free," she declared, and drank to the crunch of tires rolling over gravel.

Holden shielded his eyes from the sun as a vehicle swerved into the parking lot. Frank was back, hopping out of the Jeep and jogging toward them, Liz in tow.

Francis barked and dashed toward the ranger, and Holden jumped up at the panic on Frank's face. "What's wrong?"

Frank slowed, wiping his brow with the back of his hand. He clutched his walkie in the other. "Wildfire up on Wolf Ridge, spreading fast. I can't get a hold of Diego to warn him."

*Wolf Ridge.* Clyde and Diego weren't the only ones in jeopardy, not if Holden had really seen Siena's face on the drone feed. And wildfire could eat up miles of California forest in mere hours. Regardless of where the research team was now, they were in trouble.

"What do you need us to do?" Angel asked as Liz darted past them into the station.

"I need to make calls," Frank said. "Go run and let Zaid know. That kook can track the spread faster than the state can. We can't waste time . . ."

Frank's voice faded behind Holden, who was already jogging up the trail toward the Fort.

# CAMERON

Tucked behind a shelf in The Other Backpack's kitchen area, a small stairwell descended into a dark basement. While Ruby expertly navigated the narrow and steep passage, Cam struggled, tempted to take the stairs on her butt. Here she was, a mountaineer, thwarted by a staircase.

When she reached the basement, the sulfur stench smacked her in the face. Ruby pulled the chain on the ceiling's one barren lightbulb, and Cam finally witnessed the source.

Paper.

To the left, sheets of drying handmade paper lined floorboards. In front of the paper, various pots, containers—even a cauldron—were filled to the brim with marinating paper slurry. Nothing smelled this bad unless it was ripe with bacteria. An interesting hobby for someone so attuned to staying free of germs. Maybe Ruby somehow knew these bacteria were safe.

To the right, hundreds of handmade books covered wall-length shelves. Cam couldn't help herself, approaching the shelf without thinking and tugging one free.

"Careful," Ruby warned.

Small ornaments decorated the book's cover: a hair ribbon,

bracelet charms, a pressed leaf. A large Yosemite National Park sticker covered the back.

"You make all these?" Cam asked.

"Gotta find some way to pass the time. Other than hunting or cleaning, of course."

Cam gently flipped open the front cover, *Day 35* written on the top of the page.

"If you wanna know if it's me filling all those pages, definitely not. Though I have a few to my name."

Cam started reading.

*Ruby gave me this journal. Says I need it if I want to stay true to who I once was. I would tell you the story of how I met her, but I don't want to waste this paper on that. I am supposed to be writing memories of home.*

The page divulged a moment from childhood. Cam checked the book's spine which read *Jeremy*, something she'd missed the first time. She looked up expectantly at Ruby.

"Wanderers, travelers, transients," she said. "All those who wind up lost in these woods. I give 'em a meal and a bed for only a night at a time, and they pay me with trinkets or things to read from back home. The ones who return pay me with their stories."

Cam stepped back, admiring the handmade journals. "These are from different people?"

"Most of 'em. Some live long enough to fill a few."

"*Live?*"

Ruby actually smiled at her. "I know it's hard for you to believe. Still don't see the truth about Lee up there. No one gets how fast folks die in these woods at first, not until they experience it for themselves. And I'm sorry that's the truth. I really am."

"But you haven't died yet," Cam countered.

Ruby raised the eyebrow above her marble. Cam wondered how she did that without it falling out.

"I'm a lot smarter than most of these folks passing through." Ruby shrugged. "I also don't leave this place much. I'm lucky with the game around the building." She pointed at Cam. "Don't you dare poach anything around these parts. You won't be the first with one of my bullets through your head."

Cam didn't know where even to begin with that statement, so she didn't address it at all.

Ruby continued as if she'd said nothing offensive. "The people who end up injured to the point of dying, they are the ones always trying to find a way out. You take good ol' Lee up there."

Disgust bubbled in Cam's gut. "You talk about him like he's a corpse."

"Because he *is*. And the quicker you learn that, the quicker you can protect yourself, too."

Cam couldn't swallow it. Not right now. Maybe Ruby was right—she needed to experience more. But she'd spent months in the wilderness before by herself, even twice when she ran out of supplies and first aid. How the hell could this forest be so different from the others?

"So, why are you showing me this?" Cam waved a hand at the wall. "You hinting at how I can get a room and a meal for tonight?"

"I suppose." Ruby strode toward Cam and plucked a journal from the shelves. "And to give you this. I think you'll be needing it, if you ever decide to come back. It's fresh."

Cam took the new notebook from Ruby, appreciating the lack of hair ribbons in the cover design. Instead, beer and soda labels were shellacked to the front and back. She ran a finger over an old *A&W* label, except instead of A&W it read A&V. Must be a misprint, or maybe a foreign-country knockoff.

"I'll be right back." Cam headed upstairs to the mudroom. She tucked away the journal in her backpack, though she wasn't a diary kind of person and was certain she'd forget about it until the next time she visited the tavern.

She dug from the depths of the bag her copy of *Without a Trace*. Carefully, she tore out the flyleaves containing the photos of the Deadswitch Five and slid them behind the book, taking both with her before checking the tavern for Lee.

He wasn't slumped over on the stool where she and Ruby had left him. Cam crept down the hall to the single room tucked at the back of the tavern. Two military-style bunk beds filled the darkness, and Cam could barely make out Lee in a fetal position on the bottom bunk farthest from the door. The room reeked of his festering wound, but his torso rose and fell.

A breathing corpse. She'd believe he was doomed when he actually died. For now, her plan for tomorrow was to accompany him to The Tooth and hopefully find better care.

When Cam returned to the basement, Ruby was peeling off fresh sheets of paper from her boards. "I have payment for you," Cam said, which caught Ruby's attention. She handed *Without a Trace* to the tavern keeper. "Have you read this one yet?"

Ruby shook her head as she flipped through some pages. "Can't say I have."

"It's about a group of women who got lost in these very woods."

Ruby cracked a smile. She smiled at the strangest things. "Is that so? They ever find 'em?"

"No. Actually . . ." Cam held out one flyleaf. "I was wondering if any of them passed through." She pointed to the photo of Avery that she'd taken and sent to John Lawson. "Mostly her."

Ruby took the flyleaf from Cam and held it close to her face. Her eye flicked back and forth as she studied the different photos, then swiveled to Cam with a strange emotion. Suspicion? Surprise? She couldn't place it exactly, and Ruby was too good at quickly masking her expressions.

"You have," Cam blurted.

"I don't remember all the details," Ruby said. "It was a long time ago. Years." She gestured to the shelves. "I've had a wall of visitors since then, but yes." Ruby handed the flyleaf back to Cam. "She once passed through here."

More hope than Cam had felt in years surged through her chest. "Was she alone?"

Ruby nodded. "Think she felt guilty about that, though. Wasn't supposed to be alone. Left some folks behind—maybe those other girls—to venture off by herself. I remember that much because of how stupid I thought she was. Strange thing was she was a baby to this part of the woods—you know, the *real* woods—but she knew where to find me. Knew I'd be here. And even though I pried for the name of who sent her here, she kept insisting no one had."

"Where was she headed?"

Ruby thought for a moment, grimacing before shaking her head. "Around these parts, the only place babies go is The Tooth. They usually spot it from some mountain, or get word from a map or another traveler. The seasoned drifters know better, of course. Avoid that place like the plague."

This wasn't the first time Ruby mentioned her hesitancy—and possible disdain—of The Tooth. "Why do they avoid it?"

Ruby's marble rolled around in her eye socket a bit, or maybe that was just a trick of the dim light. "Better to be experienced to really understand, but let's just say, misery and desperation are festering wounds when they aren't nipped in the bud. And people will believe anything when scared. And that's all The Tooth is. Just a bunch of scared folks feeding off each other."

The information was too vague to be helpful, but at least Cam now knew to watch her back. She was letting her guard down far too much with both Ruby and Lee. But it wasn't like she could help it. Yesterday she had very little idea where the fuck she was going, and now she had advice. No, even better than advice. *Leads.*

"That's why you're here, then, aye?" Ruby jabbed her finger at the photo of Avery. "To find her?"

"Aye." Cam wasn't about to mention she'd left her team behind to do so.

"Well . . ." She handed the flyleaf back to Cam. "I hope she's one of the lucky ones."

"Is she up here?" Cam turned back toward the shelves. What she wouldn't give to find Avery's journal. The journal was the validation she needed.

"Hate to say I can't remember. You'd be surprised how many folks this place swallows, and how many folks I've seen pass through here." She gestured to the shelves again. "A whole wall of 'em."

"Yeah, you said that." Cam absently shook her head. Ruby couldn't be right. If Deadswitch swallowed so many people, she would have heard about it. There would be documentaries, and more books than just John Lawson's. Maybe this area would even be closed off by the federal government.

"Can I look?"

"Sure thing," Ruby said. "I didn't bring you down here just to show off. I let everyone look and search and read. If anything, hopefully they find something they like in the stories."

Cam needed no more encouragement.

As Ruby returned to the tavern's ground floor, perhaps to check on Lee, Cam went to work searching each shelf. The names on the spines were all handwritten, sometimes big, sometimes small. Sometimes upside down or all the way to one side. Names often repeated along the spines, even though Ruby had claimed only a few patrons had filled up more than one journal.

Each spine took her a moment to search, and it wasn't the quick scan she was hoping for. But she searched every single spine.

Her only glimmer of hope was finding the name *Paige*. Paige Reeves was one of the Deadswitch Five and had disappeared with Avery. But when Cam flipped through the pages of the journal, there was no sign this Paige was the same woman. Memories of childhood filled most of the journal, many abstract. There wasn't a mention of Paige's half sister, Tasha, only memories of before this Paige was a teenager, and a long passage about her parents' divorce. Cam couldn't recall if Lawson's book mentioned when

Paige and Tasha became half sisters, and she'd read the damn thing so much that she would remember. Lawson didn't like to keep his focus on anyone but Avery for too long.

Many journals didn't have names on the spines. It would take Cam days to read through them all to figure out if one belonged to Avery. She couldn't afford to stay up either, too exhausted from helping Lee get here. And she'd need to keep her wits about her if she was traveling to The Tooth tomorrow.

The smell of meat wafted into the basement, and Cam pressed a hand to her growling stomach. God, when was the last time she ate? Not at any point today.

She turned to see Ruby with two bowls of something steaming. "Payment processed." She smirked at her own joke. "Here, before it gets too cold."

Cam thanked Ruby and took a bowl. Chunks of meat and an unfamiliar root vegetable swam in an impressively thick broth. Herbs speckled the entire dish.

"Apologies if it's a little tough—I overwash and overcook everything."

Eating this stew could end up being a god-awful idea. Ruby was weird. Cam didn't know her. On top of that, if Ruby was right about infection, then eating a stew made from this forest's animals and plants could poison her, or, at the very least, give her the shits.

But this—this was very much not the end of Cam's string of potentially poor decisions. One thing her travels had taught her— even her travels through the wilderness—was to partake in local customs. In a lot of ways, it was how the street-smart survived.

Or how they wound up dead.

Ruby nodded toward the stairwell. "Gonna go eat. Thought you'd want to peruse more."

Cam shook her head. "I'm done for the night. I'll join you."

She followed Ruby up the stairs, and they sat at the table closest to the kitchen. The bulb above flickered. Cam waited, and when Ruby crammed a heaping spoonful into her mouth, Cam dipped her own spoon into the broth and sipped. The liquid was thick, earthy, and undersalted, but good.

"What's the meat?" Cam asked.

"Venison." Ruby stabbed at a meat chunk. "Most edible meat in these parts is venison. Most evolved, I think. They know what to seek out to not get poisoned."

Cam scooped up a chunk of meat with her spoon and slid it into her mouth. Ruby was right—it was tough, but fuck, Cam was hungry.

A book lay on the table next to Ruby's hand. Unlike the journals, the cover lacked gaud.

"Something I gotta warn you about, before you leave." Ruby pushed the book toward Cam. The handwritten title read *Southeast Foraging*. Cam abandoned her stew to flip through the first few pages, which were filled with sketches of plants and insects and how to prepare them.

"I know you're on a mission and all. Honestly, I haven't met a lot of new folks who want to go deeper on purpose. But The Tooth is where you'll get stuck if you're not careful. You want to stay healthy and able to find your girl, if she's still alive. Whatever you do, don't eat their food."

Cam studied the intricate hand-drawn sketches. She'd had similar Sierra Nevada foraging guides throughout her life, but they were all mass-produced. This one was made with love.

"You're giving this to me?"

Ruby nodded once. "I've made a few."

Cam closed the book, caressing its cover. "Why are you being so nice? You don't even know me."

Ruby smiled one of her smiles again. "Truth be told, baby, I'm nice to everyone who passes through, if they get past my gun. And I try to prepare 'em for what's out there. It's a sad thing that most don't take my advice. But I see something in you."

"You think I'll take your advice?" The question wasn't supposed to be as snarky as it sounded leaving Cam's mouth.

Ruby seemed to understand this. "Yes. Because you want

something deeper than saving your own skin. You're not just surviving to get out. You're surviving for someone else."

In the morning, a few sunbeams broke through the otherwise dreary sky, and Cam could finally see what glittered in the trees all around the tavern. Copper squares the size of a credit card strung like a garland in the fir tops.

"Are those solar cells?" she asked in awe.

"Made 'em myself," Ruby replied proudly, following Cam. "You'd be surprised at the amount of garbage turning up in these woods. Can't explain how or why." She sighed. "Lee, it's been a real treat. I mean it."

Lee hobbled outside. "Thanks, Rubes. Thanks for doing your best to make all this bearable." He didn't smile as he spoke.

Ever since she woke up, Cam had avoided studying him too hard. His sunken eyes, pale lips, veins bleeding like ink beneath his skin roiled her stomach not with disgust, but sadness. What disgusted her was the smell of his wound, which reminded her of fish guts rotting in the sun. Ruby was right; they'd done everything to clean it, and it didn't matter at all.

Ruby turned to Cam. "Remember what I told you."

Cam nodded, their conversation from last night returning.

*Whatever you do, don't eat their food.*

Ruby made The Tooth sound like a miserable place, but that was where Lee wanted to go. Asking Cam would likely be the last thing he asked anyone. She couldn't say no. Plus, a part of her was curious to interact with the people in this Tooth place. Maybe one of them had seen Avery recently.

"Thanks for everything," Cam said. "Maybe I'll see you soon."

Ruby grinned. "Don't forget to fill that journal. Gotta pay up when you return."

The flat and muddy road to The Tooth stretched right through the center of a valley. Still, their journey was gruesomely slow.

Lee's festering wound bled through his makeshift wrap in no time. The discharge stank worse by the second. A few hours in and he couldn't walk without help, though he refused to take breaks.

"I just wanna get there," he kept saying. "I just wanna make it."

Fortunately for her, Lee remained upright and breathing, even as the clouds rolled in and the rain picked up. Small divots that had once been footprints became more frequent, though there was no real way to tell how many people had traveled through here. Too many to have all come from Deadswitch, yet they had to have come from somewhere.

Up ahead, a sharp crag jutted behind the treetops. The *Tooth*.

"That's a little on the nose," grunted Cam as Lee put more of his weight on her.

"There's a lot of this place . . . that's on the nose," he gasped.

Lashed logs formed a perimeter, the fence roughly three times her height. While she couldn't see anything beyond the wall, its curvature gave away the commune's size. It may not be very large —perhaps an acre—but for a place like this, it was a fucking metropolis.

The wide fence gate was a concoction of chain link, parts of a rusty car body, and a few brown road signs from national forest areas. Hooded watchers wearing a mix of ratty hiking clothes stared down at them from the fence's catwalk. Cam hesitated in her approach, expecting to explain herself in order to pass. They carried no obvious weapons, though that didn't mean they weren't there.

*Hey, dumbass,* her brain politely chirped. *This looks like a bad idea.*

Upon her meeting Lee, he'd said she could find other travelers here so she didn't have to be alone. But being alone didn't bother her. Desperate people, on the other hand . . . She couldn't imagine that a commune in such a malicious forest was filled with calm, levelheaded individuals.

Maybe she was wrong. She hoped she was wrong. Regardless, she had to stay focused. Cam had fulfilled her promise of getting Lee to The Tooth. Now, she just needed to see if she could glean any answers about what had happened to Avery.

The gate to The Tooth squealed, the doors yawning open.

Cam shifted her shoulder to better bear Lee's weight. "That was easy."

"They like people," Lee said.

That didn't make Cam feel any better, though she was soon distracted as she soaked in the village.

The fang-shaped crag stood tall and proud at the commune's center, before it a smoking bonfire and a few idlers dressed similarly, clothes worn and repatched beyond belief. Grimy, but not filthy.

A ring of small cabins lined the perimeter, reminding her of buildings in national park history centers—architecture left over from early pioneer days, though these cabins weren't as well preserved. This was the fault of the rain more than anything, moss and lichen crawling over soggy beams. Someone on a ladder worked on one cabin. She couldn't get a good look at anyone's face with their hoods up and, on instinct, tugged at hers with her free hand.

The air stank of shit, the culprit possibly a lack of hygiene and plumbing.

Or wounds.

Cam glanced down at Lee's leg, his bandage so soaked with discharge that it glistened.

Lee pointed left. "That way."

Cam dragged Lee toward the cabins. "There a medic or something?"

"They can't help me."

He was so sure. Ruby had been, too. How many people—villagers—had Lee seen rot away and die from a cut? The village wasn't bustling, but more people were here than Cam had ever seen this deep into a wilderness area—even normal wilderness areas. Everyone they passed busied themselves with chores, from fencing repairs to filling in potholes with handmade wooden shovels. One of the pothole fillers looked up as they passed, his eyes hesitating on Lee's leg. His mouth hung limp, as though that was the resting state of his face. Maybe he was just focusing all his energy on staying in control of his motor functions. The way he jerked while shoveling dirt hinted at a neurological disorder.

"Here," Lee said.

Cam blinked and refocused on the cabin to her left. Few of the door's planks were recently replaced, giving an impression of a smile with only a few teeth left. Cam propped the door open and helped Lee inside, the stuffiness of the dark room engulfing her as she shut the door behind her.

"C-Cam?"

She froze and then turned from the door to a man seated on the far bed. On the stump near his feet, a wick burned atop a melted lump of wax. The light was just enough to illuminate the familiar contours of his face.

"No fucking way," she breathed. Her mind raced to jam together the pieces, but hell, why should she even try if a curveball was around every goddamn corner?

Scruffy, filthy, and tired, a young Isaac grinned at her. "You're alive."

# HOLDEN

The Fort burst with the energy of a collective nervous wreck.

Maidei and Zaid tag teamed monitoring the feeds to the cameras Zaid had set up all over Deadswitch Wilderness, trying to pinpoint locations of anyone in the woods, SAR or not. They sat at one end of the long table in the Hub while Tiffany stood at the other, a topographical map spread in front of her. The walkie perched on her hip spouted chatter from several fire watch towers. She pressed thumbtacks into the map, tracking the spread.

"If we had the drone, this would be so much easier," Zaid lamented. He still hadn't figured out a way to reactivate it remotely since it died flying over the research cabin. Wherever it had crash-landed, it was about to get a little crispy.

"Not something we need to worry about now," Maidei reminded Zaid, adjusting her wire-framed glasses as she shuffled through the feeds on her screen.

Angel sat near Tiffany, borrowing one of Zaid's laptops to build a database and dashboard for emergency response. She smashed the refresh button on an aerial image that refused to load. "This satellite internet is shit, Zaid."

Zaid still clenched his long, unruly hair in both fists, tugging. "Don't blame me, blame the billionaires."

Angel only grunted, grabbing the mug Holden passed to her. He busied himself brewing fresh coffee. After learning no one had eaten all day, he also whipped together pigs in a blanket from stale flour and cans of Vienna sausages lying around in the pantry. He fielded some of Angel's database questions as the food baked, and reviewed the spreadsheet for errors between loads of laundry. The bed linens needed to be washed in case any evacuees landed here for shelter.

As he laid out a few snack-filled plates, static burst from a second walkie lying on the table. "This is Frank. Anyone copy?"

Angel snatched up the walkie. "What's up, Frank? Umm . . . over."

"Chopper located Clyde and Diego on Agnes and evacuated them without issue. Both are fine—no smoke inhalation or anything—so they're being dropped off at a local assembly point. I'm picking them up now."

"That's good news," Tiffany said.

Frank continued. "The part of the team headed over to Lucille is in less danger, but their plan to hike north is out of the question. Diego and I will reconvene in the morning to figure out next steps. We'll need to reallocate people and resources to Warm Zones."

Hot Zone, Warm Zone . . . Holden wished he'd taken two minutes to catch up on wildfire lingo.

Maidei seemed to understand, and held out her hand for the walkie, which Angel passed over. She tucked a few braids behind her ear before pressing the call button. "Frank, it's Maidei. How big of a Hot Zone are we talking about?"

"Around ten thousand acres. Only Cal Fire allowed between Dogstooth Lake and Agnes."

Holden followed Tiffany's finger as she pointed to Dogstooth Lake west of Mount Agnes. "No one's allowed in this area except for firefighters," she said, as though sensing Holden needed a blatant explanation.

"What about the research team?" Holden asked, and caught Maidei's eyes, who frowned.

"What are the plans for the research team investigation?" Radio silence met Maidei's question, so she added, "Over."

Frank finally responded. "I . . . don't know yet. Rescuer safety needs to be taken into consideration. We'll know more tomorrow."

"Copy that," she muttered.

Apprehension filled Holden and remained after everyone called it a night. Despite his exhaustion, his sleep was tumultuous. Fed up with Holden's tossing and turning, Francis left the bed around midnight to sleep on the floor.

Contentious conversation filtered into the attic at dawn, waking Holden. He threw on clothes and hurried downstairs. Frank had arrived with Clyde and Diego, both thankfully unsinged.

Diego pressed his palms against the tabletop as he leaned forward. "Everything about our strategy needs to be reconsidered."

"The only thing the fire changes is that there should be more of an effort to find them!" Clyde paced by the windows, rubbing his eyes. "They are the only ones with a permit registered inside the Hot Zone. They're the highest priority."

"That isn't how it works," Diego said. "Highest priority goes to anyone in Warm Zones. Hikers, rangers, and anyone else surrounding the fire is at risk if the wind changes, and evacuating them won't kill my team."

Clyde dropped his hand, his eyes rimmed red. "What about *my daughter*?"

Diego raised his voice. "We were there, Clyde. You saw as well as I did. That cabin hasn't been touched in years."

"You went to the cabin?" Holden blurted.

Neither responded immediately as Clyde glowered at Diego with fists clenched, his demeanor completely different from the man who'd lent Holden his boots.

"Yes," Diego said. "We consolidated gear and hiked through the night. Made it to the cabin a little after the fire started."

If Holden was mathing right, they'd cleared over forty miles in two days. And Clyde had to be thirty years older than Holden, who'd almost passed out at mile eighteen.

*Stop feeling sorry for yourself.* Only one person here had discovered Siena's audio files. That was his strength. Not scaling mountains.

"So Cam, Siena, the others . . . they could be in the Warm Zone, too."

"That's where my money is." Diego straightened up and crossed his arms, hesitantly watching Clyde, who'd stopped his pacing and now stared at Holden. Desperation glinted in his eyes; he was looking to Holden for hope.

Siena hadn't mentioned another location in her recordings, but that didn't mean another location didn't exist. "Clyde, do you know anything about your daughter's project?"

Clyde's throat bobbed as he swallowed. "I should have been paying closer attention to her career."

"I've been over this with Frank." Diego swept his hand over the Wolf Ridge portion of the map. "He called the school. No one knows of any other location or cabin in the woods they would have wanted to visit."

"No other glaciers?" Holden asked.

"Not within hiking distance."

Tiffany entered the Hub, freshly showered and carrying her boots.

"Where are you going?" Diego's tone bordered on accusatory, prompting a raised eyebrow from Tiffany.

"Down to the station. Going to help Frank with supply runs." She sat, slipped her feet into her boots, and tied her laces. She was at ease here, in these hills. She'd been here with her father all those years ago, spending time in that little cabin near Glass Lake. Tiffany knew the woods. She was the one to ask.

"Tiffany," Holden began, "are there any other places your dad would have wanted the team to visit? Anywhere else he spent time?"

A hint of suspicion passed over Tiffany's face, disappearing so quickly that Holden must have imagined it.

She tied her second boot and sat up. "I don't know. He didn't really talk to me about the details of his work." She placed her hands on her knees and bit the corner of her bottom lip. "But Siena did, once. Not a place my dad visited, but somewhere she wanted to go."

Clyde swiveled toward her. "Where?"

"The High Sierra Conservationists' cabin—the group to which her mother belonged. Southeast of Mount Lucille, so a bit out of the way. You can't get there easily from Glass Lake Trailhead. They would have had to bushwhack through the valley." Tiffany shrugged. "But if there's no evidence the team hiked up Wolf Ridge, it wouldn't hurt to look if it's safe."

Diego nodded. "Our SAR team's north of there. Their original trajectory toward Mount Charlotte is no longer safe. I can send them south toward the conservationists' cabin." Clyde's shoulders sagged in relief, and Diego added, "There's no guarantee we'll find anything."

"But it's something," Clyde said. "I just don't want to stop looking. That's all I want."

Diego gave Holden a small nod, as if to tell him *good job*. Tiffany was the one who'd mentioned the cabin. Holden had done little but ask the right question, but maybe it was questions, not answers, they needed right now. Seeds of hope.

The solutions would come later.

Tiffany and Clyde left to hike down to the station, Tiffany to help Frank, and Clyde to call Teresa with updates. Diego took his walkie outside to relay the new orders to the SAR team, and Holden ventured upstairs in hopes of a shower. Unfortunately for him, Angel was hogging the only clean bathroom. He waited in the hall for a few minutes as she sang some pop song at the top of her lungs.

Maidei's door stood open. Now was as good a time as any to tell her about the change in SAR plans.

She folded a pile of clothes on the bed as he entered, placing each garment in an open suitcase.

"You're leaving?" he asked.

She glanced up, and then wordlessly continued folding.

"Sorry." He didn't know why he was apologizing—it just felt like the right thing to do. She was here because of him, wasn't she?

*No.* She was here because this place haunted her. Deadswitch had taken a part of her she couldn't get back, not without answers.

"I came to convince Frank to believe you." Maidei folded the last shirt and laid it in the suitcase, then closed it. "And I did that. Huang—my husband—is more understanding than I deserve. And my son is going away to college. I need to be home."

He understood, but Maidei wasn't giving herself enough credit.

"I saw our friend again," he said.

She took a deep breath when she looked at him, her eyes cautious but patient.

"Up on the trail," Holden said. "Right before I came back down. I thought . . . I mean, I could have been hallucinating."

"Your buck?" Maidei asked, and Holden nodded.

Right before Holden saw Siena in the drone footage, Holden had told Maidei about a buck made of shadow that he'd seen at the ranger station. She'd told him about getting lost in the Deadswitch frontcountry for days as a shadow stalked her. They had meant to return to the conversation.

"You aren't only here for the research team," Holden said. "And you aren't only here to help me."

Maidei jerked the zipper around her suitcase. "If this is your way of convincing me to stay, it won't work."

"No one believed you fifteen years ago. Your funding was stripped, even though you cared about what you found, didn't you? Those pines spread like a virus, and you told me—what was it? You found something that could change our fundamental understanding of biology."

"What Zaid and I found has nothing to do with what I saw when I was lost." Maidei spoke with rapid frustration. "And nothing to do with Dr. Siena Dupont's disappearance, nor the *imaginary* study you found on that drive. Even our shadows could be different things, or coincidental hallucinations."

"But what if it's all related?" If Tiffany hadn't entered the Hub this morning, Holden wouldn't have thought to ask her about other locations in the woods. They wouldn't have learned about the conservationists' cabin. "You and Zaid have studied Deadswitch in a way no one else has. You may still know things that can help."

"And Zaid is staying. He pretty much lives here."

"Zaid didn't disappear in the woods like you did." Zaid also didn't seem to care about anything other than his own tech, though Holden forwent mentioning that part.

"Correlation doesn't equal causation, Holden. It's one of the first things you learn as a scientist."

"I'm not a scientist." It was a dumb retort, but to his surprise, a smile broke through Maidei's irritation.

"No, you aren't. If you were, you'd be far less likely to act on your conclusions so impulsively." It sounded like an insult, though her eyes were soft. "You can reach me by phone via the ranger station if you need me."

"You . . ." He drifted off, shaking his head. By her expression, nothing would convince her to stay, and that made him feel . . . sad? Hollow? The emotion was almost overwhelming, and he didn't understand it. Maidei had a family. All he knew of her was what he'd learned over the past few weeks, and yet he wanted her to stay. He wanted everyone to stay. Rooming with all these people in this ugly huge house, being part of a group . . . it felt *right*. Which was silly, and borderline childish. He was just lonely. He'd *been* lonely for a long time.

"Can you stay a few more days?" he asked. "Please? I won't

ask you to stay longer than that. I just . . ." He didn't have a convincing argument to keep her here. Soon, *he* wouldn't have a reason to stay here either, especially if the fire spread and the rescue mission switched to recovery. There were no more leads, nothing he could do to help.

*Except.*

She watched him in silence, probably waiting for him to collect himself from an apparent brain fart.

"Think about it," he finally said. "Please."

She nodded. "Okay, Holden. I'll think about it."

He smiled and then hurried from the room. He still had a question, not about Siena, but Avery Mathis. And sure, correlation *didn't* equal causation, but Holden wasn't a scientist. He was the one searching where others were not.

He took the stairs by twos and sped out the front door. Dusty orange light filtered through the smoky atmosphere, somehow both subtle and overpowering. Diego stood in the clearing where Frank usually parked his Jeep, talking to the SAR team through a satellite phone. Holden waited for him to finish, and when Diego noticed him, he didn't hide his annoyance.

"What is it?" he asked.

"I have a question about what you said the other night at camp." Holden scratched the back of his head. If Diego was already annoyed just by Holden's presence, then this would really blow him away. "About The Mother."

"Really, kid?" Diego drawled. "That fire is zero percent contained, and this is what you want to waste my time with?"

Holden ignored him. "You know of Avery Mathis? She disappeared with four other women seven years ago somewhere around Wolf Ridge."

"The famous one, yeah," Diego said. "What does this have to do with—"

"Right before she disappeared, she was playing a video game set in a forest where a young girl is sacrificed to a harvest goddess called The Mother."

Diego raised an eyebrow. "The Mother isn't a unique name for a goddess."

"Weird coincidence, though, right?"

"You trying to convince me The Mother is real or something? Seriously?" Diego snorted a laugh and strode past him. "Shouldn't have told you bedtime stories, kid. Now if you don't mind, I have people to rescue."

Holden took a deep breath, the urge to let it go conflicting with the fact Diego was a complete and utter twat and didn't *deserve* for Holden to just let it go. He spun. "This may be shocking to you, but I'm not an idiot."

Diego continued his exit, waving a dismissive hand.

Holden pressed on. "I just wanted to know if there are any cult members left. Descendants or a modern branch, or whatever. It's a yes or no question, and I figured you'd know out of anyone. But go ahead. Go be important."

Diego slowed, casting a look over his shoulder. "What are you really asking?"

"The possibility of whether freaks living out in the woods have been—I don't know—taking part in human sacrifices, or something. Is it possible the researchers could have been kidnapped? That those women seven years ago were kidnapped?"

This caught his attention. Diego paused and turned back toward Holden, wearing a look of alarm. He said nothing for a moment, his brow furrowed.

Holden crossed his arms. "Don't let me keep you long. I know you're *busy*."

Diego simpered, but then said, "The cult is long gone, but yeah, I suppose there could be inspired weirdos."

"They'd had to have learned something about the original cult. Spells, rituals . . ."

"I'm sure there's some garbage on the internet. But there is a closed exhibit at the visitor center. Was open until some locals complained about it being sacrilegious and disturbing. You know how rural people are."

"Is it?" Holden asked. "Disturbing, I mean."

"Depends how much of it you believe. You run along and find out. I'm sure Frank can get the nice lady at the front desk to give you a tour."

Holden didn't give Diego the satisfaction of reacting, and the SAR lead disappeared down the trail to the station.

Even though two separate SAR teams failed to uncover anything at the cabin, Siena's audio files were proof the research team had made it to Agnes, but weren't there now. And with a wildfire raging, only one person would help him turn over every strange and culty stone.

# SIENA

Emmett paced the small interior of the outpost. "If that was The Shadow, then what does it want? Why did it lead us here?"

"The same reason he didn't come after us in the swamp." Siena sat at the table with the hand-painted map, copying every structure and trail to her own over a steaming cup of instant coffee fresh from the camp stove.

"Because it wants to lead us into a trap?" Emmett asked.

"Because he wants to show off."

Emmett stalled in his pacing, sipped his coffee, and swallowed. "You keep calling it a *he*."

"Isaac called him *he*, I think." She couldn't remember if that actually was true, but it didn't matter. The Shadow had told her what he was the first time she ever saw him, and if she explained this to Emmett, he'd harass her about taking her meds.

"Why would *he* want to show off?" Emmett asked.

"He's trying to stall me. He knows I want to figure him out."

"Maybe the more he stalls you, the easier he can use you," Emmett said.

*He will hurt you and force you to do things more horrible than you can dream.* That was what Isaac had told her. These horrible things were still undefined, which scared her more than this game The Shadow played with her.

Siena glanced up from the maps. The sweat beading on Emmett's forehead glistened in their camp light. Again, he was shaken. Maybe even on the verge of tears.

"Are you upset because you're worried he'll hurt me?" she asked.

Emmett took a deep breath. "I'm worried he has an agenda, and whatever that agenda is will inevitably slow us down. You'll die if we're stuck here too long."

So he fully believed what Isaac had said about The Shadow killing her. "You weren't like this at the cabin," she countered. "You thought we'd be too vulnerable if we left. Did Isaac's death change your mind?"

He hesitated, wiping the sweat from his face. "Isaac's a part of it. I told you, I had time to think."

"Fine." She pulled the elastic out of her hair and fixed her braid, listening beyond the outpost walls. No rain yet. No *hunger* rumbling from the forest. Nothing but crickets, the occasional rustle, and a lone howl in the distance. The howl was new; other than The Shadow, she'd yet to cross a predator in the Briardark.

She lifted the shutter near the table, the night so dark that not even the firs and maples at the edge of the clearing were visible. It was her third night traveling. One of those nights she hadn't slept, the other two spent in these outposts. Unless the black gash across the sky made another appearance, there would be no wall between them and this darkness tomorrow night.

She'd absently scraped a huge divot in the shutter with her fingernail, so she closed it and distracted herself with her bag, which needed repacking, pulling everything out onto the table. Her storm-drenched clothes had finally dried, so she folded them.

At the bottom of her pack, Siena rediscovered the mysterious deck of cards she'd taken from the research cabin. She repacked everything except the cards and the first aid kit, and sat back in her chair. From the kit, she retrieved an alcohol wipe and tweezers.

Emmett approached the table and picked up the pack of cards. "We playing slapjack?"

She smiled. "You hate card games. Plus, gin rummy is more fun." She motioned to the table. "Let me clean your cut first."

He sat in the chair across from her, peeled the bandage off, and extended his hand.

Siena studied the cut with a frown. The edges of his torn skin were inflamed, the inside of the cut glistening with a yellow patina. "How did it get infected so quickly?" She ripped open the alcohol wipe packet. "Does it hurt?"

Emmett shrugged. "Kind of."

She snapped on her kit's only set of neoprene gloves and cleaned the cut, conscious of Emmett's winces when she took extra time scraping away the pus. She liberally applied antibacterial ointment before covering and waterproofing the wound with gauze and tape.

"Do you have gloves?" she asked. "Even just knit gloves? Mine are too small for you, but you should keep that hand covered."

"Gloves weren't on my list when I left the cabin." He returned his attention to the cards at the table's edge. "So, what's with them?"

Siena picked the cards up, slid them from their delicate box, and fanned the blank faces across the table.

Emmett shook his head. "I don't get it."

Siena shuffled the cards and stacked them, trying to remember how to draw tarot cards. These weren't tarot, but the presentation felt similar. During one of her high school sleepovers, a girl named Krista drew Siena's cards, convinced they predicted a prom date in Siena's future. No one had asked her to the prom that year. There was a reason science had been her most reliable boyfriend.

She flipped over the top card. The card wasn't blank, even though they'd all shown blank faces a moment before. And it wasn't one of the two cards she'd dealt for herself in the past.

A withered old man framed by branch prison bars stared at

her, his eyes hollow and haunted. The man's face was so wizened, it looked melted.

**The Warden.**

If the man in the drawing was a Warden, then he wasn't peering out of prison, but looking in, at her. A chill ran up her arms. Her intention was to deal for Emmett, and somehow the deck knew that.

"I don't get it," Emmett repeated.

"Just wait." She drew the second card. This time, she recognized it, but it still wasn't a card she'd played for herself. She'd seen it on the table in the cabin kitchen right before she left. The face of the card was onyx, **The Shadow** written in white script across the top.

Emmett stared in bewilderment at the two cards. Siena swept them from the table and shuffled them back into the deck. She fanned out all the cards faceup, showing him they were all blank. Then she stacked the cards and dealt for him again.

**The Warden.**
**The Shadow.**

"If this is some dumb magic trick, it isn't funny," he said. "Where did you find these cards?"

"In the cabin." She scooped the cards into the deck and dealt two for herself. They were the same cards she'd dealt for herself before: the woman with the arrow in her chest—**The Butcher's Daughter;** and the upside-down evergreen tree—**The Verdantry**.

Emmett steepled his hands in front of his face. "I give up. What's the trick?"

"There is no trick," Siena said.

His voice rose. "Stop with the bullshit."

All she'd done was show him. She wanted him to wonder just like her. She wanted him to look for answers, not just demand them from her.

This was a mistake.

"I shouldn't have taken them out," she said. "I don't know

how they work, which is why I brought them with me. I want to run tests on them when we get out of here."

As she stacked the cards to put them away, Emmett's hand fell on her wrist. "I'm sorry. I'm glad you showed me, I'm just . . ." He drifted off, but she knew. He was fragile right now. Traumatized by this place, and from putting Isaac out of his misery. And perhaps something else he wasn't telling her.

Rain pattered across the roof as the storm began.

"We should go to bed," she said.

Siena lay next to Emmett on the floor of the outpost. Rain spilled from the eaves, and beyond the clearing, the trees groaned as though they couldn't bear their own weight. The familiar sounds comforted her, and eventually she dozed off, before being jolted awake by sunlight beaming through an open shutter.

It was late. Too late. She reached out for Emmett, her hand coming to rest on his empty sleeping bag.

Siena shot up and dashed across the outpost's creaking floor. As she threw open the door and stepped forward, thick vegetation ensnared her feet. She cursed, freeing herself from the vines and ferns.

"Emmett!" She scanned the dense thicket. Where was he?

The thought of Isaac disappearing and reappearing decades older careened into her mind. "Oh no," she whispered. She took a deep breath and shouted Emmett's name into the woods.

The brush to her left rustled.

"Jesus, can't a guy take a shit?" he growled.

"I'm sorry," she gasped in relief. "I thought the worst. You can't blame me, I—"

The sight of him throttled her words. His eyes were sunken, and sweat glistened across the whole of his face. He wiped his too-pale lips with the back of his hand.

"Did you throw up?" she asked. He shook his head, but she wasn't convinced. "Don't lie."

"It's probably exhaustion," he admitted.

So he had puked. Her eyes dropped to his hand. The bandage looked like it hadn't been changed in a week, yellow and red discharge seeping through the taped gauze.

She led him inside to the table. Emmett sat across from her and winced as he extended his hand. She unwrapped the bandage, trying to mask her panic at the wound filled with green pus, the rough edges surrounding the skin now black. She caught a whiff of death.

"It fucking hurts," he hissed.

Siena bent over and plucked her first aid kit from her open bag. "There must be something stuck in it." She tilted his palm toward the light, snapped on her gloves and set to work cleaning the wound. When she'd scooped out enough pus, she carefully extracted a piece of splinter they'd missed.

Emmett groaned. "Seriously?"

"At least we found the problem." Siena opened and dumped a hydrogen peroxide packet across the cut, and Emmett grunted, squeezing his eyes shut. She then swabbed a large glob of antibiotic ointment over the wound before bandaging it again.

"We can rest today," she offered. A bit of rest would be nice for both of them. She rubbed her knee, surprised it wasn't tender. The sprain must not have been as bad as she'd thought.

"I'll be fine." Emmett lowered his bandaged hand and stood from the table. "We need to keep moving."

As Siena packed away her first aid kit and tied her boots, she hoped Emmett wasn't pushing himself beyond his limits for her sake. How he rested his weight against the wall as he waited for her hinted at his exhaustion.

"I'm fine," he said again when he caught her looking. "Let's go."

They left the outpost, but their way forward was proof of Murphy's Law. Their path wasn't so much a maze as it was a wall, every tree, brush, fern, and vine symbiotic with one another, entangled like a nervous system. The canopy covered the understory like a thick layer of skin. And it was so dark in the thicket that Siena equipped her headlamp.

She kept her focus on Emmett's backpack. Despite how terrible he'd looked a few hours ago, he persistently progressed using the sheer brute force of his body. That was, at least, until they encountered a crowded grove of evergreens harder to navigate than a cavern system. The air stank so heavily of vegetative decay that Siena thought she might choke as she took off her pack and sidestepped through.

They finally emerged from the grove, but not from the darkness. Emmett's light flashed across a brook, and he voiced his exhaustion. "We need to stop."

Emmett found a sheltered site between a trio of young spruce, the patch of earth drier than anywhere else. He helped Siena roll out a tarp and anchor another between the trees to stay dry. She took out the lantern and first aid kit. Discharge soaked his bandage, but the wound hadn't worsened since this morning.

"I feel like I'm being punished," he said. "This place, this Shadow, this fucking splinter. All of it is punishment."

Siena wrapped gauze around his hand. "Punishment for what?"

"For what I did to you."

She scoffed in surprise. What did he want from her? Sympathy? For the better part of a decade, she'd trusted him with every cell in her body. The safety she'd felt with him was only an illusion. She'd carried that pain far longer than he would carry this splinter infection.

"If that were the case, then I am also being punished for what you did, which isn't very fair." Siena tucked away her medical supplies. The rain quieted, the surrounding emerald darkness deepening.

"You already know I'm sorry," he said. "I don't know how many times I need to apologize."

He couldn't be serious. "You want to have this conversation now?"

"I'll keep saying it until you believe me."

"I believe you," she said. "I know you're sorry for stealing the data."

Auditing the database logs last year, Siena had discovered a login stamp from her machine and a full database export at 4:30 a.m. She may have been Dr. Feyrer's favorite, but if he ever found out she'd exported all their glacial emission data from a secure server, he'd kill her. Except she'd never do such a thing.

A few weeks later, she stole Emmett's phone before it locked, and found the truth in an email to his boss.

**RE: Emmett Ghosh has shared 'Untitled.zip'**
**Brock Belmont <belmont@cotwo.tech>**
**Thank you.**

A tree groaned in the distance until a branch snapped, but Siena kept her attention on Emmett. "I even believe you would have atoned if I'd let you. That you would have quit COtwo and deleted the data you stole on your way out the door, even though it would have been easier to promise me a fucking planet." She fought to control her rage—her weakness. She couldn't let him write this off as hysterics, not again. "I believe you're sorry for the corporate espionage, Emmett. And I forgive you for that part."

"If you've forgiven me, then why are we like this?" He gestured to the woods, but she knew what he meant. "The reason COtwo wanted the emission data was to see if it merited a grant. I fought for you so they could invest in you. And they did. You got your money, and I've been tortured for a year. So *why are you and I still so fucking broken?*"

"Because there were two lies, Emmett. Two wrongs you committed. The lie about the research is the only thing you think you're at fault for, but you're forgetting how you lied about my paranoia. My illness." Her mind returned to the night she confronted him about the database, and everything he said to make her question her own sanity:

*Let's rewind a second. You think I went on to your laptop at four in the morning, hacked into a database, and exported everything?*

*What value does a thirty-year-old glacial emissions dataset even have? Why would I want it?*

*Dr. Reyes put you on a new med a few weeks ago, right?*

*Maybe you sleepwalked.*

*Maybe you're paranoid.*

*Maybe you're not in remission after all.*

She wished the realization crossing his face wasn't so goddamn stark, because it only proved her right. He'd never really understood the gravity of what he'd done. He'd never really known what to apologize for.

"I was sick, and you—" A tangle of grief and fury choked her. Fuck the data. He'd stolen something much more important— her ability to trust others, and herself.

He blinked and looked away. Beneath the mist—or the sweat —a tear trickled down his cheek.

Siena caught her breath, and spoke gently. "I'd die before forgiving you for that lie, Emmett, and I hope it haunts you. I hope it's the first thing you think about when you wake up every morning. Because maybe, if you ever fall in love again, you won't dare to hurt her like you've hurt me."

# CAMERON

"You don't get it," Cam said. "I watched you fucking die."

Isaac was just as haggard as Lee, and he didn't even have a flesh-eating leg wound to thank. He was paler than Cam had ever seen him, tears falling down his cheeks and soaking his sad excuse for facial hair as he tended to his brother's leg.

Lee was short for Levi. Cam vaguely remembered Isaac talking about him on their first night in the research cabin, even though she'd hardly been paying attention. She'd been envious of their relationship. Her brother Coulter would more likely beat her up than have a heart-to-heart with her, and he was forty.

"If this is death, then death sucks." Isaac wiped his nose on his sleeve and continued to clean Levi's wound with a dirty rag. It was so pathetic that Cam had to intervene, shoving Isaac out of the way and trying not to barf as she knelt in front of Levi.

Isaac pushed open one of the shutters and light flooded the room. The infection had eaten through Levi's flesh to the bone. He needed an amputation, and the only place Cam knew that was clean enough was Ruby's. Ruby hadn't offered such a service, though in fairness, the open wound of an amputation would likely not better his chances.

She toggled between Levi's messed-up leg and the fact Isaac was alive. "How long have you been here?"

"Around three years." Isaac sniffed. "Levi found me during year two."

Cam turned her face toward the open window and took a deep breath, hoping it would clear away the stench, and the nonsensical time gap. Isaac had disappeared on Mount Agnes. Emmett had found him in a sinkhole, decades older. Now, the experiences Isaac claimed he'd had still didn't align with her time in the forest. "So you've been in these woods for three years?"

Isaac pointed to a mess of tallies covering the wall. "I try to tally most days, but sometimes I forget."

"But you entered Deadswitch with me."

Isaac nodded. "You, Siena, and Emmett. And then we left, but we got lost, and I tried to retrace my steps." He wiped his face with his sleeve again, and Cam thought of all the germs living on his arm. "I swam in this weird pond and don't really remember what happened after that, just that I kept getting more lost. There were a lot of bad nights until I found this place. And there are still bad nights, just not as bad as before. Especially once Levi arrived."

"Oh, yeah. How the hell did that happen?"

"I came looking for him." Levi hissed as he stretched out his injured leg. "Our parents didn't even tell me he was missing until the rescue mission switched to recovery. I left two hours later to fly to Cali."

"People are looking for us?" she asked. No, it made little sense. They hadn't been in Deadswitch for longer than their permit stated. "There shouldn't be a team out looking for us yet."

"There *were* folks looking for you. That was years ago."

"That's impossible. We've been gone for a month at most."

Levi grimaced. "I don't know what to tell you." The sweat on his face glistened. "Anyway, I couldn't rely on someone else deciding whether Isaac was dead. I had to search for myself."

"And then you got sucked into this vortex, too," Cam finished. "Jesus fucking Christ."

"Don't take the Lord's name in vain," Levi muttered.

Out in the village, a bell rang.

"Food time," Isaac announced. "Levi, you gotta get up. You know they won't give me a meal for you unless you're there."

With his eyes closed, Levi shook his head. "Ain't happening, kid. It'll be alright."

Cam was still unfamiliar with the village rules, but she was good at picking up context. "I'll go, if they'll feed me. I'll bring back my . . . uhh . . . serving. Levi can have it."

"Are you sure?" Isaac hissed, clearly worried. "You need to eat."

Cam managed a smile. "Sure as shit."

As she stood, her eyes fell upon the room's small table, and the numbers carved into opposite sides of the surface.

*32. 33.* Something she'd ask about later.

She followed Isaac out of the shack into the muck of the village. The scent of smoked meat hung thickly on the air, and Cam's stomach growled. She pressed her fist into the cleft between her ribs to shut it up.

More people milled about than earlier; the bell must have brought them out of hiding. Most wore a strange mix of wilderness gear, casual clothing, and poorly tanned hides that reminded her of Isaac. The old Isaac. The hides were few, though. It was safe to assume that if people really died as quickly as Ruby said they did, the clothes and belongings were divvied up. Unless they were infected. She really didn't understand how transmission worked, but it was obvious this place wasn't clean. The likelihood these villagers cared seemed next to none.

A few people studied her as she and Isaac passed them, as if trying to place her. Some even gave her a nod or a wave. No one seemed suspicious of her. They should suspect her. Here they were, all lost inside some monstrous forest vortex where infection ran rampant and no one could escape, and they were fucking *waving*? Filthy, emaciated, and waving?

She wished she'd stayed at Ruby's and collected more information, because instinct told Cam she was missing something big and dangerous here. Maybe many big dangerous things.

"Tell me about this place," Cam muttered to Isaac. "It just exists in the middle of nowhere? Where did these cabins come from?"

"The cabins have been here for, well, forever. People come and go. People die. Some have been here for a decade or more, but most don't make it that long."

"Because of infection?"

"Yeah. That. And other things."

Cam stole a glance at Isaac. He looked older than the last time she saw *young* Isaac, but not that much older. A couple of years, maybe, which would match Levi's timeline and not hers. But things other than age were different about him, too. The young Isaac she remembered had a youthful and often obnoxious glow about him, like he was the kind of guy who could do a keg stand before climbing a mountain. Besides all that Jesus shit.

Did Jesus people do keg stands?

But this guy . . . this Isaac walking next to her was sick. Not how Levi was sick. It was the slow sickness one would get from eating a handful of chicken nuggets every day for the rest of their life and nothing else. Malnourished sick.

"Who runs the place?" Cam asked.

"Right now it's Bert and Tammy."

"They sound like Muppets."

"Everyone shortens their name. I go by Izzy. You already fit right in."

Isaac did *not* remind Cam as an Izzy, but she said nothing. The thought of fitting right in unnerved her enough. "So Bert and Tammy . . . are they mayors?"

Isaac shrugged. "They're called Elders."

"Sure, Elders. That's not creepy at all."

Isaac guided them on a path that led from the maze of cabins through an alley, and Cam was assaulted by the stench she'd smelled when she first entered The Tooth.

On the other side of the crag, away from the cabins, stretched a long row of covered pigsties, all occupied by—well, she wouldn't call them pigs. Hairy wild hogs scuffed about, their tusks small but sharp.

It wasn't the hogs that smelled, but the filth they wallowed in. Not shit. Something worse than shit that paired horribly with the scent of roasted meat. She gagged at the smell of them together and tried hiding her reflex. Isaac didn't seem to notice.

"So that's what you eat?" Cam sneered at the hogs as the two of them funneled into a line a few dozen yards long.

"Yeah. We take turns caring for them. And killing them."

*God.* "And what if you don't want to take your turn? What if you don't like the idea of killing an animal?"

Isaac glanced out of the corner of his eye and swiped a finger across his neck.

Cam halted in her tracks, the guy behind her almost stumbling into her. "Shut the fuck up."

"Shh," Isaac hissed, gesturing for her to keep walking. "They kick you out. If you put up a fight, that's when things get violent."

"So you do your job, feeding and butchering . . ."

"And guarding and cleaning and fixing," Isaac said.

"And in the end you don't die."

"And you stay dry."

The staying dry bit Cam could understand. It hadn't stopped raining since she entered the valley.

Night was deepening, the sulfurous torches along the perimeter doing little to brighten the village. A part of her hoped to glimpse Avery amid the crowd. She was also terrified of the same thing. Would Avery be Cam's age? A few years older, sped up along a timeline Cam didn't understand?

Dead?

Most likely dead.

Levi was literally rotting away in the hut behind her. Clearly there wasn't a doctor or a medic here, or Isaac would act with more urgency. Right?

They approached the front of the line. The serving station looked like a booth stolen straight from a small-town carnival. The woman who served roasted pork from a variety of old tins and take-out platters looked like she'd survived a battle. The left side of her head was burnt, and she was missing a patch of hair. Cam couldn't tell if she was thirty or sixty, but beneath all the marks and the scars, she'd once been beautiful. She wore a thread-bare sweatshirt and jeans, and a bloodied coffee shop apron.

The woman smiled with unsettling confidence. "Welcome."

Cam recalled her earlier conversation with Isaac. "You Tammy?"

Tammy flashed a scar-crooked smile. "I see you've already met the folk around here."

"You could say that," Cam said.

"You a newborn, or a returner?"

Ruby and Levi had also called her a newborn, but she was unsure what constituted a returner. Tammy's grin deepened, a sign that Cam's hesitation gave her an answer. "This should serve you good." Tammy scooped some slop into a wooden bowl and pointed to a Big Gulp cup full of mismatched spoons. "Happy to have you. Up for a tour in a bit? You can hang around here until I'm done, and I'll show you the place."

*Play the part,* a little voice whispered. She was here for information. This was the easiest way to get it.

Cam took the bowl. "Sure."

Tammy winked at her. "I'll come seek you out." She pointed to the plate of slop. "Enjoy that."

Cam handed the slop off to Isaac as soon as Tammy wasn't looking in her direction. As he returned to feed Levi, she waited in the rain, meandering around the bonfire near the canine-shaped crag. Here, the woodsmoke and wet soil masked the hog stink.

Despite making everything soggy, the rain wasn't that cold.

She hadn't been cold at all since embarking from the cabin. Warm, wet environments were breeding grounds for bacteria, maybe the source of such lethal infection. But this was just an assumption. This place would terrify her once she knew more.

The other villagers hurried back to their cabins in groups to eat. Had they reached this place in a group, or grouped up after arriving? How many people could fit into those tiny cabins?

The villagers shared their houses and their food. So many of these people looked emaciated. Thing was, when people starved, they acted more desperate than those in this village. Fights broke out. Factions were organized. Not here, at least, not from what she'd seen so far. Everyone politely lined up to receive their one daily serving of slop. Violence could create such obedience, maybe. Malnourishment and weakness could as well.

A couple sat across from Cam at the bonfire, a pale woman and dark-skinned man both in their fifties. The man reminded her of a reed in clothing. The word *BASTION* was written on the patch over the brand label of his jacket. The woman had dumpling cheeks and wore a vintage hunting coat that must be heavy with rain. Neither carried a bowl of stew.

The man smiled hesitantly at Cam, and then his eyes lit up and he waved. She lifted her hand in return. Did he think he knew her?

"You're new here," the woman announced, elbowing the man. "What's your name?"

"Cam," she said.

The woman pointed to herself. "Dee." Then to the man. "Star."

*Be cool.* "Hi." Would it be too weird at this point to whip out a picture of Avery and ask if Dee and Star knew her? *Patience.* She'd be here tomorrow morning. She could ask then.

In the meantime, she had to placate Tammy.

The couple muttered quietly to each other, and it felt weird to stick around, so Cam returned to the food shack. Tammy was hanging up her apron, a group of thin men and women scrubbing rusted pots in buckets of water behind her.

When Tammy spotted Cam, she motioned her closer with the crook of her finger. "Let's go somewhere dry, shall we?"

Cam nodded, following Tammy deeper into the village. Tammy walked with a subtle limp, but Cam couldn't tell if it was age-related or an injury from the elements.

At the very back of The Tooth stood a building much larger than any of the cabins. Less shabby, too. Their government building? *Elder* building? The term would never stop creeping her out.

Tammy escorted Cam to the double doors at the closer end. "The Tooth is more than just a few cabins for lost souls. It's our home, and our sanctuary." She pushed open one of the heavy double doors. The air inside the enclosed hallway smelled of mildew. Oil lamps flickered softly along the walls.

"Lost souls," Cam repeated. "How the hell do so many people get lost out here?"

Tammy slid off her soaking patched jacket and folded it over her arm. She looked up at Cam and grinned crookedly again. She was such a small woman, commanding leadership in ways other than her stature.

"It's our purpose. All of ours. I can't believe anything else, with how magnetized our community is. Our faith beckons people from the outside."

The hairs on the back of Cam's neck prickled. "Faith in what?"

*Oh*, she could tell Tammy had just been *waiting* for that question.

"The same faith that sustains us." Palpable pride tinged Tammy's voice. She turned and walked down the hallway, and Cam followed her. "It keeps roofs over our heads and fills our stables. Prayers are our bricks, and belief is our mortar."

The weathered wood and crumbling stone that made up The Tooth defied Tammy's metaphor. Was it faith that held this place together? Or a collective delusion?

The hallway opened to a cavernous room and the bulk of the building, and Cam halted in front of a statue of a majestic antlered woman.

She didn't know how long it had been since she was standing in the research cabin's lab with Emmett and Siena, Emmett having just retrieved old Isaac from the mysterious reappearing tunnel beneath the cellar. He'd taken pictures on his phone of a grotto within the mountain, and a statue exactly like this one.

*The Mother Reigns.*

This statue was much cleaner and well taken care of, the floor of the building constructed around The Mother's feet, as though she'd been here long before the village of The Tooth.

"This is The Mother." Tammy spoke with hushed reverence. "She who blesses our bounty, our families, and ensures the continuation of The Tooth."

"A harvest goddess," Cam said, trying to hide the disgusted, sarcastic tone rising inside her. The blessing of such a goddess wouldn't come so easily—at least not without something in return. Goddamn, she fucking *hated* religion, and weird religion even more. She tore her eyes from the statue to Tammy, who watched her carefully.

"I'm sure The Mother isn't a selfless goddess," said Cam. "What do you offer her in return?"

Tammy didn't seem offended by this question. "We care about her well-being as much as she cares about ours, and believe in a harmonious cycle of giving and taking."

*Don't roll your eyes.* "So *what* do you offer her? Those pigs out front are pretty fat. You sacrifice your food? Resources?"

Tammy pursed her lips like she was trying not to laugh. "Of course not. Her needs aren't the same as ours. She requests one of us every year in autumn to join her in the forest and be nurtured."

*Oh. Great.* A human sacrifice—no big deal. Something told her panic wouldn't go far here, so she kept her expression even despite her dire need to gasp for air.

"Is joining them in the forest code for—"

This time, Tammy did laugh. "Of course not, sweetie. We don't *kill* the one she chooses."

Cam cast her eyes at the statue. "The Mother *chooses* the person?"

"Well, yes. When I arrived in the village years ago, she would request a child. Though I've known no one to bear children successfully in these woods. So we'd offer a pool of our youngest for her to choose from. But the Mother is particular, and she no longer asks for children. The past few years, she's requested a lover . . ."

Cam tuned Tammy out as memories thundered through her.

After Avery's disappearance, Cam had obsessively searched the internet and collected every video, every article, every social media post on Avery Mathis, hoping the threads of her online life would weave together and form a clue—any clue—as to what had happened to her.

It only took seven years, but here Cam was, in some mystical forest, standing in front of an effigy as a brainwashed woman casually explained the human offering required by The Mother.

The thing was, Cam had heard this all before. Seen it, really, in the last video game Avery had played. She couldn't remember the name of the damn thing, but the premise was exactly this, wasn't it? A child cast away from the village after a great harvest feast, a sacrifice made to the forest and The Mother in exchange for prosperity.

*Some sicko could have set this up to mimic the game,* she rationalized, though it felt false the moment she thought it. Deep down, she knew the game was based on this place. Avery had disappeared into these woods after playing it. Cam just didn't understand what it all meant.

Siena could figure it out. Though, as a nauseated foreboding filled Cam, she was so fucking thankful Siena wasn't here.

"Aren't you curious how The Mother chooses her sacrifice?"

Cam blinked, refocusing on Tammy. The woman had been

talking this entire time, but Cam didn't care what she had to say. She needed to get the hell out of here, but before she went . . .

Slipping her hand into her back pocket, Cam retrieved the flyleaf from the back of *Without a Trace*, unfolded it, and showed Tammy the photo of Avery. "Was she ever a *sacrifice*?"

Tammy scrutinized the photo, scratching her chin.

"Would have been a few years ago," Cam elaborated.

"You know, she may have been the final child sacrifice," Tammy said.

"She wasn't a child," Cam retorted.

"But young *enough*. The youngest out of the villagers."

"What happens to the sacrifices?" Her voice hitched, this news getting the best of her calm facade.

"We release them into the woods the night of the feast, and The Mother takes them."

*Like the game.*

Tammy's smile tightened. "I think you should meet someone." She gestured to a small open door. The room beyond was dim, but that was all Cam could see.

"Bert, our Soothsayer. The wisest man I know."

Cam didn't wait for Tammy, but crept toward the room herself. It was the size of a closet, wall shelves lined with bottles, books, and melting candles. *Bert, the Soothsayer.* She expected some wrinkly old man sitting in front of a crystal ball, but this man looked barely forty. Built like a lumberjack, he had a matching beard to boot. He sat at a small table in the center of the room, next to him a large half-finished bowl of stew—not the slop fed to the villagers, but something akin to what Ruby had fed her the night before.

He wore a dark sweater with a blue patch on one elbow that he rested on the table. As he ate, he read from a handwritten book. Recognition flashed in Bert's eyes when he glanced up at Cam. He looked vaguely familiar, like someone from her recent past. Maybe one of the Caltech faculty. But Cam was terrible with faces.

"This is Cam." The tone of Tammy's words harbored a secret, and when Bert nodded, it was like Tammy had spoken something else.

Alarm thrummed through Cam, and she stepped backward. "I'm not feeling well," she said, but when she spun, Tammy wasn't who stood directly behind her. Instead, she was confronted with two men and a woman, all the size of Bert.

These fuckers had clearly been fed more than slop, too.

"Go on, Cam." Tammy stood behind these—these *sentinels*—sounding like a mother encouraging her kid to approach the *Free Candy* van.

Cam's heart hammered in her throat. Her curiosity was about to kill her.

"Sit down," Bert ordered.

Cam whipped toward Bert, forcing her expression stoic to match his, and sat opposite him.

"I apologize, I am not one for pleasantries," he rumbled, like an engine revving in slow motion. "That's Tammy's expertise. But I promise you, this won't take long."

"I haven't been told what I'm doing here." Cam's voice was thick. She was failing at the whole biting back her fear thing, but Bert didn't seem to notice, nor care. He stood and meandered toward the nearest wall, fluttering his fingers before plucking something off the shelf. He returned and set it carefully on the table.

A deck of cards. Cam recognized the sketch of antlers on the back, but couldn't remember from where.

Bert sat again, pushing the cards to the middle of the table. He did not shuffle them, instead drawing the top card and placing it faceup, near him.

A sketch of an open hand, eye in the center of the palm: **THE HAND.**

"Loyalty, patience, obedience." Bert drew another card with a sketch of a woman with antlers. **THE MOTHER.** "Fertility, abundance, and sacrifice."

What was this, a fucking tarot reading? Was he kidding? No . . . he looked way too serious to be kidding.

"These are my cards, and now we'll read yours." Bert flipped over the next card. In the sketch a skeleton lay twisted on the ground, jaw agape, in its chest a bleeding heart.

**THE LOVER,** the card read. The second card Bert pulled was also **THE MOTHER**.

Behind Cam, Tammy muttered something fiercely. A prayer?

"We've completed all readings of our new community members this year. A Lover had yet to emerge, but I kept my faith. The Mother has always guided us."

Cam burst out laughing, but it was only to hide the knee-jerk terror. "You've got to be kidding me."

Bert smiled at her, and she hated how warm and inviting it was. *Sincere.* "This is an honor."

"I'm not a part of your fucking community," Cam spit. "I met someone on the road who needed help, so I brought him here."

"And yet you're still here." Tammy pushed past the guards and stepped into the room. "Asking questions about a woman who was sacrificed to The Mother years ago. If you're searching for her, then we're your only option."

Cam had already come to this conclusion herself, that the prospect of this ritual was the missing link—the only link—to the path that led to Avery.

But being The Mother's *Lover* carried its own set of horrifying implications. "You believe so strongly in your cute little fortune cards, and yet you've brought the cavalry. Why?"

Beneath his beard, Bert's lips twitched, but he said nothing.

"The Mother has chosen me. If I run away, will she smite your village here? Or will she smite me?"

"She won't smite at all," Bert said. "She will find you no matter where you are and take you as her own. But to keep our community strong, and The Mother invested in our prosperity, the ritual of the Feast must happen."

"So I have to stay here."

He nodded. "Unfortunately, any escape attempts must come with consequences, though that is not an ideal scenario. You won't need to escape, because the woods are far more dangerous than what's between these walls." His eyes gleamed like he was sharing a secret with her. "We'll take good care of you."

Cam swallowed. "How far away is this *feast*?"

"Two months."

*Two months.* Two months in a place Ruby said was full of misery and desperation. Two months in a place she wasn't supposed to eat the food. Did she have enough dehydrated meals to last that long? She couldn't remember how many she'd thrown in her pack, but it wasn't two months' worth.

She'd have to ration, or eat the meat. She didn't want to fucking eat the meat.

But being spit out into the forest after the Feast, on a trail Avery had taken years ago, wasn't too bad. If Avery had survived for seven years, she could survive two more months.

Cam's chair squealed as she stood. "I'd like to go back to Is— Izzy's cabin now."

"I'll keep you company," Tammy said. Cam pushed between the trio of goons, who didn't join them.

Cam's resolve crystallized as she and Tammy walked back to the cabin in silence. Night had fallen, and the rain had slowed to a sprinkle, though mist hung thickly in the air, every building a soft but dead-black silhouette against the muffled torchlight. Quiet, too. Only the occasional hog snort accompanied their squelching footsteps.

Cam had to be smart about this. She needed to formulate an escape plan for the next two months in case this place became too dangerous for her. The Mother would not come find her if she ran away, because there was no Mother. But that didn't mean she wanted to escape; she was closer to Avery than she'd ever been.

Either that, or she was a desperate idiot on a wild goose chase.

They reached Isaac and Levi's cabin, and for the first time, Cam noticed there wasn't a lock on the cabin door. Not odd for a culty village, but something she needed to keep in mind.

Stepping into the shack's dim interior, the stench of rotting flesh assaulted her. The room was silent and cold, the candle in the corner burnt out.

"Lee?"

Cam fished the flashlight from her pocket and clicked it on. Her stomach lurched.

Levi lay dead atop the covers of his bed, his eyes open and mouth agape. Black ooze covered his infected leg, which had been severed right beneath the knee.

Levi's foot was on the ground. The infection had eaten straight through his entire limb.

Tammy, who had slinked in behind her, muttered a prayer beneath her breath, and Cam fought the urge to wheel around and deck her in the face.

Where the hell was Isaac?

"Stay here," Tammy said. "We need to take the body away from the cabins and disinfect this one. I'll go get help."

So Tammy knew of the dangers of infection, too.

Tammy left. Cam covered her nose and mouth with her sleeve, following the beam of her flashlight around the rest of the small cabin. She refused to look at Levi again; the longer she soaked in the viscera and fucked-up contours of his gaunt body, the more overwhelming the dread became.

How did anyone survive here? How would she survive?

The beam of Cam's flashlight fell upon a note atop Isaac's threadbare bedding. She picked it up. The paper was handmade, like Ruby's.

*Cam—*

*I can't stand The Tooth without him. I don't know if I can live with myself knowing I'm the reason he's here, and the reason he died.*

*Don't come after me.*

*—I*

*P.S. They feed the bodies to the pigs.*

# HOLDEN

The sky grew hazier, its orange glow an unavoidable omen, and Holden was dead sick of spending his time only cooking and cleaning instead of doing something meaningful to help. Frank was understandably busy orchestrating fire efforts, and it took him three days to get permission for Holden to visit the closed exhibit in the visitor center.

Holden drove himself and Angel down the mountain range to the center, located down a cracked paved road somewhere between the ranger's station and the nearest town. He parked at the front in a lot that needed as much repaving as the road, before them a hodgepodge of '70s architecture and wilderness lodge aesthetics. A lonely Dodge Stratus sat a few spaces to their right, the only other car in the lot.

Holden turned off his car as his phone buzzed repeatedly in his pocket.

"Oh god, we have service," Angel groaned. "I'm afraid to look."

"I think we're obligated to look. I need to see if I still have a job."

"*We* need to see if we still have jobs."

Holden slid his phone from his pocket and checked his texts. None from Chelsea, the woman he'd been sleeping with for months. They'd never broken up because they weren't officially together, but still . . . weird that she hadn't even bothered to check if he was alive.

He opened his work email and tapped on a message from his boss with Angel cc'd.

*Chase relayed to me you all took the initiative to cut hours during the summer. While I'm sure you were well intentioned, please confirm with me first before taking extended leave. Make sure you're back by the 24th.*

The 24th was the day after tomorrow.

"It looks like we won't be meeting that deadline," Angel muttered as she read the message from her own phone. "I called out for the both of us. You want me to quit for the both of us, too?"

Holden exhaled and stared out the grimy windshield, burnt light beaming through the tall pines behind the visitor center. Twenty thousand acres already, Frank had told them before they left the station this afternoon. The fire wasn't even a week old.

He'd tried helping the rescue team once, when the stakes were a hell of a lot lower, and failed. Now he was about to give up his job so he and Angel could keep playing Sherlock and Watson. And he wasn't even Sherlock.

Angel snapped her fingers. "Earth to Holden."

"No, don't quit for me. I'll do it myself."

"So you *are* quitting?" she asked.

They exchanged glances. Angel's face was blank, like she was looking to him for guidance on what to do. He didn't want to be responsible for her decision, especially if it ended up being the wrong one.

"You need to do what's right for you," he said.

Angel rolled her eyes. "No shit. I'm quitting regardless of what you do."

Holden smiled pathetically. "Maybe when all this is over, I'll move to Portland or something. Better jobs." The self-confirmation loosened the knot in his chest. Whether or not they found the research team, his time in Deadswitch would end. He had options beyond his old life. Infinite options, as long as he could get over the thought of being alone for a bit.

"That's the spirit." Angel unbuckled her seat belt and pushed her door open. "But really, if you want to copy my resignation letter, I'll forward it to you."

"Better do that now while we're back in the 21st century." He got out of the car and followed her to the visitor center's double doors.

The air inside smelled like mildew and a Febreze plug-in. Dead critters stuffed before Holden was born peered at him from behind glass walls, the shellac on the exhibits' wood frames sticky looking, like it never fully dried. Rumpled and faded forest backgrounds hanging behind all the taxidermy showcased dense groves and lakeshores, too idyllic to feel real.

Other than the whir of the AC unit, the lobby was dead silent. Even the woman manning the desk said nothing as she watched Holden and Angel over a pair of delicate spectacles. She had the appearance of a burnt-out kindergarten teacher who should have retired a decade ago. Her brass-plated name tag read *Marilyn.*

Angel cleared her throat. "Ummm, hi. Frank called about us."

Marilyn released a melodramatic sigh and thumbed through the keys on the lanyard around her neck. "You're lucky Frank is a good friend. I'm not supposed to do this." She swept around the desk toward a dim hallway.

"Are we supposed to follow?" Holden whispered. Angel shoved him with her elbow.

"So . . . you never give tours of the old archives?" Angel asked as they followed Marilyn at an awkwardly long distance.

"No," Marilyn said. "Bureaucratic nonsense. The state won't

employ another staff member, and we'd need at least two with a building this large." The reason conflicted with what Diego had said about the exhibit being too disturbing. Then again, Marilyn didn't seem fun enough to tell them the juicy truth, if there even was a juicy truth.

Marilyn approached a door at the end of the hall. "Opening the exhibit for the two of you is technically illegal, but Frank was adamant. Said you two were helping with something important as he's tied up with that horrid fire. Sure hope they put it out quickly."

*Something important.* Frank could have been bluffing to get Marilyn off his back, but it was nice to think that someone Holden liked thought he was doing something important, even if Frank only knew Holden had a lead involving the cult. Frank hadn't even asked questions.

Marilyn unlocked the door with her jangly set of keys and propped it open. A mostly empty hexagonal room awaited them. A scattering of paintings on the farthest wall were the only ones uncovered, but with one window, the room was too dark for Holden to make out what they were. Empty display counters atop cabinets lined the perimeter, as if guests were supposed to start and end at the room's entrance.

"Any remaining artifacts are in the cabinets to keep them clean," Marilyn said. "The rest have been redistributed to descendants and native organizations. You can open the cabinets, but *touch* nothing. It's twenty-five cents for each photocopied page of the documents. You can ask me for copies at the *end* of your visit. Until then, I will be busy. Please shut the door when you leave." And with that, she was gone.

"She wasn't loved as a child," Angel said.

"Be thankful she let us back here and don't talk shit." Holden glanced around.

Angel flipped the light switch near the door, but nothing happened. "Looks like we're doing this in the dark. I'll start on the far side." She beelined to the far cabinets, and Holden began searching through the ones to the left of the door.

There wasn't much. Most of the "artifacts" were shoddily glued together dioramas depicting pioneer life. Possibly made by fourth graders. Diego was right—this exhibit *was* disturbing, but not for the reasons Holden had imagined.

The actual artifacts comprised a couple of tools found on an excavation and broken arrowheads. None of it seemed relevant to the pioneer cult.

Angel distracted him as she piled stuff from her cabinet on top of the display counter.

Holden stood. "I thought the lady said—"

"Oh, come on. She's clearly the kind of person who gets more pleasure from scolding people than actually protecting *precious* artifacts." Angel huffed as she stood, then picked through the pile on the display case.

Holden joined her, studying the collection. A couple of books with laminated, unmarked covers, a plaque that had once been on a wall or display case . . .

"Is that a flute?"

"Four of them." Angel laid the flutes next to each other. Other than the natural grain of the wood, they looked identical, their bodies as smooth as driftwood, though the design was crude.

Something didn't look right. "Aren't flutes supposed to have more holes in them?"

"I'm not a flute historian." Angel pointed to the plaque resting above the flutes.

*Local pioneers renounced their Methodist faith to create one of their own. This cult worshipped a goddess they called The Mother, handcrafting instruments from cedar to play a hymn known as The Mother's Prayer.*

A terrible screech scraped across the room, and Holden jumped as Angel lowered a flute from her lips.

"You'll get us in trouble. Or worse," he said.

"What do you mean, worse?" Angel asked. "You scared I'm gonna summon her?"

"The Mother?"

She shrugged. "Why would someone craft an instrument specifically to make that screech other than to summon some eldritch god from a distant realm?"

Fair point.

Angel tapped the top of a book. "I think this is a copy of the pioneer leader's journal. Why don't you snap pics of the pages?" Angel snorted. "*Photocopies.* I'll do a sweep of the other cabinets."

Holden did as Angel asked. The glossy pages were scans from an old book, the dates erratic. Pages were missing. Maybe they were inappropriate for the public, though he doubted Marilyn would let him in on the location of the actual journal.

He checked the back of the book for the publisher.

"The High Sierra Conservationists . . . Is that the group Dr. Dupont's mother belonged to?" Holden asked. "They published this book."

He handed the book to Angel, and she frowned, studying the stamp on the back. "Why would a conservationist group publish documents from a historic cult?"

*And how is Siena's mother connected?*

He heard Maidei's voice: *correlation doesn't equal causation.* How many coincidences did he need to run into for the connections to no longer be just correlation?

He thought about Angel's question. *Why?* "Any chance the cult influenced the environment in Deadswitch?"

Angel flipped through the book. "I don't think we have enough information to figure that out."

Holden pulled out his phone and typed "High Sierra Conservationists" in the search bar on his browser. "What's the name of this cult?"

"This looks like the journal of some priest or leader, and he keeps mentioning 'The Church of Bounty.' Try that."

Holden typed it in. As the results slowly loaded, he glanced around the dark room, then made his way to the paintings hanging over the far cabinets as his browser loaded. A quick scan of the links showed nothing related, all results about the High Sierra Conservationists displaying a crossed out "~~church of bounty~~" beneath the listing.

Holden squinted at the uncovered paintings on the wall, stepping closer. Even with little light, he could tell the paint texture wasn't typical. It looked like mud, which explained why the paintings were all so dark. Abstract, too. Seemed unlike the popular art at the time, though he knew nothing of art history.

He shone his phone's flashlight at the largest painting. The image shimmered with bronze and flecks of minerals, the paint caked on thick and creating a dimensional texture, like the painting was meant to be touched. He relaxed his eyes, the once-abstract shapes sliding into focus.

Antlers.

Sweat prickled the back of his neck, and the tang of iron flooded his mouth—not real blood, but he could still taste it, like a memory.

"*Holden.*"

Holden blinked and turned back toward Angel, who crossed her arms.

"I said your name three times, and you were totally spaced out. What's going on? Low blood sugar? You need a snack?"

*Correlation, not causation.* "I've seen this before."

Angel approached him, staring up at the wall. "What, the painting?"

"What's *in* the painting."

It took Angel as long as him to make sense of the image. "A deer? You've seen a deer? I hate to break it to you, but—"

"Not a deer. *This* deer. This buck . . ." He hadn't told her yet, because the first time he'd seen the buck, he'd been ashamed and thought it had been the product of a nervous breakdown. And then he'd told Maidei, but both their shared experience and the surrounding mystery felt like it was supposed to be kept secret, until now.

Because this painting was evidence that what he'd witnessed twice wasn't a figment of his own imagination.

Holden and Angel sat with Maidei and Zaid around the table in the Hub, Francis snoozing in fiery sunlight trickling in through the window.

An unfamiliar game lay unfinished on the table, black and white pieces on a board with a cross through the center. Holden looked upon it with a strange remorse, like he'd missed someone's birthday. He wanted to be around for the fun, even if the only fun to be had at the Fort was a board game, and not just the tension that now filled the room.

Angel sipped her coffee, lost in thought. Holden had just recounted both experiences seeing the shadow buck to the group. He'd expected Angel to crack some joke about his mental health, but she'd grown quiet and contemplative, which meant she believed him.

"So is this the same thing you saw all those years ago, Maidei?" For once, Zaid had shut his laptop, enraptured by Holden's story and the painting they'd found at the visitor center.

Maidei sat with her arms crossed, scowling at the edge of the table. "Similar. Not the same. I never got a good look at the shadow that followed me. It hovered just out of sight, which is why I spent so long trying to convince myself that trauma had rewritten my memory of what had actually happened." She said it so matter of fact, as though it was the only way she could talk about those few days lost in the woods.

"Three times," Angel said. "You said you saw it twice, Holden. But I saw it once, too. With you . . . the day we drove up here. We almost ran into it."

He'd forgotten about that day—the black blur flying across the road. His car skidding across gravel as he stopped short. And Francis, in the back seat, releasing a string of vicious growls.

He asked the obvious. "So, what is it?"

No one spoke. Maidei wrapped a few of her braids around a finger and tugged, still glaring at the table's corner.

"Sounds like magic," Zaid said.

Maidei refocused her glare at him.

"Oh, come on, Mai. Don't look at me like that. You know I was talking this way from the beginning with those lodgepole pines growing fast enough to break laws of biology, chemistry, physics. Magic was the closest thing possible to a rational explanation. Still is, especially now that there's a cult involved."

"Speaking of . . ." Angel held out her hand toward Holden. "Can I see your phone? I want to look over those journal pages."

Holden passed his phone to her, and she got busy flipping through the images.

"There was someone at the visitor center, right?" Zaid asked. "Met her once. Lovely lady."

"Lovely isn't the word I'd use to describe her," Angel muttered.

Zaid ignored her. "She have anything to say?"

Holden shook his head. "She refused to answer questions when we were done looking around. Said she wasn't a historian." Marilyn had acted like the fact Holden and Angel had tried questioning her at all about the cult was a personal affront. She clearly wanted no affiliation with them. "I don't know where else we can get more info at this point. Maybe Diego, but I don't want to bother him again. He was annoyed enough with me the first time."

"Hoolyyy shit, listen to this." Angel pinched the screen of Holden's phone to zoom in. "These are journal pages from one of the cult leaders. Date reads 1882.

"*Blessed newcomers. Everyone has been fraught with worry. All the children have drawn their cards and The Mother has yet to choose her prize. But three families arrived today from the southern hills. Eleven children in all. Their cards shall be drawn tonight. The Mother is still good to us, and through her love, we will not starve."*

"I'm not following," Maidei said. Holden wasn't following either, and Angel staring at him with wide eyes, waiting for him to *get it*, wasn't helping.

"*Cards*, Holden. Didn't you also draw cards?"

The night of the party in the woods flooded back: annoyance, inadequacy, but more importantly the fortune teller between the trees. The oil lamp, the cigarette marks on the wooden table.

"*What* is going on?" Maidei's eyes were sharp as she watched Holden's expression, suspicious of his reaction to Angel's prompting.

"It's . . ." Holden sighed. "A long story."

"Try me." The muscles in Maidei's crossed arms clenched.

"A couple of things happened when Angel and I were looking into Dr. Dupont's recordings back in Corvallis. The first was that Angel bought and read the book *Without a Trace*."

"That's the book about the Deadswitch Five, right?" Zaid leaned toward him. "I think I have a copy."

"Did you read it?" Holden asked.

Zaid waved a hand in front of his face. "I don't read."

Angel rolled her eyes. "Really, *scientist*?"

"Not for pleasure, anyway. Got it because those girls went missing around Wolf Ridge. Thought it was odd, given what happened to Maidei. But I never got around to reading it." A light turned on behind his eyes, like he was finally putting together the Deadswitch Five, the research team, and Maidei's story. "You don't think—"

Maidei cut him off. "Let Holden finish."

"The book was mostly about Avery Mathis, the famous content creator. Anyway, I looked into the game she was playing right before she disappeared. It was about *this* cult—a village in the woods, and a girl cast into the forest as a sacrifice to The Mother."

Maidei's expression dropped in surprise. "You can't be serious."

"Trust me, it gets better," Angel said, perking up.

"A few weeks later, I went to this party in the woods between Corvallis and Newport. This woman . . . she knew I'd be there. Sent this guy to look around the bonfire and find me." Holden shook away the chill running up his back. "She was out in the woods, all set up with a lamp and a table. I sat down, and she pulled my cards like a tarot reading, but it wasn't tarot. She drew two cards, the first a faceless man in a cloak. She gave some hokey interpretation, like I wasn't supposed to be a hero. Then she pulled another card: The Mother. A woman with antlers. She told me the card meant we were on the same side of the apocalypse."

Maidei pressed her lips into her knuckles, now glaring at the table like she was trying to melt it.

Zaid lifted the lid on his laptop and started typing furiously. "We need to cross-check everything with what we learned fifteen years ago. We may find more connections."

"I don't know if I want to get too deep into this, Zaid," Maidei said.

"I know, Mai. But I can." He tore his eyes from the screen to look at Maidei. "Hey."

Maidei glanced up.

"You can go home," Zaid said in an unusually gentle tone. "I got this."

Maidei blinked and straightened in her seat. "I can handle it. I just don't want to."

Holden wished he understood why Maidei was so allergic to searching for the truth. Was it only trauma? The fact she was a scientist and so much of what was happening in Deadswitch was inexplicable? He wanted to ask, but she closed up before his eyes.

She would tell him if she ever became ready. And if that didn't happen, he'd have to be content with saying goodbye, for now.

Static shot from the radio on the table. "This is Frank, anyone there?"

Maidei seized the opportunity and picked up the handheld. "We're here, Frank. Any news?"

"One of the choppers made another successful rescue. The woman is recovering at the station. She's asking for you, Maidei."

"Me?" Maidei stared at the radio like she couldn't trust it.

"Yes, you. Holden and Angel back from the center? Tiffany is driving her to the Fort. You'll want to listen to what she has to say."

In the beginning, The Shadow created the world.

The mountains, the valleys. Virgin forests and the rivers cutting through them. Rock threaded with shimmering ore.

The Shadow created the plants, animals, and fungi, and said to them, "Feast upon the world."

But The Shadow wasn't satisfied with a world only he could see. As if his world were a tapestry, he tore through the fabric small holes only a few could find.

The Mother was the first to enter.

The Shadow loved her so deeply that he gifted her a piece of him. From the gift, The Mother created a weapon—a fierce, antlered creature tasked with seeking out those most loyal to her.

For The Mother knew The Shadow's power could destroy the mountains, the valleys. Virgin forests and the rivers cutting through them. Rock threaded with shimmering ore.

The Mother knew The Shadow could destroy her, too.

*—First Sermon, Church of Bounty*

# FOUR DAYS AGO

Emmett had never bought into the sexy *Indiana Jones* fantasy of academic field research, not even as a teenager. The field offered little other than a nature excursion. It was boring. Uncomfortable. Often fruitless. Yet he was here anyway because of his boss, tromping through the middle of a forest thicker than a jungle.

The danger was here and real, not a fantasy. A nightmare. He'd just killed a man. He may have looked ancient, but Isaac had entered Deadswitch at twenty-three. As far as Emmett was concerned, Isaac was twenty-three when Emmett blew him to pieces with a shotgun.

Just a kid.

Isaac had been suffering, and Emmett had put him out of his misery. But that didn't make the atrocity better. He'd cried for the past two hours, the longest in his life. He'd given himself that. Now, he had a job to do.

Soaked and exhausted, Emmett's hunt for Brock's mysterious cache continued, the note with the map from his boss in his grip. This cache could answer all Emmett's questions, and once he had answers, he would escape with Siena.

He'd hiked all night by the light of his headlamp, his skin

crawling at the wilderness whispers and animal cries. And now, he was close.

At the bottom of a small shadowed gorge, a crevasse yawned from a rock wall. The map Emmett carried didn't signify the cache would be in any cave, but that would make the most sense, especially if the contents needed to remain dry. Even after a whole day's and night's worth of time to himself, he couldn't imagine what was in it. But he'd find out soon enough.

Before Siena, he wanted to be a corporate climate scientist. Cam may have called him a shill, but if that was the case, then he'd been a shill from the very beginning.

Shill, shmill. He was practical. Nothing to be ashamed of.

In graduate school, Emmett entered academia for the sole purpose of being around Siena. When he had her, and when she stayed with him despite his career choice, he no longer had to pretend academia was endgame, so he returned to the usual paid programming.

Stealing Dr. Feyrer's research had not been a part of that plan, but an opportunity to secure both his and Siena's future. A bonus for him, a grant for her. Even then, he hadn't realized COtwo—Brock—intended for him to act as staff on Siena's project if she accepted the grant. Given that stipulation, he was shocked when she accepted it, especially because Brock had implemented Emmett as a babysitter.

A large part of him—most of him—hated that Siena had taken the money. It meant if COtwo had just proposed the damn grant to her in the first place, without making Emmett sniff around, she would have taken it.

And he'd still be with her.

The gorge was silent save for his own feet on the forest floor and the occasional skitter of rodents. Emmett slid his flashlight from his pocket, clicked it on, and shone it into the crevasse. The grotto looked safe, so he turned sideways and shimmied through the crack in the rock.

Inside, his light bounced off the walls of a dry and temperate cave until it landed on a steel storage crate.

Emmett's survival instincts flared up, his subconscious worried any movement would trigger the crate to blow up or something. He knelt next to it carefully. While the crate bore no logo, a four-digit lock was built into the front. **Date of Entry** was engraved beneath.

*Date of entry?*

Emmett tugged his phone from his pocket and turned it on. August 14th. He was sure that date was wrong, given he couldn't trust his phone to have tracked the time correctly when they were trapped in the cabin. Still, he tried plugging in 0814. The latch remained locked.

If the code wasn't the day he entered the cave, then it had to be the day he'd entered Deadswitch.

He set the lock to 0713. The mechanism clicked, and he lifted the lid.

Objects filled the crate in organized stacks, the items so familiar that he almost forgot where he was. Emmett picked up and unfolded a track jacket, thumb gliding over the stain from a ballpoint pen. Up at Lake Garnet, the pen had exploded in Siena's pocket after she finished her field notes.

How had the jacket ended up in the crate? She'd brought it with her into Deadswitch. She'd been wearing it when he left yesterday.

He pressed the jacket to his face and inhaled. It still smelled like her.

Rage tore through his chest. What the hell had they done to her? Had they taken her?

*Who are* they?

His head spun so fast that he couldn't calm himself down enough to make sense of anything, and then he spotted something that confused him further. Beneath Siena's track jacket, the same neatly folded garment waited. Same ink stain. Emmett made a fist around the fabric and lifted it to his face.

Same Siena.

Beneath the jackets sat a few neatly stacked Macbooks, all the same make and model. Six, seven tape recorders filled another compartment within the crate; two pairs of her hiking boots, one worn and the other destroyed beyond repair, were tucked along the edges, the crate like a costume trunk for Siena. All her extra garments and belongings tucked inside, waiting for her.

No. Waiting for *him*. Why was he here? Why had COtwo replicated Siena's stuff down to her very smell?

He lifted the laptops. An unfamiliar book rested beneath. It looked like something a child would have handmade in class, *Siena* scrawled across the spine, her name traced repeatedly with a ballpoint pen.

He flipped through the pages, all dirty with mud and dried blood. Siena's handwriting brimmed within them.

Emmett's thoughts quieted. Whatever he'd uncovered wasn't comprehensible. Turning to the center of the book and starting to read felt like submission.

The faded, smeared writing was almost illegible.

*Caught me . . . a few days left . . . discovered something . . .*

No dates marked the pages, but she hadn't written in the journal this trip. Maybe the one after they broke up, though it wasn't like Siena to tote around something so chintzy. She bought Field Notes journals in bulk.

A large, dark smear filled the final page, along with the line: *I didn't think I'd die with so many regrets.*

Some sick joke. Had to be. Emmett dug further into the crate, uncovering a row of neatly filed plastic evidence bags. Old socks, a drained pen. Dried herbs bunched together with an elastic hair tie. A knife carved from a deer antler. A homemade arrow. A Deadswitch Wilderness map. An empty tube of cherry Chapstick, Siena's favorite. Drawings of cells—bacteria—scribbled on scrap paper.

Emmett tugged free a black binder. Everything else in the crate was in various states of wear and tear, but the binder was new. The outside bore no label. He flipped open the cover, an envelope with his name on it tucked in the pocket. Behind the envelope, a printed sticker on the inside of the binder's cover read:

**Variable: Siena Dupont**

A plastic protector encased each binder page. Emmett scanned the first one.

**Entry dates listed in Alpha Timeline. Timelines in correlating dimensions are not parallel.**
**Variable #01**
**Alpha Timeline Entry: November 11th, 1987.**
**Confidence: 59%**
**Contents:**
**Artifact: Sunglasses, missing left arm and hinge**
**Artifact: Cellphone, broken screen, missing SIM card**
**Field Notes: copied, processed, and annotated. See index.**
**Length: 76 days**
**Cause of Death: Exposure. Confidence: 11%**

It was like reading a foreign language.

**Variable #07**
**Alpha Timeline Entry: February 6th, 1998.**
**Confidence: 82%**
**Contents:**
**Artifact: Macbook, hard drive exported and processed**
**Photo: Crude effigy made of twigs and unknown substance. Possible biohazard.**
**Photo: Several reagent jars containing various berries and herbs**
**Photo: Tool set made of bone, for cleaning animal hide**
**Length: 651 days**
**Cause of Death: Infection. Confidence: 64%**

Emmett flipped to the last page before the index.

**Variable #13**
**Alpha Timeline Entry: April 7th, 2020.**
**Confidence: 98%**
**Contents:**
**Artifact: Cellphone, intact and functional, exported and processed. See index.**
**Photo: Misc. gear, including backpack, clothing, and first aid. Stored in #013 cache. See index.**
**Length: 14 days**
**Cause of Death: Homicide - strangulation. Confidence: 100%**

His ribs clenched down on the white-hot fury in his chest. He couldn't breathe enough to think, so he instead ripped through the envelope and yanked open the folded paper.

Emmett read the letter. Then he read it again, and again. A slither of terror killed his anger until all that filled him was a dark, seeping cold.

It was a lie. It *had* to be a lie.

Emmett—

If you're reading this, then you've surpassed my expectations. Well done.

I didn't want to send you out here to find this letter. I wanted to tell you in person what you were up against, but the risk was too great. What makes you perfect for this mission is the same reason why you're volatile and unpredictable. You care too much about the variable. I don't believe I could have persuaded you into accepting the truth and assuming your role. You had to witness the Confluence Region for yourself.

There are many cross-dimensional instances where the variable's team, more often than not including you, entered Deadswitch Wilderness on the perceived date of July 13th, 2023 to collect and analyze data on the Alpenglow Glacier.

I know you're a man of science, though perhaps not physics. However, if you're familiar with string theory, you'll know that to solve mathematical inconsistencies within our theories of space and time, we must assume there are dimensions smaller than an atom that house the tiniest particles in our universe.

Perhaps this theory is correct. However, it doesn't account for an anomalous vibration pattern: a dimension curled into the size of Yellowstone National Park.

This is where you are right now, Emmett. You stand where I once stood many years ago, when I discovered the truth.

The Confluence Region isn't a place accessed only by our universe. Instead of universes existing in parallel, the Confluence Region layers time like a delicate confection. We can study the previous experiences of others, and ourselves.

We've traced the variable historically. With each entry, she discovers another piece to the jigsaw of the Confluence Region: how it exists, operates, manifests. This is the largest discovery humanity has ever made, and we must ensure she continues to have opportunities for breakthroughs.

Why her? Whether it's her intimacy with Wilder Feyrer's

research or the way she analyzes organically, I don't know. We need more data, especially on the unstable factor she calls The Shadow. This figure may be our key to understanding more.

It is finally 2023 in our world, and we can have a direct impact on the variable from our dimension, referred to as Alpha Timeline within the literature. She must remain in the Confluence Region, and must stay alive for as long as possible. Any efforts by her to leave, while likely fruitless, still need to be corrected. We know from our historical data that the longer she remains healthy and within the region, the more she will learn, and the more our organization will inevitably learn.

Your job is to copy or capture her notes and deliver them to this cache, as well as the notes you write on her. The faster the variable makes breakthroughs in Wilder Feyrer's dataset, and the more she discovers on her own, the better, though we cannot extract you until she is dead, usually between eighteen and thirty-six months, though longer if you can protect her.

This also means you'll be risking your own life. Please understand that I have complete faith in your survival. You've survived many times before.

I am a generous man, Emmett. Survival and extraction won't be your only rewards. As soon as we've gathered enough data from both our own agents and the variable on the Confluence Region, we will open this project up to investors, and your compensation will be handsome.

We believe our firm's influence within the Confluence Region is unique. COtwo Industries is anomalous so far. The next variable that enters from another timeline may come from a place where our firm doesn't exist. The next Siena Dupont, and the next, and the next, may still be in love with you, or at the very least, a version of you. If you live and prove valuable to this mission, I will use what resources we have to isolate her for you. I know how much you care about her.

I am offering you a reset, an opportunity, and a life you've always wanted. Do not disappoint me.

I've left further instructions and your expected schedule in the binder. Good luck, and we appreciate your sacrifice.

*—BB*

I've left further instructions and your expected schedule in the binder. Good luck, and we appreciate your sacrifice.

*—BB*

# EMMETT

Emmett arranged the contents of the cache just as he'd found them, stood, and stumbled to the cavern exit.

Outside, he sank to the ground, his pants soaking in the mud. The gorge smelled of rot.

This *place*. He didn't give a fuck what this place was. He didn't care what its existence meant.

He howled until he tasted blood at the back of his throat.

Every sacrifice, mistake, selfish whim had made him malleable. Usable. He'd helped pen Siena's death sentence. He'd signed the fucking paperwork.

Again, he cried.

Isaac had been right, pushing Siena to escape. Isaac had been the better man. He'd told her the truth about her danger. He hadn't hesitated.

Emmett still had time. He could get Siena out and to safety. And if COtwo had a problem with that, then they'd have to find him first.

He'd never believed he could sacrifice himself for someone else, even Siena. But now he was certain. He'd die for her. And he'd fight for her, even if COtwo killed him for it.

Now, he had to get her the hell out of here.

# SIENA

Beneath their hung tarp, Siena and Emmett slept next to each other in their separate bivies. Siena couldn't see Emmett, but he was quiet. If he were asleep, he'd be snoring.

She'd waited a year to tell him he could never earn her forgiveness, which she regretted, clinging to hope that one day she could learn to trust again. Even after Feyrer's betrayal, and Cam's.

*Cam.* Siena's fury couldn't mask her worry for Cam, mostly because she didn't know how long it would take for Cam to give up on her search for Avery Mathis. Giving up and hiking out of the Briardark or dying in her search were Cam's only two options, because Avery was dead.

*Inconclusive.*

Inconclusivity led to hope. Hope led to trust.

Trust could kill.

The rain fell through the night. At some point she woke to a deep groan in the forest. She unzipped her bivy and pointed her flashlight into the brush beyond their clearing.

Nothing.

The sense of being watched prickled the back of her skull. The Shadow didn't always announce himself. He could be there, right beyond the tarp: an onyx tear in the world, floating and speaking in silence.

After that, the rest of the night was fitful. She choked down an energy bar when morning came. Emmett looked a little better than the night before, the bags beneath his eyes less purple. He changed his bandage without her help, and she was relieved that he seemed to be on the mend, albeit slowly.

As they packed up, Emmett said nothing about their conversation from the night before. And that was okay, too. He needed time to process, and they had enough of it as they traveled.

If they even *could* travel.

It was like the ecosystem had flagged them as an infection. Branches clawed at them as they passed, Siena's feet tangling in ground vines every time she took a step. She shielded her face with her forearms to protect her eyes.

Emmett fell behind her, so she faced the brunt of the attack, which was unlike him. Even yesterday he took the lead. But she didn't question it, not even when he refused to stop for a water break, instead drinking from his bottle as they moved.

The rain didn't let up. Her boots hadn't been dry since before the swamp, her heels hot and rubbing uncomfortably through two layers of socks. The sole on her left shoe kept peeling away from the toe, and she had no real way of repairing it.

The forest floor before them tilted downward and deeper into the valley. With the foliage so thick, she didn't know how much more of this they could safely take. And that wasn't even considering how much time they were losing.

"Sen," Emmett muttered.

Siena stomped down an oversized fern to clear the path before them.

"*Sen.*"

She spun.

Emmett stood still a few yards behind her, his expression hidden by the bandanna across his face for protection.

"What is it?" she asked.

He swayed, reaching out to grasp the nearest tree before he stumbled and collapsed.

A wildfire of panic swept through her.

"Emmett!" Siena dropped to her knees and rolled his limp body until he faced upward. Holding his hand, she shoved his sleeve up.

Black. The whole bandage, pitch black like tar.

Rain pelted them both, and once she'd dragged Emmett beneath the shelter of a spruce and out of the storm, she hastily brushed wet strands of hair from her face.

He was still out cold. The color in his lips was all but gone. Her hands trembled as she reached out for his pulse point, but when she touched his neck, her fingertips grazed a lump.

Siena tugged down the collar of his shirt. Purple nodules embedded Emmett's clammy skin. Gnawing trepidation settled deep within her chest.

She needed to wake him, but didn't know how concussed he was from the fall. After fumbling around in her pocket, she retrieved her flashlight, clicked it on, and peeled open one of his eyes, crying out at the milky film veiling his cornea.

*Sickness.* A sickness she'd never seen before. Inflamed abscesses, cloudy eyes . . . If bacterial, the infection was severe.

She tentatively unwrapped the bandage around his hand. The fabric clung stubbornly, sticking to the black discharge beneath.

The wound ate away at the necrotic black flesh surrounding it. A fungal growth, feathery like kitchen mold, sprawled from the bit of bone that glinted in the center and left a whisper-thin pattern across tendon and tissue.

Her fingers trembled with unchecked fear. Not only did she lack the ability to treat him, but she didn't even know what she was treating. The illness played by rules she couldn't discern, and Emmett's shallow breaths mocked her impotence.

His eyelids fluttered open. Mostly milky and unreadable, the dark blobs of his pupils and irises darted back and forth, trying to latch on to something familiar.

"I'm here," she said. "Emmett . . . Emmett, can you hear me?"

His eyes swiveled in her direction, pale lips forming her nickname. "*Sen.*"

"Hold on," she whispered.

His face contorted. With his good hand, he reached out to grip her arm with a strength that belied his condition. "Brock. He . . . he told me about them. About *you*." From the corners of his eyes, tears the texture of wet sand dripped down the sides of his face, leaving a gritty residue.

Why was he talking about his boss? Was he trying to apologize to her again? She couldn't have this conversation right now, not when she needed to figure out how the hell to keep him stable.

She hushed him. "I need you to stay calm. Can you see anything? Emmett? Can you see me?"

He didn't answer, and his gaze never truly fixed on her, always wandering and searching. His disjointed muttering intensified. "*You died,*" he kept saying. "*Brock tricked us.*"

His fingernails dug into her coat, the sheer intensity of his fear paralyzing. All she could think to do was whisper reassurances and hollow promises. "You'll be okay. I'm here."

Emmett's ramblings and movements suddenly halted. The cold, humid air stilled as the forest took a breath.

"Siena," he whispered, voice hoarse but strangely serene. "I love you."

Her throat constricted. She wanted to say something, anything, to break the oppressive silence. To tell him she understood, that she forgave him, that she felt the same. Perhaps those words were what he needed to hang on. To stay with her.

And then, as suddenly as the clarity had come on, Emmett's body convulsed. Siena, caught off guard, fell back into the mud as he lunged at her, fingers clawing, milky eyes wild and frantic.

"I've killed you," he gasped, words distorted and mangled. His grasp slackened, and the limp weight of his hand fell away.

He was still once more, and she didn't know when she'd get another moment to act.

*Amputation.*

No matter how she tried treating him, his infection would not clear unless she stamped out the blight that fed it.

*Don't think. Do it.*

She lunged toward her pack and dug through it until she found her med kit and a lighter. Creating a sterile environment here was impossible. Holding down Emmett, a man nearly twice her size and delusional with fever, while she sawed through the joint of his wrist was impossible. But she refused to sit here inert and helpless. Fuck this place. Fuck the Briardark.

Fuck everything.

It took three alcohol wipes to scrub the tarp beneath his infected hand. She rolled his sleeve to his elbow and fished a tourniquet from the bottom of her med bag. The device took up a quarter of the kit's space, but she'd brought it anyway. Never had she thought she'd actually need to use it.

It took Siena far too long to swallow her panic and remember how to place a tourniquet. Once she slid the band through the buckle two inches above Emmett's wrist, she began twisting the windlass. She didn't know how tight she was supposed to make it; the tourniquet came with instructions for stopping blood flow, not cutting off a hand.

She twisted the windlass as tight as she could before securing it. Emmett hadn't moved. Unconscious again, most likely. She just needed to sterilize her hunting knife and ready the gauze.

Siena glanced up. Emmett had turned his head to watch her, mouth open, about to speak more nonsense. Tell her he loved her again.

A grainy tear dripped from his cheek onto the tarp.

He didn't blink, nor speak, but she kept waiting for the shock etched in his features to morph into something else.

She said his name once, quietly. Again. *"Wake up."*

If she just reached out and checked his pulse, she'd know. For once in her life, she didn't want an answer. She held two of her fingers stretched out in front of her, watching them tremble and collect mist.

*Two fingers. Carotid artery. Level with the larynx.*

*No.*

She grabbed Emmett's shoulders and shook him. "*WAKE UP!*"

His head flopped to the other side and thudded against the ground.

She'd spent her whole life studying the way glacial melt carved paths down mountainsides, but hadn't understood gravity until now. The way it weighted her spine, harnessed her to the earth. No longer would gravity release her hand so she could press her fingers to Emmett's neck. Not that it mattered. She could no longer track the movement of blood through his body, gravity once more a victor, blood pooling in veins and capillaries, coagulating at the small of his back and beneath his ass and in the back of his knees. She knew this not from her studies of science, but from the day she was at the hospital, still on the phone with food delivery, trying to figure out where they'd left the goddamn takeout for Mom, who hadn't eaten in two days. Returning to a flatline and the chaos of doctors. Gravity had tried to teach her a lesson then, inflicting its ruthlessness as it dragged her down, dim sum spilling across the linoleum as she collapsed. But she hadn't listened.

She'd committed the same mistake with Emmett—so desperate to fix him, only to miss the moment of his departure.

The rain's alien patter bounced against her skull like a mallet. *Gravity.*

The forming stream of mud bubbled over the edge of the tarp. *Gravity.*

The flood of grief. *Gravity.*

The boundary between her and the wilderness blurred. Sound stretched and bent, the forest's insistent hum deepening. She stared into the woods, her eyes sliding out of focus into a kaleidoscope of green and umber. Vivid, rich, trembling. The woods embraced her with its rhythm, the strangeness repelling and beckoning her at once. Either a comfort, or a warning. She could no longer tell the difference.

She floated adrift, and time lost its hold.

She returned to suffocating darkness, the smell of her own piss, and rain thundering against the tarp above her head.

Lifting her hand, she ran it blindly up the length of Emmett's body, and pressed two fingers into the cold flesh of his neck.

She was alone.

# HOLDEN

Dr. Jane Clevenger sipped on the Earl Grey Holden had made for her as she perched on a sofa chair near the fireplace. She looked like a tourist coming back from a safari gone wrong, all linen and canvas, midsixties, a gray braid falling from her sun hat and down her shoulder. She'd been camping alone near Triplet Lakes when the fire started.

Maidei sat on the table's bench facing the Fort's new arrival, a quiet fury burning behind her eyes. "You didn't return my calls."

Clevenger lifted her chin toward Tiffany, who leaned against the far wall with her arms crossed. "Nor did I return hers, if that makes you feel better."

"It doesn't," said Maidei.

Holden and Angel tossed glances back and forth, silently arguing about who would be the first to speak up and ask questions.

"Who are these two?" Clevenger nodded in Holden's direction.

Holden opened his mouth, but Maidei interjected. "My assistants."

Clevenger narrowed her eyes at them. "I see."

Great. Holden had no idea how to act like a scientist.

"And Jane was my dad's research partner," Tiffany said.

*Research partner.* Jane had studied the same glacier in the same cabin as Siena's team.

"Please, call me Dr. Clevenger."

Tiffany cocked her head. "Sure, *Auntie.*"

The tension was suddenly so suffocating that Holden had to look away and at Zaid, who sat on the floor behind the table, sifting through a stack of papers he'd just brought into the room. An odd thing to do now, but he didn't understand Zaid's intentions half the time.

"You both called Dr. Clevenger about Dr. Dupont?" Angel asked.

"Yes," Tiffany and Maidei said in unison.

Maidei continued. "When the team disappeared, I wanted to know whether there were other places Dr. Feyrer would have sent them. Somewhere else we could look. But instead of divulging anything to me, you came here in secret and ventured up the mountain yourself. Why?"

"I don't speak of the research over email or phone." Dr. Clevenger said. "I signed an NDA for Dr. Feyrer."

"My dad's dead," Tiffany said.

"Just because he's dead doesn't mean I shouldn't be quiet and careful."

*Quiet and careful?* "Weren't you studying the same thing as Dr. Dupont?" Holden asked. What was so secret about glacial emissions?

Dr. Clevenger was quiet for a moment, her eyes roaming over Holden like she was contemplating his existence. "We were studying the same thing, but I don't think Dr. Dupont or her team knew this. I don't believe Feyrer told her the whole truth before he died."

Holden's fingers itched in anticipation. Whatever Clevenger knew was about to link his carefully aligned pieces or smash the puzzle to bits.

"Is that why you hiked into Deadswitch alone when you

knew she was missing?" Maidei asked. "Is *the whole truth* why we can't find her?"

Clevenger smiled coyly at Maidei. "I suspect you know more than I thought."

"What the hell is going on?" Angel muttered.

"I ventured into Deadswitch because I have a suspicion where Dr. Dupont's team went," Clevenger said calmly. "I went alone hoping to collect research we left at the cabin all those years ago, research Dr. Feyrer wouldn't let us take off the mountain."

"Why wouldn't Dr. Feyrer let you take the research back to the university?" Holden asked.

Clevenger lowered her tea and saucer to her lap. "Because what we found was dangerous and challenged our understanding of the world, and we didn't know who we could trust with the information."

Holden had heard something like this before from Maidei, when she'd shown him the old files from her own research project.

*We were on the brink of a discovery that would have changed our rudimentary understanding of life.*

"Here." From inside his fort of papers, Zaid passed Maidei a few folded pages. She unfolded them, stole a glance, and set them in her lap.

Tiffany paced near the window, and Holden's heart raced as he watched her. "So, if you weren't studying the glacier . . ." he began.

"We were," said Dr. Clevenger. "But it was the nineties. Climate science was changing, and skeptics abounded. Alpenglow Glacier was melting too fast, and we were sent there to prove the melt wasn't related to geothermal or biological activity. We took samples of everything: soil, plants, core wood." She nodded toward Maidei. "Some of our findings matched Dr. Chari's a decade later, but nothing made sense. We scraped animal cells from trees. It was like we were being tricked.

"Then one morning, I woke to this awful ringing in my head and left the cabin to fill my canteen in the outside barrels, but the surrounding alpine environment had changed to one green, dark, and full of ancient growth. Unlike any temperate rainforest I've ever seen, let alone the Sierras."

Tiffany stopped pacing, her expression so horror-stricken that Holden did a double take before he could even process what Clevenger had just said.

*Ringing.* He and Tiffany had heard a ringing in Deadswitch, too.

"I don't understand," Angel said.

"Neither did we," Clevenger replied. "We panicked and fought a lot that first day, unable to agree on where we were or how we'd gotten there. Days passed and we still couldn't decide what to do. Instead of working together, we grew suspicious of one another. Started stealing clothing and food, going on walks into this new strange wilderness alone instead of in groups. We acted like children. I'm not proud of . . ." She looked down at her tea, brought it to her lips, and drank slowly. She swallowed. " . . . of anything, really. And then one of our postdocs went missing. Wandered off into the forest. We split up trying to find him. Sent up flares. I never saw him again."

"Tell me you reported him missing," Maidei said. "You must have found a way out. Tell me you sent more people to search."

Startled by Maidei's demand, Holden picked apart her rising anger. This same thing had happened to her, lost in a wet, dark, unfamiliar forest. Frank had found her sleeping on the ground. He'd searched for her.

Dr. Clevenger clasped her hands on the table near her tea, her expression reserved and unreactive to Maidei. "We found a way back, or I should say the way back found us. Two weeks later, we returned the same way we'd entered—a sharp ringing upon waking, a seemingly random event out of our control. We hiked out of Deadswitch within the hour, and Feyrer made us sign an NDA before returning home."

"And what about the postdoc?" Maidei pressed.

"We lied," Clevenger replied matter-of-factly. "We reported

him missing after we made it home. We told officials he never arrived at our meeting point the morning of the trip."

The revelation stole the air from the room. Maidei clasped a hand over her mouth and stood, moving toward the windows.

Disgust twisted in Holden. The postdoc's family deserved to know the truth about where he'd gone missing. And everyone visiting Deadswitch deserved to know what could also happen to them.

"Mai," Zaid said softly, still on the ground. Concern etched his face as he watched his research partner.

Holden had forgotten Francis was in the room until he whined, padding over to Maidei and sitting near her feet.

"Did you ever find out more?" Angel asked quietly. "Where you actually went?"

"Yes," Clevenger said. "Wilder had theories, so the next time we entered Deadswitch, we took a theoretical physicist with us. This time it took four weeks for us to be transported. Same forest, same place we were before. Our physicist culled from the chaos what he believed to be the most important element of it all: the frequency we heard upon arriving, and when leaving. The ringing in our ears."

*Ringing.* Holden searched for Tiffany, but she was absent from the room. Where had she gone?

Dr. Clevenger took a long sip of her tea. Her fingers trembled around the porcelain.

Angel huffed, and Holden knew it was from impatience. He was not impatient, wishing for some cosmic pause button he could jam down and take a few breaths.

"Our physicist theorized the frequency was not just a sound but a signal, the harmonic resonance acting as a gateway. His hypothesis was heavily influenced by the theory that extra dimensions are required for the consistent vibration and interaction of the particles in our universe. We'd stumbled upon a rift. That's why our data was inconsistent during our first trip. We were collecting samples from two different worlds."

A hush blanketed the room. Holden sat to combat his dizziness.

"Two different worlds," Maidei slowly reiterated. "And you kept this a secret."

Clevenger scoffed. "We had to. Imagine if this reached the public—or even the *government*—before we fully understood everything about the place beyond the rift."

Maidei sneered at her. "You mean you could no longer exploit it in secret?"

Clevenger raised her voice. "Ill-equipped people would try to find it. They would get hurt. Lost. *Killed*."

"That's already happening." Maidei marched toward Clevenger and flung her arm out, the folded papers between her fingers. "A police report. *My* police report."

Clevenger warily took the pages and unfolded them, holding them away from her face as she read. "You've been there." She swiveled from Maidei to Zaid. "And you were searching for these pages before I explained my story. Both of you knew what I was about to tell you."

"Zaid knew of my experience from the beginning. I wanted to forget it ever happened, but he kept the documentation."

Zaid pulled himself from the floor to a seat at the table. "At least one of us needs to be a hoarder."

Maidei continued. "I called to tell you Dr. Feyrer's mentees were missing, left messages, and you never responded. I sensed from that point you knew where they were, and that it wasn't as simple as pointing out a location on a map."

No, not a map. "We found Dr. Dupont with the drone," Holden said. "I told you I saw her, because she was standing *there*, just not on Agnes. She was already through the rift. That's why I only saw a flash of her before the feed went dead." This was as close to proof that he'd actually seen Siena as he would get.

"Dammit." Zaid buried his face in his hands. "And now the drone is toast. We could have learned more."

Holden tugged on his collar, the room too hot.

"This frequency," Angel began, wringing her hands on top of the table as she stared at them. "Were you able to—I don't know—manipulate it somehow to open this rift?"

"We tried amplifying it," said Clevenger. "Sometimes we amplified the frequency and the rift immediately opened. Other times it would take months. We never identified the other variable."

Angel's hands froze on the table before she dug into her purse on the seat next to her.

"The technology is better now." Zaid's eyes gleamed with excitement. "Amplifiers and transmitters are more portable and powerful. Maybe you just needed a stronger sig—" A shrill screech through the air cut him off.

Francis barked. Holden whipped around to Angel and saw what she held in her hands. "Tell me you didn't."

"They won't miss it." Angel looked down at the wooden flute she'd stolen from the visitor center, and blew on the flute again. Francis howled.

"What is that horrible thing?" Clevenger asked. Zaid's eyes widened like a five-year-old in a toy shop, and Angel handed him the flute.

"Ever heard of the Church of Bounty?" Holden said.

Maidei crossed her arms. "I'm guessing you didn't check out that artifact through any official channel."

Holden held his hands up. "Angel stole it. I didn't know."

Dr. Clevenger's face had fallen sheet-white. She picked up the small satchel she'd brought with her, rummaged through it, and pulled out her phone. After pecking on the screen a few times with her finger, she held it up. A high-pitched shriek emitted from her phone's speaker, perfectly in tune with the flute. "Sixty-eight hundred hertz," Dr. Clevenger announced. "Same frequency as the one we heard."

The cult knew about the frequency. They'd created instruments to match it. Was their entire religion based on what they'd found beyond the rift?

"Holy shit," Angel breathed, and slumped in her seat.

Holden shook away a shiver and stood. "We need to tell Frank."

"And then what?" Maidei watched him like he was an unpredictable zoo animal. "Frank has been at his post long enough to understand that something is terribly wrong with the wilderness area he oversees. He knows my story, and at least ten others have gone missing in the past decade under his watch."

"Exactly!" Holden cried. "He needs to know the truth. He needs to prepare for something like this to happen again."

"He is one man," Maidei argued. "A ranger. What is he going to do? No one can reach the cabin right now. No one even knows if it still stands."

Holden took a step back. "So what are you saying? We do nothing?"

Maidei visibly swallowed, and then straightened her shoulders. "I've already told you I've done my part. I'm leaving tomorrow. I need to go home."

*Unbelievable.* He swung his glare to Dr. Clevenger.

She jutted her chin. "I never had the intention of returning to that place beyond the rift. I came to Deadswitch this time to find the only proof I know of, in the research cabin on this side. I planned to contact Dr. Chari once it was in my possession."

"Your plan was to hand the responsibility off to strangers? I . . ." Holden shook his head, stunned into silence. A revelation this big was supposed to get them closer to finding Siena. Now, he only felt hopeless.

"What do you think we should do, Holden?" Angel asked.

As he shifted his attention to her, Angel lifted her hand to chew on her thumbnail.

What had she told him, right before the fire started? *We're not the A-Team of wilderness rescue. We're here for the evidence protocol misses.*

The evidence protocol misses. He knew of another place where this frequency occurred.

"Did anyone see where Tiffany went?" he asked.

"I suppose I upset her with my story," Clevenger said. "Her father never told her."

"I'm going to look for her." Holden hurried from the room with Francis on his heels. He opened the front door to check outside, Frank's Jeep parked in the dirt clearing. Unless she'd walked to the station, she was still here.

He shut the door and climbed the stairs past the second floor to the third. Tiffany's room was empty.

Francis yipped softly and barreled up the pull-down stairs to the attic, more acrobat than dog. Curious, Holden followed, and found Tiffany sitting on his bed.

She jumped up and turned toward the window, wiping her face. "I'm so sorry. I was trying to find somewhere where no one would look for me, and panicked." She took a deep breath and faced him, her eyes rimmed red.

"What's wrong?" he asked. "Other than the obvious."

Tiffany deflated and sat again, and Francis hopped onto the bed to lick the tears from her cheek. She smiled and pushed him away, and the dog lay his head on her lap.

Tiffany reached out to stroke Francis's ears, her gaze averted from Holden's. "I've been there. To this place Jane and my dad were trapped."

Holden's lips parted in surprise. He wanted to respond, but his mind raced too quickly.

"This was before Maidei's research group. Even before Frank. I was a kid. Nine. My mom was with her boyfriend in Greece, so Wilder . . . he didn't really know what to do with me. When he went out into the field that summer, he dumped me at the cabin with a stack of books and VHS tapes."

"Wait, you were *nine*?" Holden reeled. The cabin by Glass Lake was no place for a nine-year-old to stay by herself for weeks with no bathroom, no water, and no kitchen.

"I was alone," Tiffany said. "And lonely. I missed my friends and real food. Dad idiotically trusted me with a camp stove, but all I had were granola bars and cans of Chef Boyardee."

"Jesus Christ," Holden said. That was the reason she'd been acting so strange when they visited the cabin together. "Your cabin transported you to the other forest, too?"

"Yes," Tiffany said. "And if the timeline is right, it was also at the same time as Dad and Jane. Couldn't have happened to everyone in Deadswitch, though. There are a couple of hundred people in the wilderness area throughout summer. Someone else would have said something. But I didn't, and apparently my dad made his team sign an NDA."

Tiffany fell quiet and looked down at Francis, who lay there patiently waiting for more pets. "You're a very good boy, aren't you?" she whispered.

"What was it like?" he asked quietly, hoping his tone implied he didn't want to force her to say anything she didn't want to.

"Dark," she said. "Impossibly dark. Everything beyond the cabin was overgrown and soaked. Nothing like Deadswitch. It . . . I don't know. It terrified me. I went outside once, walked around the cabin a bit, and then went back in and locked the door. I went to the bathroom in a bucket. I rationed my stock of soda and water bottles Dad had left me, not knowing if I would ever be brave enough to leave. Two weeks . . . yeah, that sounds about right. And the ringing Clevenger mentioned to you—"

"We heard it while we were there." He'd sat inside the husk of a dimensional rift, only a few miles away from here, drinking a Coke and utterly clueless. And Tiffany hadn't said a word about it.

She could sense his thoughts. "You have to understand, I was looking to prove what happened to me was a figment of my imagination. If I had said something, it would have given power to possibility. It's so much easier for things just to stay impossible, Holden."

He understood. Tiffany had been trying to protect the part of her that was still that little girl. But now, given how many lives were on the line, someone had to be brave enough to go up against a tear in reality. The thought sent a bolt of terror straight through his heart.

And yet, everything he'd gone through, everything he'd discovered, had led to this. He thought of his dream the night before he and Angel had driven to California—sewing up Siena's leg with catgut somewhere in the wild. The confidence he'd felt in that moment, albeit imaginary.

Frank and SAR were entangled in the tangible emergency of the wildfire. Those who'd witnessed the dimension themselves didn't want the responsibility of their knowledge. Not only that, but it was possible opening the rift would take time. Weeks.

He had time.

No, he wasn't built to take this on by himself. But no one was built for anything at the beginning. Grit was equal parts strength and stupidity.

Tiffany whispered his name. Holden blinked and refocused on her.

"Whatever you do next, you need to be careful," she said. "There will be no rescue if something goes wrong. No one will be there to hike you off the mountain."

# LAUREN

Lauren Vega ran her thumb along the mouth of the Schlitz bottle, watching the door of the pub from her booth.

This was the only bar in Oregon that sold Schlitz. The beer tasted like burnt rubber, but something about the old label design comforted her. She was a glutton for comfort—soft old t-shirts, ugly small dogs, labels that made her nostalgic even if she didn't know why. The grease splatter on the menu. The Christmas string lights hanging over the crusty bar counter. Any reminder she possessed some concept of a soul fueled her tank, and right now she was running on fumes.

The door squealed open and shut. Chelsea Morton stood there, wringing the strap of her designer bag, and Lauren took comfort in how nervous she looked.

Chelsea spotted Lauren and beelined for the booth, before sitting across from her. She adjusted herself in the seat and tucked a lock of highlighted hair behind her ear. "Well?"

Lauren took a swig of her warm beer. "Relax."

The bartender had already swooped upon their table, a woman too old and jaded for manners. She waited with her arms crossed.

"She'll have a tequila soda," Lauren said.

Chelsea held her hand up. "Just a club soda, please." The bartender rolled her eyes and left, and Chelsea turned back to Lauren. "I stopped drinking."

Lauren took another sip. "Good for you."

"I can't stay long."

A smile crept across Lauren's face. "Unless you plan on pulling a gun out of that purse, you'll stay as long as I want you to stay."

Desperation flashed across Chelsea's face. "I already did my part. *Please.*"

The thing with depravity was that everyone involved deserved to be a little nervous at some point. A little scared they wouldn't get what they'd signed up for. Those were the rules, and as far as Lauren was concerned, Chelsea had gotten her part of the job done with hardly a hitch. There was that part at the beginning where she'd gotten so drunk at the college bar that she almost blew it with Holden, because Holden was too damn *good* to take advantage of a fly.

She'd had a nice recovery after that fumble. Lauren would give her credit for that. She had expected her little catalyst here to be a larger liability.

Chelsea jumped when the bartender slammed the plastic cup of soda water on the table and left again. She pinched a brown napkin from the plastic holder and wiped away the spill, then tucked the soggy napkin to the side, folded her hands in front of her, and bounced a bit in her seat.

Lauren slid the banded bills from the inside of her leather jacket and tossed them onto the table.

"What if someone sees?" Chelsea whispered, eyes darting wildly around before she swept up the money.

"There's no one in here except for a bartender who wouldn't care if we pulled off a heist right now."

Chelsea bit her lip and glanced down at the money in her lap.

"You can count it if you want," Lauren said.

"Is he okay?" Chelsea asked.

*Oh, please.* Chelsea hadn't hesitated when Lauren first offered the proposal and a payment of twenty grand. Distract a nice, vulnerable man for a few months and heartlessly ditch him. Easy for a broke young girl who didn't understand the meaning of relationships.

"He's fine."

"Why . . ." Chelsea tucked the cash into her purse and nervously took a sip of her soda water. "Why did I need to do it?"

Now she cared. "That answer will cost you five grand."

Chelsea straightened her shoulders. "Fine." She stood, brushing down the front of her blouse. "There are apps for these kinds of transactions, you know."

"You're not that stupid," Lauren said.

"What am I supposed to do with a *wad of cash*?" she hissed.

Lauren shrugged. "Don't spend it all in one place. People will think you're a criminal."

"Whatever." Chelsea spun on her heel, struggled with the front door a bit, and left.

Lauren sat back in the booth and drained the rest of her beer. She glanced over at the bar, and the bartender shot her a smile full of dead teeth.

"Bad Tinder date?" She seemed very proud of herself for knowing what Tinder was.

Lauren smirked. "Sure."

She pinned a twenty beneath her empty beer bottle and left, lighting a cigarette as she walked to the truck she'd bought off a farmhand. In the cab, she rolled the hand crank and took a long drag before exhaling out the cracked window.

Cameron Yarrow hadn't registered Lauren's influence on her decisions, but what Lauren had done to Holden made her feel bad. At least he wasn't a sacrificial lamb. Neither of them were. They were just pieces, and to move across the board, Holden needed to feel unwanted and have no reason to come back home.

She slid two cards from the pocket of her jacket and fanned them between her fingers.

**The Martyr.** A woman on a pyre, skin melting from her bones.

**The Mother.** Her means of revenge.

Lauren took another drag of her cigarette before tossing the cards into the cup holder and starting the engine.

# THE WAY BACK

**Variable #05**
**Alpha Timeline Entry: January 24th, 1995**
**Confidence: 23%**

**Contents:**
**Artifact: Lighter, no fuel**
**Artifact: Sports bandage (biohazard - used as tourniquet)**
**Field Notes: copied, processed, and annotated. See index.**
**Length: 32 days**
**Cause of Death: Fungal infection on right foot. Confidence: 19%**

# SIENA

Four or five days after Emmett died, she found a meadow.

The ground squelched beneath her feet. She rested her bag on a rotten stump to relieve the burning ache in her shoulders.

The sun was out. She tilted her chin until warmth baked her face. When was the last time she'd seen the sun? She'd grown careless with tracking days. Everything between leaving the mountain and now was a blur of color and trees accompanied by stabs of grief.

After he'd died—after she'd finally pulled herself together—she'd dragged some branches and lichen over his body and left him on the ground. She didn't know if what had killed him was contagious, but if it was, she was likely infected. Time would tell, and she felt powerless against the possibility of dying like him. She'd traded out her bag for his because it fit better, and would have taken his digital watch if it weren't strapped to the rotten hunk of flesh that was once his hand.

Then she'd left and followed her compass south, her nubuck gloves permanently fixed to her hands. Emmett's death played on a loop in her head until the recollection devolved into a surreal memory with little emotion attached. She wasn't sure if this stage of grief was supposed to be denial, or acceptance.

She dropped her chin to gaze across a sea of high grass and mustard-yellow flowers, her breath hitching at a small deer with dark spots and hook-shaped tusks. The deer blinked at her and ducked its head beneath the grass, foraging for something. Insects, maybe.

A compulsion crawled over Siena to unstrap Isaac's bow from her bag and shoot the deer. Her subconsciousness had known to not part with the weapon in hopes of a fresh kill.

Her mouth flooded at the thought of meat until a flash of fungus growing from Emmett's hand made her dry heave.

*Enough.*

She gained some semblance of control, and felt guilty for wanting to shoot the poor thing, which was just minding its business. After sitting on a stump, she drew her field journal from her pack, and poorly sketched the deer. She'd compare the drawing to Feyrer's research the next time her phone worked. For now, it lay dead alongside Emmett's at the bottom of her bag.

She also carried with her the remainder of their food, a tightly rationed month of dehydrated dinners, energy bars, and MREs. If that wasn't enough to get her home, she had bigger problems.

Her eyes scanned beyond the meadow to the next woodland edge. She blinked a few times against the sun. A lump formed in her throat, and she pulled her map from her rain shell and unfolded it, even though she was certain she'd copied no landmarks other than the trail and the outposts for the rest of the journey.

Less than a quarter of a mile away, ancient growth cut the land from east to west, more absolute than the wall of a military base. The trees grew upward of ninety meters—impossibly tall— and from where she stood she could make out an impenetrable canopy and the beginnings of fatally thick growth.

She'd stolen Emmett's batteries—seven triple As in various used states—and had a sense her headlamp would remain on at all times through the next leg of the hike. Hopefully a short leg. The damp darkness she'd traversed since Outpost 2 continued to eat away at her nerves. Not only that, but a scratch from a wayward branch could be the end of her, for all she knew.

The sun dipped behind the clouds, and she zipped her rain shell to her neck and tied a bandanna over the lower half of her face. After throwing on her pack, she crossed the meadow and found a trail, following it until the forest swallowed her.

Siena took a breath of drenched air. Her headlamp beam swept over the bracken hugging the narrow trail. Moss and maidenhair painted giant slick trunks while fungus ate away at crumbling deadwood. Water splattered over her hood, falling as thick as rain, though it hadn't been raining when she entered.

It was beautiful. And then, less than half a mile in, the forest fell darker than fucking midnight.

If it weren't for all the growth—and the rain—she'd think she was in a cavern. The perpetual nighttime biome echoed, cacophonous hoots, caws, and chitters casting back and forth beneath lichen-drenched boughs. Every so often, her headlamp caught the tail of a mouse or the flutter of a bat.

Before her stretched only the promise of black forest. Siena followed the thinning trail deeper, kicking through ferns and lunging over tree corpses. She strained her ears for the sound of lurking predators, or the hungry rumble that signaled The Shadow.

A few miles later, she glanced up at the sweet relief of stars.

*No.*

Horror pulsed through her as thousands of eyes reflected the light of her headlamp. Bats, owls, rodents. Pale mammals with big ears, for which she didn't have names. Lizards. Snakes. Spiders hanging from their webs, eyes quadrupled. An infestation.

A fight broke out somewhere between her and the canopy, a creature shrieking in death. Sets of eyes zipped away, scrambling from the noise. Siena gripped the straps of her bag so tightly, she felt her panicked pulse beating in her palms.

To hell with making camp here. She'd keep walking until she died.

She lunged forward when branches snagged her bag, scanning ahead for any sign of light. Her attention caught on trash scattered between the ferns—a cluster of plastic bags, an old tire.

How did a tire get here?

When she slowed to investigate, something from beyond the darkness rattled. She picked up her pace again, leaving the tire alone. Better to not piss anything off.

But hours later, both her determination and caution waned, and exhaustion slammed into her full force. If she kept walking like this, she'd run her body down until she was stuck here forever.

So much for walking until she died.

She shook her ground tarp out on the driest patch of moss she could find in the dark, then struggled with her bivy, fingers fumbling to connect the poles. Water pooled in her hanging tarp mere seconds after she strung it up, but she was too tired to care. At least she could filter it for her bottle in the morning. She wriggled inside her bivy, laid flat her damp clothes, and spent as much light as she could waste tearing up her field journal with notes.

*How does life evolve to survive without the sun?*
*Chemosynthesis*
*Bacterial or fungal symbiosis*
*Soil nutrients—leaves and rot*
*Gets warm enough to sweat here, between 15–20°C.*
*I understand the plants more than the animals. Their noises never wane or change, like nothing in this biome sleeps.*

Light had yet to break through the forest by her third camp.

The rain wavered between mist and downpour but never stopped. She gave up on the pipe dream of drying out in her bivy. No amount of shaking out or blowing on her hands could unprune them. Her feet were in a worse state, both macerated and inflamed, her heels as tender as raw chicken. She'd used all her aspirin on her knee sprain, a laughable injury compared to this. The soles of her boots drooped from the toe like flapping mouths. She duct-taped them shut and set them aside, then swept her headlamp over the troughs and ridges of her waterlogged skin to check for infection. Nothing yet, though her luck had to run out eventually, like the fuel of the camp stove she'd abandoned this morning. There would be no more instant coffee. She could still taste it from when she and Emmett made cups back in Outpost 2.

When she turned off her light, it was too dark to see her hand waving in front of her face. Her rib cage tightened around her lungs, and she couldn't expand her chest enough to breathe. She reached out and touched nothing other than her cold sleeping bag.

After her diagnosis, when Emmett still slept by her side, she'd wake up in a panic and reach out to touch him. He'd wake up every time, roll over, and hold her. He'd done the same at the research cabin when they were trapped there. A reflex.

Over the sour and putrid stench of her own body, she could smell him, here in the dark. Their bed, his sweat and deodorant. She could smell him even though there was no one around her for miles, no one to reach out and touch, not even if she needed touch to keep living.

She wrapped her arms around her body and pretended they belonged to someone else, and in the morning, she ate half a package of glutinous rehydrated Alfredo, packed up, and kept moving.

She fantasized about the sun the way she used to fantasize about good sex, almost too distracted to notice that her ribbon of trail had finally thinned to nothing. Her light flashed over beads of water dripping from thorny briars. She took out her compass and shook it a bit until the trembling red-capped needle pointed to her right.

Assuming her compass even worked in the Briardark, the trail had been leading her west, not south.

Her feet snagged on roots, and saplings clawed her pants, the light from her headlamp unhelpfully trembling like it was afraid of the dark. She sank to her calves in a sea of soaking detritus, backtracking when fallen trees blocked her way.

Any sign of a trail or a break in the suffocating canopy eluded her. She stomped down enough growth just to make camp, and did this over and over again, and again, and again, taking her meds diligently each time she thought twenty-four hours had passed, until the last twelve pills rattled around in her bottle.

Then her feet started to bleed, and she lost track of time.

When Siena was a kid, she watched a cartoon movie about a boy who drove monsters and goblins away by singing. So she tried it now, oscillating between Spice Girls and John Denver.

Her mother had owned a cassette of *Back Home Again* that never left the deck in her car. It had played on repeat, flipping to side B and back to side A again as they drove to Lodgepole in Sequoia National Park. Mariposa Grove near Wawona. The idyllic little village of Mammoth Lakes. They'd drive up those slow, winding roads that glittered with mica as her mother sang "Annie's Song," heading toward tourist-trodden visitor centers that smelled like pine needles and ice cream.

Siena had played that album on her mother's last day in the hospital, right before she went to get lunch.

She shoved herself southward long after "Sweet Surrender" died on her lips, fighting off spiky new growth until the nocturnal foliage parted for the vaguest sliver of a path. Hope pulsed inside her, and she followed the path eastward and around a bend until the dulling beam of her headlamp caught the remains of a structure. She ventured through the thicket and wet pulp to a sign hanging crookedly from one of the remaining beams.

*Outpost 4*

Outpost 3 was somewhere behind her, probably passed by the first time she lost the trail. The dank atmosphere had eaten this outpost whole, gutting her chances of drying out and healing her skin for one goddamn night.

Her singing had warmed her voice up for a shriek of anguish.

Farther down the trail, she threw down camp and crammed the last of her remaining batteries into her headlamp. She unfolded her damp map and located Outpost 4, then brushed her rippled and peeling finger back and forth across the paper valley before clenching her fist.

Halfway. Halfway to the last outpost and the ring with two slashes through it. Halfway between Mount Agnes and home, if she could even get out of this place.

Halfway.

She was half-fucking-way.

Did this midnight biome stretch all the way to the last outpost? Was the pitch-black canopy merely The Shadow, ingraining into her the lesson that what he giveth, he taketh away? The light, the sun, a clear path forward. All of it, merely a privilege.

She finished her MRE. Two more, along with ten mangled and squashed energy bars, remained at the bottom of her pack.

Not enough.

She woke screaming, despair thundering through whatever emotional valve had finally broken inside her.

She gasped and sobbed, frantically feeling around until her sticky fingers found the strap of her headlamp. She clicked it on, the light shining on her nails caked in blood.

She stared at the red crescents in a daze, snot dripping from her nose, until a tender spot on her back itched. Flipping over, she lifted the blood-smeared hem of her shirt. Broken pustules clustered along her flank. They hadn't been there the last time she camped. She'd scratched them open in her sleep.

Numbly, she dug through her pack for her deflated first aid kit, and cleaned the area and her fingers with her last alcohol wipe before bandaging her side with tape and gauze.

How long had Emmett lived after the splinter? One day? Two? This rash wasn't the same infection, but she couldn't trust it would be any kinder.

She took a small bite of the energy bar in her pocket and folded the wrapper over the rest. One and a half bars. Four pills after rationing. No more antiseptic.

She licked the open cracks of her lips and fell back into her sleeping bag. This was better than dying in a hospital like her mother.

A branch snapped outside, close to her tent. Something from the woods had heard her scream and had arrived to scavenge her corpse.

She unzipped her bivy and shone her light into the forest and a gnarled claw of thorns. A small lizard skittered away.

Nothing.

She sang out the first line of "Annie's Song." The darkness ate the melody whole.

Six or seven or eight camps later, she was still alive.

Her antipsychotics were gone. The rash had spread across her greasy flank. Her headlight had petered out, and now she dragged the bloody stumps of her feet through the darkness by only the soft beam of her pocket flashlight.

She passed garbage every once in a while. Tangled chain link fencing, a soggy fast food bag. What the trash signaled, she couldn't know for sure, but clung to a fragment of hope.

*Hypothesis: I'm reaching the end.*

Pale rodents the size of enormous rats hopped and skittered through the bracken and leaf rot, weaving courageously between her feet. She caught only flashes of them with her weak light. Their behavior differed from when she entered the pitch-black forest, when thousands of creatures watched from the safety of the tree branches. She committed their features to memory, their large ears and puckered eye sockets, the purple fungus that grew on their backs. Parasitic? Commensalistic?

One latched on to her pant leg, and she shook it off with an angry yowl.

This happened two, three more times until she duct-taped her pants to her shoes for fear they'd get beneath her clothes and bite her.

The rodents weren't the only creatures getting braver. She dodged a snake and a spider the size of her hand, both so bullish in their approach, like hallucinations. Maybe they *were* hallucinations—products of her paranoia.

When Siena was still getting her PhD, she'd dreamt of traveling to the arctic and studying subglacial lakes, overwintering with her team at a station. She'd even written a draft of the proposal, and had researched how to prepare herself physically and mentally for the months of unending darkness, when the sun never breaches the horizon. Cabin fever. Isolation. Hijacked hormones and circadian rhythms. Disorientation and delusions. She read about the researcher who'd plunged a kitchen knife into a data manager for eating the last of the station's chocolate stash. Early explorers stripping naked and sprinting across the ice until they froze to death. Wooden barracks full of sleeping technicians and engineers, lit on fire by a deranged supervisor.

Siena's dream had fizzled out when she was diagnosed and could no longer pass a psychological screening. But she still often thought of those scientists and explorers who caught winter-over syndrome like one would catch a cold. A spark of madness was all it took, a fire poker to the brain, sending thought patterns and emotional intelligence aflutter, like ash.

The same thing would inevitably happen to her. Better Emmett died before she could brain him with the rod of her bivy, strip naked, and walk through the fetid abyss until the rats ate her. There was still time for the latter to happen. She couldn't think of a better way to kill herself. Maybe pills, but she'd eaten all of hers.

A clearing interrupted her path, the fire pit in the center covered in moss and slime. A skull sat on one stone, fungus eating away at the eye sockets.

She sat near the ring, resting. The tremors in her muscles wouldn't stop, not even when she slept.

"I can't decide if I'm jealous of you," she told the skull. She swept her light from its eaten eye sockets to an equally eaten canvas bag to her right. Pushing the fabric away, her hands closed around a metal cylinder. At first she couldn't believe it. She dragged the can toward her face, her dull light falling on the label.

*Pennyman's Pork and Beans - Campfire Style*
She laughed, and then she laughed harder.

She checked the can for bloat, then pried open the lid with her knife. Raising it to her lips, she shut her eyes as the sludge slid into her mouth and down her throat. Brown sugar and slime with chunks of ham. It was gone before she could even enjoy it, and she cried as she licked the inside of the can clean.

Siena tossed the can aside and wiped her nose with the back of her wrist. She found one more can in the rags of the canvas bag, which she took, but nothing else to identify the poor soul who'd lost their head by the fire ring.

At a snap, Siena glanced up and lifted her light. In the dull yellow orb, a deer picked at the leaves of a spiky bush on the other side of the clearing, its milky eyes bulbous, hairless flank threaded with inky veins. Its little knees bulged with white cartilage. Pustules like the ones on her back covered half its body.

Was this what she would turn into? A walking scab?

She could shoot *this* deer. It suffered from the same thing that infected her, so why the hell not? Put it out of its misery and eat the meat. All tinder and wood near the clearing was too wet to start a fire, but at this point she'd eat the meat raw.

She'd also never dressed a deer before. Cam had. They'd taken a duo trip around the Tahoe Rim a few years ago, and somewhere between their shared joint being a quarter smoked and two-thirds smoked (she'd noted this intently), they'd begun co-creating a survival scenario where they were stuck in the woods, Bear Grylls style, with nothing but a hunting knife and a fire source. Foraging and creating small traps for prey was priority one, of course, but *what if* they saw a deer?

*"Clearly at this point in my life, I'd have taken knife-throwing lessons,"* Cam had said.

But it wasn't just the knife throwing they needed to ponder. There were a hundred and ten ways to fuck up dressing a deer.

The two most important ones Siena remembered: don't puncture the intestines. And don't puncture the bladder.

*"You have to cut out its asshole."*

*"Christ, Cam."*

*"What? All the meat you eat once had an asshole."*

*"Yeah, why do you think I don't eat a lot of meat?"*

*"Because you think about asshole too much?"*

There'd been a lot of incessant giggling. She missed the joy of deranged conversation. A dry sleeping bag. The soft orange of sunrise. The voice of another.

She licked away a tear that rolled past her mouth, then the surrounding foliage shook, and something struck out from the darkness. The deer screamed as it fell forward, feeble hooves digging into the mud as it scrambled to find purchase.

Siena jumped up as the deer was dragged through the thorns, fumbling with the straps holding Isaac's bow to her bag. She finally freed it, sliding an arrow from the elastic side pocket and nocking it for her own defense. She wouldn't get far through the thicket if she tried to run.

She pulled back on the string, and it snapped apart, the arrow tumbling into the mud.

"*Fuck!*" She held her breath in the stifling dark, straining to listen beyond the pattering rain.

In the distance—she didn't know how far—the deer released a death shriek.

A predator.

She waited for primal fear to surge through her body, glancing at the dim flashlight in the mud near her feet. She wanted to know —*needed* to know—about the creature in these woods strong enough to snatch a deer from right in front of her.

She picked up her light and hobbled toward where the deer had stood, then peered into the woods. The flashlight beam shook along the ground. No drag marks, no animal tracks. No tang of iron in the air.

The scream of the deer echoed in her skull.

She returned to her bag, lugged it onto her weak shoulders, and pressed her fingers to the belt pocket containing her empty pill bottle. She fished it out and held it before her, shining her light on the bottom of the empty bottle until it glowed like the sun.

"Wake up."

Siena opened her eyes to darkness and the patter of rain, her face slick. She blinked, sniffed, then slumped once more against the half-rotten tree she leaned against.

She'd stopped to rest when the muscles in her calves wouldn't stop clenching and trembling, and must have fallen asleep. Her head drooped, and she let it hang there, contemplating every shallow breath.

Did she have enough energy to set up camp for the last time? Her belongings had finally surrendered to the rain, her bivy and sleeping bag soggy and moldering. Slipping into them would be worse than just sitting here. She couldn't feel much anyway, her legs pleasantly warm and numb.

"I expected more from you."

Her head bobbed as she tried to lift it. The voice was her own, yet her lips hung limply open and wordless.

"Drink."

Her teeth clattered against something plastic. Siena lifted her head and gulped cool water. Fingers plucked a leech from her neck, and another from her forehead. She'd lost the energy to keep fighting them off hours ago.

"Nothing waits for you back home," her voice said.

Siena swallowed for the last time, her head falling back against the tree. *Her father*, she wanted to say. Her father was still alive. As far as she knew. In his cabin up in the Yukon. No phone. No internet.

When would he learn of her death?

A bright orb burned up the darkness.

Tears streamed from her sensitive eyes. She blinked until her vision adjusted and settled on a silhouette holding a lantern. Light flickered over blurry plastic lenses, a long, hazy tube snaking from their mouth. She processed just enough of the figure to recognize the man in the gas mask. The man from the other cabin on Agnes. A severed mule head, a message in blood.

*The Mother Reigns.*

Terror seized her, her body trembling uncontrollably as his familiar deep voice rumbled.

"*Don't be afraid.*"

# CAMERON

Little pink mushrooms.

The color reminded Cam of the ring of mildew that formed around the bathtub drain. An unappetizing, soft peachy hue.

They were her lifeline. The core of her diet. The first page in Ruby's foraging book.

*Pebble mushrooms: abundant within a thirteen mile radius of The Other Backpack. Source of fiber, protein, probably vitamin D. Never pass up a patch. You will regret it.*

Cam hated mushrooms. She didn't understand why anyone would enjoy eating a dirt-flavored sponge. The texture was still terrible after two weeks of consuming them. That was when the last of her backpacking food ran out.

Pebble mushrooms grew in patches along the fence of The Tooth, and every few mornings, when Cam was assigned moss and fungus scraping duty, she'd collect them. She loved the satisfying *pop* they made when she plucked them from the ground. The patch that had cropped up along the eastern side of the fence could feed her for a couple of days.

She unzipped her fanny pack—something she'd taken from Levi after he died—and stuffed it with the mushrooms instead of dumping them in the gunk bucket next to her. Her fingers moved quickly and inconspicuously before sweeping up her scraper from the ground. She stood and focused on digging out the slimy green growth poking from the wood wall.

The Tooth had no rules against collecting and eating mushrooms. There were no rules against foraging at all, especially for the folks who could come and go as they pleased, because why would anyone forage for dirt-flavored fungus when slop was freely available every night?

Cam concealed her mushroom gathering because that was easier than explaining why she did it.

*Haven't you heard? Those filthy, hairy animals butchered for dinner are fed rotting corpses.*

Plus, she didn't want anyone getting wise and stealing her mushrooms before she could get to them.

"Mornin'."

A few meters down the wall, a gaunt woman named Spice waved her scraper at Cam before starting on the patch of moss in front of her. Everyone at The Tooth was gaunt, but Spice looked like she'd used her scraper to shave the fat from her own cheeks.

Cam returned her attention to the wall. "Sun's out today." She inwardly cringed. Small talk was worse than eating mushrooms.

"Lucky us," said Spice. "Got an outside job."

Cam scraped the log clean and stepped over to the next. The catwalk above jangled, and she glanced up at one of the wall guards leaning against the metal rail and staring right at her.

*Subtle.*

Cam knew they reported her every move to Tammy, because Tammy would tell Cam during the evening slop dish-outs, when she'd smile unnaturally wide and ask Cam if she'd had a good day cleaning the exact section of the wall she'd been working on. If Cam sneezed during her shift, Tammy would ask if she had a cold coming on. And Cam would always smile unnaturally wide back, and say something like "Good day indeed" or "Right as rain" or "Never felt better."

And then, from Tammy: "Will you join us for prayer around the bonfire tonight?"

Cam answered with that same shit-eating grin on her face: "Plan on getting to bed early."

She had a little dignity, after all.

But Tammy never seemed concerned by this answer as she flung hog slop into Cam's bowl. "Surrender will happen in time."

If by surrender, she meant forcefully offering Cam up as a Lover in some weird sexual sacrifice to a goddess who didn't exist, then sure. Cam would surrender eventually. Tomorrow, in fact, at the Harvest Feast.

Ever since her cards were pulled seven weeks ago, Cam had been such a good little chosen sacrifice. She never fought or pled or attempted escape . . . yet. She showed up for her shifts, scraping the walls and manning the medical cabin. She was pleasant to the villagers even though it killed her on the inside—most were terrible conversationalists and never had dirt to offer on Tammy or Bert.

For the first time in her entire life, Cam did everything she was supposed to do. The Tooth was an atrocity of secondhand cannibalism, but she was exactly where she needed to be, in the same place Avery was years ago. Handpicked for The Mother, a sacrifice cast into the woods the night of the feast.

Unless *cast into the woods* was a euphemism for *fed to the pigs*. She thought about this often—whether this Harvest Feast was a show to keep folks faithful, and Bert and Tammy merely planned on killing her. But Tammy gave her more devout-fanatic vibes than evil cult engineer. The woman truly believed in this sacrifice bullshit. Bert was the wild card. Cam hadn't seen him since her cards were drawn. A shepherd who kept his distance from his flock was one with secrets.

Even though she'd willfully ignored her danger radar since leaving Agnes—a habit of hers that would inevitably define her demise—she'd have to keep her wits about her before this feast.

She still had time to escape if the urge presented itself. But for now, she was closer to Avery than she'd ever been.

She thought of Siena. She'd had a lot of time to think of Siena over these past weeks, and how appalled she'd be at the mess Cam had gotten herself into. Siena would have been morbidly fascinated by The Tooth and gleaned more answers from her surroundings. Harassed more of the villagers, gone to the night-time masses to soak in as much information as she could about the cult, gotten on Tammy's every nerve. She would have come up with plans beyond going through with the sacrifice or escaping.

But Siena wasn't here, and Cam would have to figure her own way out of this mess.

When she was done with her section of the fence, she headed toward the bonfire to dump the contents of her bucket, the guards' eyes shamelessly burning into the side of her head. Did they even know why they were supposed to keep an eye on her? She hadn't been announced as The Sacrifice to the public yet. That was a reveal for the Harvest Feast, to leave no time for friends or family of the sacrifice to doubt The *Mother's will*.

She stole a glance at the catwalk. A young woman with an unfamiliar face stood amongst the guards. Her skin was vibrant, cheeks flush and plump. *Newborn.* Those stern, watchful eyes would soon house an untethered gleam, and her gums would recede until her smile was full of dark, bleeding gaps. And then she'd be taken off guard duty when she developed the shakes.

The shakes happened to everyone who ate the pork. At least, that was what Cam gauged with a control group of one: herself.

One thing she knew for certain was people who took refuge at The Tooth died quickly, most often from infection fed by a weakened immune system. Cam had seen enough wounds to make this conclusion.

Tammy did a good job at shuffling those who died out of sight. There was always vacancy for the newcomers to The Tooth.

Cam veered left around the crag and away from the hog pens, dumped the contents of her bucket in the fire, and stored the bucket and scraper in a nearby toolshed. She continued toward the cabin that had once been Isaac and Levi's and entered stuffy darkness. Kneeling near her bed, she jiggled a floorboard free and deposited the contents of the fanny pack inside the makeshift compartment, rotating the older fungus to the top of the pile. Her hand brushed against a folded piece of paper—the letter Isaac had left her.

Every time she thought of Isaac, a sick weight filled her gut. She hadn't forgotten her final days in the research cabin, Emmett dragging in a borderline decrepit Isaac to the couch. He'd been old. Which meant that no matter what, Isaac had to live long enough to reach that age.

Right?

She still had no idea how this time-loop bullshit worked. She'd contemplated for weeks whether she wanted to ask someone here if they knew anything about it, but every time she thought of doing so, a warning flickered inside her.

*Trust no one. Listen. Don't speak.*

Not like anyone would give her a straight answer, anyway. Probably some religious horsecrap about how The Mother controlled time, or whatever.

She resecured the floorboard, tugged the frayed hood of her rain shell over her head, and returned to the muddy street, weaving between cabins and past waving strangers with familiar faces. She waved back with a grimace for a smile.

The rare morning sun slid behind a soft blanket of gray. In the distance, the sky loomed black. *Storm.* Big fucking shocker. There was never a day it didn't rain, and never a handful of them where the sky wasn't darker than a city night—just enough light to make her feel like an abyss wasn't holding her hostage. The one thing this place had in common with her home—her real home—was pattern. Storm every two days. Three days. Two days. Every day until her skin was pruny even after she slept. And then a break of sun. But not long enough. Cam had never known such a craving before. She'd turned into an antivampire, desperate for light.

*Eat the mushrooms. Get your vitamin D, bitch.*

The clinic looked like another cabin, and upon Cam entering, the cloying stench of infection slapped her in the face. Three cots and a stool filled the room, and melting candles made of foraged beeswax lined the floor near the walls. Only one bed was occupied, by a woman who whimpered when Cam entered.

Fresh rainwater funneled into a basin in the corner, and Cam washed her hands, still wearing her jacket. "What happened?"

"I f-fell." Youthful vulnerability filled her voice, though she looked a little older than Cam, with pale skin and jet-black bangs that stuck to her forehead. Her watery eyes were too big for her head. Familiar eyes, though Cam couldn't recall her name.

Cam picked up a glass bottle on the lip of the basin and rinsed her hands with an herb-based astringent. From her pocket, she tugged free a pair of neoprene gloves, one of the few she'd packed in her first aid kit all those weeks ago. She'd been so damn careful not to rip or lose them, and gingerly eased a hand into each one before turning back toward the woman. "Let me see."

The woman presented Cam with an upturned palm and a shallow gash. Blood rolled between her thumb and index finger.

*Splat.*

Great. Now she would have to scrub the floor.

She retreated to the basin and returned with the bottle of astringent. "Keep your hand steady, this will sting."

The woman hissed before Cam had even tilted the bottle. Maybe this would be easier if she distracted her. "How long have you been at The Tooth?"

"A couple days."

"What's your name?"

"Thia," she said through gritted teeth, her hand jolting when astringent flooded the wound.

*Thia?* No, that wasn't right. Cam remembered now. The woman she was thinking of had lived in The Tooth for a whole ten days with her husband before taking off into the woods in search of a way back home. She'd volunteered in the clinic for a few days with Cam.

"You remind me of someone I knew who lived here for a bit, but her name was Cynn."

Thia's eyes darted from the hand she cradled to Cam's face. "*Cynn?*"

Cam nodded slowly, trying to make sense of the alarm on Thia's face. "You know her? She left a bit ago . . . probably before you arrived."

"How did you—" Thia's head shivered, and Cam couldn't tell if she was shaking it or trembling. "That's my name," she whispered. "The first part of it."

"Cynn . . . thia?" Cam said dumbly, and then repeated, "Cynthia."

"But I've told no one. I thought I was supposed to shorten it, like everyone else. How did you know?"

Cam stared at her. She swore to all fuck this woman had introduced herself as Cynn and left The Tooth a couple of weeks ago. "Weird coincidence, I guess," Cam muttered.

She was aware enough of her fellow villagers that she'd figured out the patterns and flow of how many came and went, just like the weather. Every time new folks wandered to The Tooth from the woods, their faces either looked familiar or so plain that they *felt* familiar. Their one-syllable nicknames often contained only a handful of letters. *Pill, Star, Dee, Jon, Maz, Chess, Clem.*

It was like she was stuck in some fucking simulation. *The Truman Show: Cult in the Woods* edition. That thought slid into her mind at least once a day, both outlandish and perfectly plausible. Was Thia some actress, having played the part of Cynn a couple of weeks ago? Did some higher power think Cam was too stupid to notice? Or was this the inexplicable time loop at work again?

Thia said nothing as Cam contemplated this, her attention fixed on the cut in her palm welling up with blood once more.

Cam tested her. "How's your husband?"

Thia's head shot up, her eyes full of bewilderment. And then Cam gleaned pain from her expression.

"Dead," she choked. "Out there. Out in the forest. Before I made it here."

*Oh, shit.*

"Did I . . . did I tell you I had a husband?"

No, she hadn't, but Cynn had a husband, and Cam had been trying to call Thia's bluff. Now she just felt like a monster.

Cam avoided the question, sliding an old tin from beneath the bed and opening it. She selected a long strip of fabric sterilized through boiling and wrapped Thia's hand. "Cut's not deep enough to waste stitches on. Keep it dry and clean. I mean it. Come back tomorrow to get the bandage changed, unless it gets wet, then you come back immediately." Cam stood, carefully tugging the gloves from her fingers, rolling them together, and tucking them into her pocket.

She didn't say goodbye to Thia as she left.

*Ignore it,* she thought. After tomorrow, she'd never see Thia again.

The stench of roasted hog hung heavy in the air. Her evening ritual was almost upon her: fixing a meager dinner, counting her remaining calories, and then working on her plan before the bell for the slop line rang. It would keep her mind off Cynn and Thia, too.

And, of course, the Harvest Feast.

A raw-throated voice scraped the air. "Hey there, Lover."

Cam skidded to a halt, mud sloshing over the front of her boot. A casual phrase. A stupid nickname for a friend, or actual lover. If only there hadn't been so much intention behind the word.

"That's right, I'm talking to you."

According to Tammy, no one was supposed to know about Cam's cards, and that she was the sacrifice.

Morbid curiosity got the best of her, and she swiveled toward the smoking bonfire. A handful of folks sat on the logs surrounding the pit, but the sky was already dark and their hoods cast shadows over their faces. She couldn't tell which of them had called out to her, but the voice had been older and feminine.

"Come here."

The person who spoke sat farthest away, on the other side of the fire. Cam craned her neck and spotted Dee's smirking face. Dee—one of the first villagers to introduce herself around this same fire all those weeks ago.

"We don't bite," Dee said. "Unless The Mother's Chosen thinks she's better than the rest of us."

"Heh, heh." The man across from Dee ended his laugh with a choked cough.

"How did you know?" Cam blurted, unable to help herself. God, she hated being surprised.

"You think Tammy can keep her flapper shut for half a second? Probably the reason folks respect Bert more than her. Swear to god, she'll never learn."

A few of the others around the fire hummed in agreement. Cam counted five in all.

*Thump, thump, thump.* Dee slowly slapped the empty patch of log next to her. "Sit."

Cam resisted the urge to run, and then questioned the impulse. Was she afraid of these people? Maybe, but it was more than that. She didn't trust anyone who stayed in this place for fun and without an ulterior motive.

Then again, how would she know what they really felt if she kept her distance?

Cam took another step toward the fire, and then another, choking on the wet-wood smoke. The ends of Dee's smile twisted victoriously into her dumpling cheeks as Cam sat.

Dee was one of the few villagers who didn't look hollowed out. Neither did her lanky partner, Star, a man with youthful dark eyes. The others around the fire had faces both gaunt and haunted. She recognized them, but couldn't place their names.

"Hanging in there, Lover?" said a woman much younger than

Cam, face scarred and voice petal-soft. When Dee said the nickname, it had surprised her, but this time, the word slowly grated against her insides.

"That's not my name," Cam said.

"Your name doesn't matter," Dee replied. "You'll be gone in a day, won't you? Thrown to the trees like the others." She offered a rusty flask to Cam.

Cam stared at it. The thing on its own would give her tetanus, and she didn't know its contents, or who'd put their filthy lips on it.

"No, thanks," she said.

Dee snorted. "What you trying to preserve? Your dignity? Health? Trust me, none of that's gonna matter."

The omen filled Cam with apprehension. "Why not?"

Dee shook the flask, and the liquid inside sloshed around. Information for a drink . . . that was the bargain, and Cam was both desperate and impulsive.

Cam pinched Dee's flask from the woman's hand with two fingers like it was covered in shit. She made sure it didn't touch her lips while carefully pouring no more liquid than absolutely necessary into her mouth, expecting some pisswater moonshine like what she'd drunk at Ruby's.

Smoked caramel hit her tongue, followed by a kick of black pepper. Goddamn, she missed whiskey. She let the liquid melt through her mouth before swallowing. "This rye? What brand?"

Star chuckled. He was missing a couple of teeth, his upper lip split in a scar. She hadn't paid enough attention to him to notice.

"How long have you been in these woods, Lover?" Dee snatched back the flask as though she suspected Cam would steal it.

Cam roughly calculated how much time had passed since she'd entered Deadswitch on July 13th. "Three months, give or take."

"And how far did you travel before settling here?"

"A hundred miles, maybe," Cam said. Dee grinned, and Cam

felt the need to clarify. "Came from the south. Walked north until I found this place. Didn't have to wander around in circles much."

"I'll let you in on a little secret, Lover." Dee passed her flask to the younger villager. "Wherever you came from to where you are now ain't nothing but a sliver of these woods. There are darker places. Safer places. Villages, settlements, raiders. All different and yet all sharing one thing—a sea of wilderness that keeps them separate."

Cam didn't know if Dee was talking out of her ass, but others around the fire nodded like she spoke gospel.

"You see these places yourself, or just hear stories?" Cam asked. She wished she'd drunk more whiskey when she had the chance.

Dee's smirk softened. "I've been in these woods longer than you've been alive."

"Hard to believe," Cam retorted. "Because if that were true, you wouldn't be *here*. This place is a fucking hospice."

"I haven't always lived in The Tooth, Lover. I've been all about these woods. It's what keeps me alive. But you're right, I have settled down for a few months. Tam's needed me here."

Something inside Cam clicked, and she suddenly saw it— Dee's resemblance to Tammy. Sisters, maybe. She couldn't be sure, but they were definitely related.

"Only a few months?" Cam asked.

"This time around. Been back every couple of years."

"You've been around for the Harvest Feast?"

Dee chuckled. "Oh, you bet."

"If you're so close to Tammy, tell me what happens to the sacrifices. Really." Even trying to keep a neutral tone, Cam came off desperate.

A strange quiet fell over the group. She swallowed and read the others' faces. Star looked uncomfortable, but the others were curious.

They didn't know.

"You go out in the woods," Dee said. "You go out in the woods during the night, and then you never come back. No one does."

"I won't get murdered and turned into pig feed?"

Dee's laugh hissed like a sparkler. "There's enough pig feed already."

So she knew what happened to the bodies. A chill ran up Cam's spine. "Do you believe in The Mother?"

Dee's expression fell, delight leaving her eyes, almost as though she suddenly grew uninterested in the conversation.

"There's no believing. There's no faith. There are folks with power to do whatever the hell they want to the rest of us. And then there's the rest of us. You're the mouse, Lover. The Mother is the cat. The second you get out in those woods, I suggest you run . . . and you find a place to hide."

Cam returned to the cabin and started a fire in the tiny pit, her meager supply of wet firewood smoking more than catching flame. Preparing food in the cabin was so arduous with a piss-poor fire, especially because she always boiled the water before running it through her hiking filter. Seemed pointless, though, after drinking from the flask.

She should have drunk more deeply. Maybe whiskey would have eased the leftover tension inside her from her conversation with Dee.

*The second you get out in those woods, I suggest you run.*

She retrieved rainwater from the collector outside and tossed it into the cooking pot, studying her hands in the light—the pallor of her skin, her brittle nails, the way her spindly fingers twitched like spider legs. *Run . . .* She was far too weak to run. A few weeks of malnutrition had already fucked her up this badly. How was that even possible? She'd never dreamt, not in all her years of training, that a place like this could weaken her so quickly.

She'd murder someone for a cheeseburger. At least, a cheeseburger made from a cow fed grass, not body parts.

She filtered and separated the water when it was done boiling, half to a mug with added herbs for tea, the other half back to the pot. In went mushrooms, the product slightly better than hot mud water. As it cooked, Cam sat on the floor and shut her eyes, rolling through her plan once more.

The Harvest Feast: a communal meal with the villagers. Cam would be announced as the sacrifice—The Mother's new *Lover*—and cast out into the woods for The Mother to find. Every now and again, Cam had asked some veteran Toothers about the feast details while waiting in the slop line, but they'd more or less said the same thing. Food and Sacrifice, Mother and Prosperity. Dee had talked in riddles, but at least gave Cam a little more information.

*There are folks with power to do whatever the hell they want to the rest of us. And then there's the rest of us.*

Dee spoke as if The Mother were the one with power, but Cam knew better. The Mother wasn't the one who'd trapped her in this village for two months, because The Mother wasn't real.

At least all this would be over soon. And once cast out, she'd be on the path Avery had taken.

Cam wasn't allowed to take any belongings, but rules wouldn't stop her. She'd already sewn hidden pockets into her clothes, which contained Ruby's guide, the empty pouch of her water filter, her knife, and Avery's map. Which would have to do; any more and the bulges would be suspicious.

But she felt like she was forgetting something.

Her mind drifted to her bag and the supplies she kept stashed there—just her tent.

*And the journal.* Ruby had given her a handmade journal before all this, and Cam hadn't cracked it open once. She was always terrible at writing things down anyway, but maybe if she could make a list of all the things she needed to remember to do and take with her before this Harvest Feast bullshit, she could calm her nerves.

She dug for the bag beneath the bed and yanked it out, the wilted sack depleted of her store of food and clothing. The journal and pen were tucked beneath her bivy. Sitting on the floor, Cam opened the journal, and frowned. The page was full of very familiar handwriting.

*When everything evolves at such a rapid pace like this, there is no top of the food chain. Mammals, reptiles, bacteria, and fungi are in a constant fight to be the top. The risk to their species is high. Everything is trying to kill or run from all the threats, and every-thing is a threat.*

*I am innately aware of this threat, too. The cut on my arm isn't healing. The blisters on my feet are turning yellow and fat and I feel like I'm walking on needles. Injuries a backpacker expects, and yet my instincts scream that I'm in danger. That if we don't find real shelter soon, we'll both be in serious trouble. But Cam won't listen.*

Cam reread the last sentence two, three times. She stared at her name, or the word she thought was her name, willing the curves of the letters to spell out anything else. But the hand-writing was neat.

Siena. This was *Siena's* journal.

Cam flipped the page so quickly that it tore between her fingers. The next few were filled with mediocre sketches—Siena had never been an artist. Leaves and plants, fungi and trees, birds and rodents. Siena had labeled them with question marks and notes: *strange, doesn't present like its species.* On animals, she'd drawn arrows to lumps along bellies, spines, and wings. *Tumor? Infection?*

Siena's documentation of life in the Briardark. Except, when Cam had left Siena a couple of months ago, they'd only really been in the Briardark for a handful of hours.

Cam had left Agnes Cabin while Siena remained with

Emmett. What if Siena had come looking for Cam instead of leaving?

*No.* Even if that were the case, the timeline didn't add up. This journal entry featuring Cam would have had to occur before Cam left Agnes.

Unable to come up with a theory that made sense, she kept reading, hoping context would align things.

The next entry was brief.

*Scabs keep ripping open.*

Jesus Christ.

There were more drawings, but they were haphazard, and some pages were smeared with so much grime that Cam had a hard time deciphering them.

More entries.

*She's so obsessed that she'll leave me to die.*

Cam swallowed and turned the page, but there was nothing. She turned the page again, and again, but the pages were all blank. Half the journal was empty.

*She'll leave me to die.*

No . . . Siena couldn't be talking about Cam. Cam would never . . . ever.

Fire roared in her chest, and she blinked away tears when she remembered Ruby had given her this book, claiming it was empty. There was no way she'd done this by accident. Ruby knew this journal was Siena's, which meant she knew of Cam's friendship with her. Ruby had lied.

And Ruby also knew Siena's fate.

But Cam couldn't think about that now. She needed to let her anger drive her, and figure out how the hell she would escape The Tooth to ask Ruby herself.

Variable #12
Alpha Timeline Entry: November 15th, 2018
Confidence: 85%

Contents:
Artifact: Pair of military-style gloves
Artifact: Empty prescription bottle, label scratched off
Field Notes: copied, processed, annotation TBD. See index.
Length: 98 days
Cause of Death: Suicide. Confidence: 92%

# SIENA

*"Don't be afraid."*

Maybe she was already dead, and this was the last of her neurons firing.

The masked man loomed over her, lowering his lamp and blinding her with white light.

"Get up," he said.

Her thick tongue filled most of her mouth, and she couldn't speak long enough to tell him she was too weak. She tried lifting her head from the trunk she was slumped against, but her neck couldn't handle the weight, and she fell forward.

His hand landed on her shoulder and slipped beneath her arm, yanking her to her feet. The muscles in her legs convulsed.

The moment he released her, pain shot up her spine and darkness tunneled her vision. The man didn't stop the momentum of her fall. The sounds of the woods dwindled to a muffled hum as she collapsed. She blinked, but the haze of darkness remained, her body unbearably heavy.

The man muttered something. He grabbed her arm again and rolled her to her back, then tugged her into a sitting position by her wrists.

She couldn't remember what happened after that.

Time was funny in her head, in this forest. It played by its own rules, and for a while it turned into smoke and slipped right through her fingers. But now she *was* time, a pendulum swaying back and forth. Beneath her, the ground crunched and splashed, the noises sometimes faint, sometimes sharp.

He carried her.

She couldn't remember, but by the way her body ached, his shoulders had been carrying the burden of her for miles. As she grew more lucid, she faintly recalled him stopping several times to rest as she slumped against a tree or stump or slimy boulder. Not some "god" like The Shadow. Not the grim reaper. Only a man who groaned and swore every time he picked her up to continue.

What did he want with her?

There were many possible horrifying answers. She attempted to ask him during her brief moments of lucidity as they traveled, her voice mostly leaving her in unintelligible grunts, which he ignored. She was too tired to fight or run, and even if she could get away, he'd catch up to her. He moved too easily through the darkness, and she'd spent a long enough time in these woods to know how unforgiving the thicket was.

She had nowhere to go. Death by the forest or death at the hands of this man—Siena didn't have enough information to know which was worse.

She drifted in and out of consciousness, and woke again to the creak of wood and echo of dripping water. The lantern was off, gone, or she'd lost her eyesight.

The masked man groaned as he sat her down, this time on a bench or a chair—she couldn't control her own muscles to feel around, nor could she stay sitting without his hand supporting her.

They were in a dark, dank enclosure. A hut of some sort. After a squeak of metal, the sound of rushing water filled her ears.

The man spoke over the noise. "I'm sorry." His tone carried no inflection. He then said something about *trust* and *time*, his voice oddly gentle. He made quick work of undressing her, the stagnant air and his touch against her skin so distant until his grip strengthened, and she was dragged into the shock of cold water.

Siena thrashed, pummeling his arms with her fists. His hold tightened, and he pushed her down until her back hit something hard and flat.

He was drowning her.

*Figure a way out of this.*

Her brain spurted back nothing helpful other than that drowning was a better way to go than what had happened to Emmett.

When her lungs burned, his fingers dug beneath the base of her skull, and he lifted her by her neck until she surfaced. Siena coughed and sputtered, then drew a deep breath to scream, and he dunked her again.

Her pulse hammered an alarm throughout her body. Not enough oxygen.

This time was shorter, and when she surfaced, she coughed out acrid water.

"Please—"

"Breathe!" he barked.

She gasped and gasped until he threw her beneath the surface again, but it wasn't enough time.

The rush of blood filled her ears, then nothing.

Siena came to with a leather strap between her teeth.

She lay on her stomach somewhere hard. A floor, maybe. Or a table. She was dry, something she'd never thought she'd feel again.

The relief was short-lived. When she tried to move, straps bit into her wrists. She opened her eyes to the glow of flame and a closer silhouette, though as much as she blinked, she couldn't focus.

A hand pressed to the small of her back.

"What . . . do you want?" The words dragged like sandpaper across her throat. She had nothing but her body, which she wouldn't give up willingly, not even strapped down.

"I'm sorry," he said again. But she knew he wasn't, not really. Men were never sorry for the animalistic things they did.

Siena heard the hiss and smelled her own flesh before she felt the hot iron against her side. She screamed until blood flooded her mouth, red pulsing behind her eyelids.

The shock of hell-bright pain died. Flesh gone, nerves dead.

"Twice more," he said.

She pled quietly with herself to fall unconscious, except this time she stayed lucid and unable to fight as he held her down and pressed scalding hot metal into her side again, and again.

When it was all over, he removed the bite strap and wiped the snot and tears from her face.

She inhaled the char of cooked flesh and hungered for meat.

She woke again, still on her stomach but against a softer surface. Her mouth tasted like blood and bile, and she tried swallowing but couldn't. Pain arose like it had been hibernating in her bones. She groaned loudly enough to rouse the dead.

"Don't move."

Siena quietly sobbed, the only thing she had enough energy for. The past several years of her life flicked through her head like some demented flipbook. She'd done something to deserve this. Not stood up for herself enough. Spent too much time at work. Let her relationship with her father fall apart. Maybe those Christian fanatics were right, and this was eternal damnation, a punishment for her atheism and torrid love affair with science.

All her schooling, all her published papers that detailed the current state of the world and not a way to fix them. All the effort and stress, the time she'd spent not enjoying food or sex or the fucking sunshine. The months pathetically wallowing after she split with Emmett instead of convincing herself she deserved better. The years feeling guilty for not being by her mother's side when she died.

The pain forced her to be more present in this moment, even more so than all those cathartic trips to the woods that she'd taken by herself to lick her wounds. Both a slow death, and a reminder of everything she'd missed.

His shadow passed back and forth in front of her. She shifted her body just to spite him. To her surprise, she was no longer tethered down.

His hand returned to the small of her back. "I said, don't move."

There was something between his skin and hers—a blanket. She rested on a cot, or a bed. This new information confused her. She blinked again, eyes focusing on a fireplace beyond the man, flame crackling softly.

His hand fell away. "You took a beating out in the dark."

Bits and threads filtered back to her from the past—days? Weeks? *Months?* A claustrophobic fever dream filled with the unending midnight woods. And then the torture she'd endured from this man.

"The next couple of weeks will be rough," he said. "The blight entered your bloodstream, which means the burn hasn't fully stopped the spread."

*Blight.* He meant the rash on her back. The night she'd woken in her bivy to the bloody, broken pustules along her flank.

He hadn't burned her for the sake of torturing her. He'd burned her to kill the growth crawling across her skin.

"You should have told me that—" The first few words left her in an incoherent mess, so she licked her lips and tried again. "You should . . . have told me that was . . . why . . ."

"Why I was burning you?" he finished. "I did. I couldn't tell when you were conscious, and I didn't have time to wait."

She had so many questions, but even breathing was difficult.

His fingers slipped beneath her chin and lifted it enough so she could drink water from a flask. Her throat and chest throbbed as she swallowed, and before she could recover enough to ask who he was, she was asleep again.

The next time she woke, her vision had sharpened enough to make out more of her surroundings, though from her angle, it was difficult to see much. Her arms burned and ached upon stretching them, and she struggled to flip to her back beneath the itchy wool blanket. Her whole body spasmed in pain.

Everything *hurt*, like she'd been mowed over by farming equipment. Shredded up and pieced back together. This must be how Frankenstein's monster had felt when it came to life. She hurt like an abomination.

But instead of burning through all her energy and falling unconscious once more, she gained enough mobility to run her hands along her body. She was naked except for the cloth bandage wrapped around her torso.

Other than the crackle of the fire, the room was silent. She cleared her throat and waited for the shift or approach of the masked man, but neither came.

After tucking the blanket beneath her armpits, it took several tries to prop herself in a sitting position against the wall near her bed. Siena looked around. The room was bigger than the other outposts she and Emmett had found, but smaller than the cabin on Agnes. Across from her, a cooking grate sat within a small clay fireplace. Threadbare blankets lay twisted on the floor between her bed and the fire. The man had been sleeping there, though he was nowhere to be seen.

To the right of the fire stood a table covered in junk—an old radio, a pry bar, a pair of leather gloves, and an iron that was likely the culprit of her burn.

Above the table was a—window?

Faint light a green between emerald and pond scum glowed through clear plastic. It was too dark to see much of anything. Either it was night, or she was still in the primeval forest.

A counter lined the back of the cabin, cluttered shelves covering the wall. She spotted utensils, a cluster of mugs, and a stack of books.

The door squealed open. The masked man entered carrying a shriveled rib rack from a mystery animal.

"You need to rest." His voice was muffled; he must have not been wearing the mask when he was tending to her before. Either he only wore it when he went outside, or he was trying to hide his identity from her.

She thought of Isaac returning decades older after years spent in the Briardark. Did she know this man? She didn't recognize his voice, though her brain lit up like with déjà vu.

Siena cleared her throat. "I am resting." She sounded like a frog, but at least she could talk. "How long have I been out?"

He crossed to the back of the room. "Three days."

*Three days.* Coma levels of sleep.

The man set the slab of meat on the back counter. With his back to her, he unfastened two clips at his shoulders and ducked his head out of the mask, then hung it from a hook near the window. He did the same with his dark coat before pinching the gloves from his fingers and tossing them into a drawer. He got to work, pulling utensils from drawers and bottles from shelves.

His hair was dark, gray-streaked, and tied in a knot at the base of his skull. He wore a knit sweater, the fabric frayed along the bottom hem. The winter tree pattern of the fabric was far too cute and left her uneasy.

The first time she met this man had been up on Agnes, when Emmett found the tree as large as the ones in this forest. Siena had crawled through the tree's hollow, and then a tunnel, to emerge in the Briardark. In the few moments she was there, she'd met this man.

*You shouldn't be here.*

There was something deeply wrong with his presence here. If she'd had any choice in the matter, she'd try fleeing now, while his back was turned. But she didn't have the strength to even stand, and hunger gripped her stomach like a vise.

"Have you been following me?" she asked.

"I needed to make sure you left." He shook powder from a jar onto the meat.

"The mountain?" she asked.

He reached up and grabbed two mugs, and then another jar of something that looked like dehydrated mushrooms. "The Briardark."

She teased apart the questions flooding her brain. "What . . . why . . ." She took a breath. "If that were true, you wouldn't have let me almost die."

"I didn't want to intervene unless I had to." He slid a kettle from a shelf, placed it in a basin and turned a squealing valve. "You were doing okay until the groping blight got you."

Water flowed from the spigot above the basin. *Running water.* "How . . ." Her teeth clacked together as she slammed her mouth shut. She needed to stay on track; asking about the water would have to wait. "I was starving and falling apart, but you let me be because you didn't want to intervene?" He sounded like a nature photographer witnessing the struggle of a dying animal. Her stomach twisted at just how long he'd been following her. "You let Emm—my partner die."

He turned toward her. Her pulse leapt as her eyes roamed his features, searching for familiarity.

The planes of his face were both strong and carried a soft kindness, his narrow eyes warm. She guessed he was in his fifties. His jaw was unshaven, tan skin weathered from the elements, but not like Isaac's. Perhaps that was the point of the mask.

His eyes flicked back and forth as he watched her, expression briefly coy.

"You're disappointed," he said.

She was. "I figured I knew who you were if you were willing to stalk me for weeks just to make sure I escaped."

He took the meat and the kettle to the fire. The rack sizzled when it slapped the grate, much like her skin had when he'd laid the iron on it.

"I'm sorry about your partner." He stoked the fire as he spoke, some of the ash fluttering onto the meat. "I lost you for a while, after the swamp. Didn't catch up again until you were in the Edge. Your partner was gone by then."

"The Edge. You mean this biome." She adjusted herself against the wall, though nothing could ease the deep ache in her shoulders and spine. Sooner than later the last of her energy would drain away, again.

"The darkness, yes." He slid the kettle atop the grate, picked up a fire poker, and prodded at some coals.

It was time to ask the obvious. "So, who are you to me? This place is desolate—am I supposed to believe that you and your cozy oasis magically appeared just to guide me home?" She was fading. If she didn't speak quickly, she'd soon lose the strength to do so. "I met you before I knew what the hell . . . what the hell I'd gotten myself into. You beheaded a mule just to . . . write a message."

*The Mother Reigns.* She could still see it written in blood.

He opened his mouth as if to argue, then shut it again. His jaw flexed as he stared at the coals.

"There's so much of . . ." She coughed, then wiped her phlegm on the blanket. "This purgatory that makes no"—she gasped—"no goddamn sense."

He finally looked at her. The flame flickered in his brown eyes. "You recover from this blight, and I'll tell you everything I know."

# CAMERON

Cam never did well when she had free time. She always broke shit or got into trouble, even in her thirties, post-PhD, when she ran out of grant money. She wasted time, broke hearts, hurt feelings, made dumb decisions like trying to fix her own car and critically fucking it up. That kind of trouble.

Other than a few hours a day scraping moss and manning the clinic, Cam's residency at The Tooth had been responsibility free, and she'd had ample opportunities to break shit, like the lashings on the fence near her cabin. Plan A was available to her whenever she finally decided that fucking around The Tooth and finding out was no longer a viable option.

Cam had only called escaping Plan A because she'd never actually gone through with any of her Plan As at any point in her life. But with this journal of Siena's implying her death, things had changed. Now there was a strong reason to escape, if only to travel back to Ruby's and yell at her. Hopefully in return, Ruby would admit to slipping Siena's journal to Cam on purpose, and explain how she knew of Cam's connection to Siena.

There was also the small fact that Siena couldn't have died in the way this journal implied, because Cam had left Siena very much alive back on Agnes. She did not cause Siena's death. She'd left Siena behind for that very reason.

Hadn't she?

Siena's safety had always been more important to Cam than finding Avery.

*She's so obsessed that she'll leave me to die.*

Even the fake fucking journal knew.

*Not fake.* Couldn't be, not unless Siena had faked it herself. She'd learn more once she reached Ruby's tavern, The Other Backpack, three miles and a straight shot away. She could clear the distance in a couple of hours, even in the dark.

After giving her slop away to a newborn sitting around the bonfire, Cam returned to her cabin to eat as much mushroom soup as she could stomach before filtering water from the boiling pot into her bottle. She clipped the bottle to her belt, filled her rain shell pocket with her knife and flashlight, and tucked Siena's journal near her chest. She wouldn't call her light packing smart, but her very limited time and desire to not get caught meant she needed to hurry.

She doused her fire, pulled up her hood, and slipped out the cabin door.

The broken lashings were only a few paces from the back of her cabin. She'd cut them one day during scraping duty, fixing them to hide the loose boards. The damage was difficult to spot unless you knew what to look for, and the only reason she knew she hadn't been caught by the guards was because Tammy hadn't mentioned it—and Tammy mentioned everything.

The walkway between the back of Cam's cabin and the broken fencing was deserted. She soaked into the shadows beneath the eaves of her cabin while listening for any movement. The Tooth was lively after the shared meal. With it being the night before the feast, she'd have watchers.

Her eyes slid across the catwalk to the right, where two sets of feet faced each other. To the left was another guard, legs in her direction.

She leaned forward until she could see their head turned toward the gate.

Now or never.

Cam dashed across the walkway and beneath the catwalk, then pressed her back against the fence and listened. Conversation drifted from her left. No metal clang of footsteps to her right. She squatted and pushed the loose log aside, then ducked her head through the opening, releasing her breath as she squeezed through. The seam of her pants popped, snagging on the rough wood.

She swore beneath her breath. In the dark beyond the fence, she examined her pants the best she could without a light, hoping to shit they hadn't torn. Exposure brought more risks than water-logged skin.

Her attention soon drifted to her surroundings. It was dark where she crouched, light from the torches casting a soft glow across the forest. As long as no one spotted her movement from above, she was golden.

Every rustle and snap rang louder than a smoke alarm as she slipped between the trees. When she was deep enough, she looked back. The guards hadn't noticed. She'd escaped unscathed.

Tonight could be one of those nights Tammy checked on her. Surely it would be, given tomorrow's events, but she hoped to be far from The Tooth by that point.

When it was safe, Cam slid the flashlight from her pocket and popped it on, navigating through the brush in a wide circle around The Tooth until she found the road, the village far behind her.

She ran. Or at least her version of running. Goddammit, she was out of shape—out of shape *and* malnourished. Before long, dizziness slowed her down.

*Just three miles. You can handle this.*

The trail was clear in her memory, a flat muddy path through the center of a valley almost as wide as a road. It remained that way until she needed to veer off toward Ruby's tavern, The Other Backpack. Easy.

Mist crowded her flashlight beam. The forest was quiet. So strange how a forest brimming with so many noises—crickets, water, wind, birdsong, skittering—could fall so utterly fucking silent all at once, as though it weren't made of many parts and plants and creatures, but the parts and plants and creatures were made of the forest.

They sensed something she didn't know.

The mist cleared, and then her flashlight beam caught the start of a thick sheet of rain. In seconds, Cam was soaked to the bone.

"Dammit," she hissed. Less than a quarter of a mile later, she could hardly see in front of her face.

*No.* This was a good thing. Once they realized she was gone, they'd come looking for her. The rain made her harder to track—not that any of those buffoons could track a person. They rarely left their safe little walls.

Maybe they would be too afraid to come looking for her.

The guards posed no threat, something she'd realized not long after Bert pulled her cards. The most he'd ever done was coordinate some tall people to block her way before she was *selected* as The Lover. She hadn't been shackled or confined to her cabin, and never strongly felt the need to escape.

Everything at The Tooth felt too easy.

*That's why people don't leave.*

But Cam differed from all the others at The Tooth. She knew her way around a mountain, a forest. She knew how to survive in the wild. The Tooth had been a means to find Avery, and a morbid curiosity.

A part of her deeply wanted to know what happened the night of the feast. She wanted to prove she wasn't a pawn in their game, that she was no sacrifice, that she could walk away from The Tooth free from the hold of this *Mother*. Prove she was better. Prove Tammy was nothing more than a fool.

Prove she could outsmart this whole damn Briardark.

The rain didn't let up for the whole three miles, and by the end, Cam was nearly swimming. She almost missed the offshoot to Ruby's, but eventually The Other Backpack's beer sign cast a neon glow across the trees.

The silky warmth of comfort washed over her. Did she actually miss seedy bars? Yes . . . she missed their familiarity. She missed their disgusting toilets and snarky bartenders and paying real money for greasy food and a cold beer. She missed how generational they were, how she saw no one younger than her, especially in country dive bars. Maybe that was why she'd always dated older women. If there were a lady patron in The Other Backpack right now, Cam would probably try to date her too.

Hell, Cam always enjoyed hurrying into casual relationships when she felt most shook up and vulnerable. That was what had happened with her and Lauren, when she met her at—

Cam halted on the porch, peering through a rain-drizzled window. No one inside.

The second she yanked open the door of the tavern, the rotting stench of meat assaulted her.

Cam buried her nose and mouth in the crook of her elbow. It smelled like Ruby had left raw venison sitting on the counter for days. She blinked through watery eyes and looked around the place. Despite its wear and tear, the tavern was as spotless as when Cam was here two months ago.

Dread crept over her.

She dropped her bag and didn't bother taking off her shoes like Ruby would order. Cam ran, and skidded to a halt in front of the room with the first set of bunks, and then the second. Both empty.

She returned to the front of the tavern, slid behind the counter and into the kitchen. Not a single dirty dish or glass, and yet . . .

Cam slammed her eyes shut. The smell was worse than when she found Levi.

*No.*

When she heaved open the basement's trapdoor, the stench worsened. There was only one outcome waiting for her in the basement. She steeled herself and kept her face buried in the crook of her arm, slowly descending.

Nothing could prepare her for seeing Ruby, or what used to be Ruby, lying amid a scattering of homemade paper, corpse covered in little pink mushrooms, the ones Cam had been living on for the past two months.

Her stomach lurched and she leaned against the wall. *Don't you do it. Don't you dare puke.*

She took a few deep breaths, which weren't so bad. Somehow she was already getting used to the stench.

*Ruby.*

The damn woman had spent her entire life being dead careful, and it still didn't matter. An infection killed her anyway. Not like Cam would be able to tell if Ruby had died from anything other than infection. The fungus ate away most of the viscera, the rest gelatinous. Her eyes were gone, lips eaten away, skeletal smile wide and hideous.

Horrifying. And yet Cam made room inside her body for self-ishness. To grieve the answers to Siena's journal she'd never learn.

She shouldn't stay here. She still didn't know for certain whether this infection spread from one body to another, but the way Ruby had been so careful around Levi made her think it could.

Cam's own breath was hot and wet. She spun toward the shelves packed with stories and journeys and secrets. Ruby had known who Cam was. Who Siena was. Was her knowledge an outcome of the time loop bullshit Cam still didn't understand?

She yanked a random journal from the shelf, skimmed a few pages, and then threw it to the ground. A stranger. Another, this one pink and covered in dried flowers. A few lines proved to be those of a much younger woman. Stranger. She threw it to the ground.

She searched for nothing other than familiarity. Siena, Avery, Isaac . . . fuck, even Emmett. One of them had to be here, to provide the answer of Siena's fate—that Cam hadn't left her to die. She tore through journal after journal, some of their delicate bindings breaking when she tossed them to the ground. It didn't matter. Ruby was dead, dead, fucking dead. No one to man The Other Backpack, to care for the lost. All the work she'd put in, the anxiety she'd borne to stay safe and clean didn't matter.

Cam choked back a sob and threw another journal on the ground.

She lost track of time, cleaning off one shelf after another. She searched by the armful, flipping open a page and then sliding the journal from the stack and letting it fall onto the cluttered floor. Every fucking nerve inside her body burned with adrenaline, and yet she'd never been so tired in her life.

She opened the next cover, and her fingers froze on the page. Surprised, she gasped and then choked on her own spit. Her arm that carried a fresh stack of journals fell, the books falling bent, broken, and open atop the heap. Cam took the only journal that mattered and sank to the floor.

She had the handwriting of a twelve-year-old boy whose hand was tired from copying sentences in detention. Doctors had nothing on her. On top of it, Cam was left-handed, the tilt of her letters uncomfortable to everyone who had to force their way through her scrawl. But she took pride in the fact that her words were illegible. No one ever tried copying her or asking her to write notes on the whiteboard. Her handwriting got her out of so much bullshit.

This was her handwriting, but this was not her.

No, it *was* her, just nothing she remembered writing.

*So I'm supposed to be writing in this journal, not about what's happening but about my fucked-up childhood or whatever . . .*

It was just like Ruby had said: write about home. In the journal, Cam described her childhood, though it wasn't that fucked up. At least, not compared to many people. She'd been chronically ignored by her parents in favor of her older brother Coulter, and the only person who'd paid attention to her, Grandma June, had died when she was twelve. If being ignored was abuse, then it was manageable abuse. It was easily survivable.

And then there was everything after childhood. Seventeen fucking years of it. Jesus, had she really been alive for so long?

Maybe she'd written this. No, maybe she *would* write it. In the future. Because that was what Siena had done, hadn't she? Siena's older self had written something Cam had read in the present.

Except this journal wasn't written by future Cam, because it began detailing a present that contradicted Cam's past.

*Siena won't let go of her guilt, but that's typical. She's still worried about Emmett because she thinks he can't make it home without her. I keep reminding her he wanted to stay up on Mount Agnes anyway. He was trying to keep her there, trapped. But I guess she thinks he is helpless up on Agnes too. Imagine wanting to marry a guy who can't even survive in his own profession.*

*I am taking this out on Siena when I shouldn't. It isn't her fault. I'm just, I don't fucking know, irritable right now. Scared. I feel like we're trapped in some nightmare I can't get out of.*

The next entry began several days later.

*There's a weird fucking commune Ruby warned about. Siena and I traveled around the outskirts and continued north, but now she's wondering if we made the right choice not stopping by for a visit. Not because we should stay awhile or anything, but because there are people there. Lots of people. Which means we could learn more about this Briardark place, maybe ask around about Avery. But I don't know—something tells me to trust Ruby.*

A world where Cam never visited The Tooth. Another timeline.

She didn't know why the hell she hadn't thought of it before. Maybe because the idea was crazy, but then again, she'd experienced enough wild shit since entering Deadswitch to last her the rest of her life. Teleportation, portals, rapid aging . . .

*Holy fuck.* Isaac.

Isaac hadn't traveled through a time loop or aged in a matter of hours. Older Isaac was another person.

The Isaac from The Tooth wasn't her Isaac either, because he'd been trapped in the woods for three years. Her Isaac could still be alive.

But what the hell had happened to him up at Agnes? Why had he disappeared, and why had older Isaac appeared a couple of hours later?

Just the thought of trying to figure it out gave her the hives. Siena was the one who was good at this brain-twisty shit, not Cam.

Then again, she'd read the other Siena's journal. Lots of hypotheses, no answers. Maybe this other Cam would be more helpful.

She read the next entry.

*Siena wants to go back, return to Ruby's. Says she isn't feeling well. I never told her to come with me. I wanted to do this on my own. Avery isn't her obligation, but mine. Now she's slowing me down.*

Another entry. All this one said was: *She can't walk. I'll have to carry her back to Ruby.*

Cam turned the page.

*I fucked up, and now she's gone.*

She glanced up at the mushroom-covered corpse in the corner, now used to the smell of its rot.

Why hadn't Ruby told her? Why hadn't Ruby let her know how easily Cam could turn into the worst version of herself when she became so obsessed?

No, she was the worst version of herself now. She'd abandoned not just her colleague, but her best friend in order to traipse through some haunted forest to find a woman she'd known for a year and had been deemed dead for over six. Sure, she'd found leads that Avery had existed in this place, too, and she'd risked her life chasing those leads. She'd probably risked

Siena's life too when she left the research cabin without saying goodbye.

Isaac had told Siena that Cam and Emmett would only hold her back, but maybe Isaac had been speaking from his knowledge of whatever timeline he was from, not theirs.

A wave of panic rose inside her. Cam tried flipping the page, but two of them were stuck together. She carefully peeled them apart.

*I went through Siena's things and found a deck of cards. All the cards are blank until I stack them and draw two from the top of the deck. No matter what, the first card I draw is a skeleton with the name of The Lover. The second is a lady with antlers named The Mother.*

Cam barked a horrified laugh.

*I try drawing more cards, and they're all blank. I shuffle the cards, and I get the same two, no matter what. What kind of fuckery is this, and why the hell was Siena carrying the deck?*

This version of her—the one who had never been to The Tooth—was also The Lover. This version of her, as far as she knew, had never fulfilled her *destiny*.

Cam held her palm out. Her fingers trembled. She clenched them into a fist.

If this Mother was so desperate to have her as a Lover, then she'd have her.

Cam's body shook so much that it was hard to climb the stairs, but when she was back in the kitchen, she threw open cabinets and drawers. She found a skinning knife with a polished stone handle far sharper than her own and grabbed it, along with a cloth bag filled with venison jerky.

When The Mother failed to show up and take Cam—when Cam found out what really happened out in those woods after the feast, she'd tell everyone at The Tooth the scam they were falling for.

This was her *real* destiny.

# SIENA

The man's name was Ren, his safe house Outpost 5.

Though Siena couldn't pinpoint why, his name bothered her, a feeling she blamed on the intuition goblin she continuously failed to exterminate from her brain.

"Tell me about yourself . . . *Ren*," she asked as they sat and ate at the table he'd cleared off and pulled away from the window. Smoked and salted meat kept appearing to close her nutrition deficit, both tough and utterly mouthwatering. At mealtimes it was accompanied by an herb porridge and a mushroom tea that almost satisfied her coffee craving.

Across from her, Ren chewed carefully and swallowed, setting his fork and knife on the plate. The utensils were unexpected given their wild surroundings, and he held his set properly when he cut and ate, like he'd taken an etiquette class.

"What do you want to know?" His voice was hesitant and mellow, like it had been with her since she'd regained enough strength to hold her own body up.

"You weren't born in the Briardark." Not a question, though she wanted him to confirm it.

"No."

"What was your life like? Before?"

There was a long pause as he watched her. "Simple. Often lonely."

She waited for him to continue before realizing that was all he would provide. Simple and lonely. It seemed, well, it seemed more palatable than busy and complicated, and she understood the lonely part. Life had been lonely for her too after she broke off her engagement. Sure, there was Cam, but Emmett had been Siena's person. Confidant. Keeper. The one she'd reach out and touch at night to ground her. And she'd been so lonely after they'd separated.

In a way, that loneliness had prepared her for the loneliness she'd battled as she navigated the black forest alone.

"Did you get trapped here by accident?"

"I was looking for someone who went missing," he said. "That's how many of us end up here."

*Many of us.* The promise of others intrigued her, especially given how isolated she'd been on her journey.

"Did you find them?" she asked.

He took a long sip of tea, set down the chipped floral-patterned mug, and glanced out the window into the faint green light. "I did. But they're gone now."

A lump formed in her throat. She wanted to know more about this missing person, but sensed the topic was painful for him. "You know the way out, but you're choosing to stay. Why?"

She chewed on a piece of greasy fat as she waited for him to say something. Today, Ren was dressed in another knit sweater, this one navy blue and unpatterned. His clothing came from a large trunk behind the bed, which she'd missed upon studying the room for the first time. Inside were not just clothes that fit him, but an array of sizes. She currently sported worn UCLA sweatpants and an oversized baseball tee, both from the chest and left by *others*.

"There are a few of us who have been here so long, we feel beholden to it." He returned his attention to her. "It's dangerous . . . You know this better than anyone could. It's evolv—changing."

*Evolving.* He stuttered on the word like he was afraid to use it.

She tucked the fat between her gums and her cheek. "Are you trying to learn how this place is evolving? Searching for answers?"

"I have enough answers, for now." The firelight glittered in his dark eyes. "I know that's not the same for you." He stood and brought back two small bottles, then set them in front of her. They were shaped differently; one looked like it had once held a skincare product, the other a hot sauce. Murky concoctions filled both.

"This is what I've been giving you for your infection." Ren pointed to the hot sauce bottle. "Fungal compounds that kill cellular processes." He pointed at the skincare bottle. "Hybrid plant-animal antibodies."

Siena blinked at the bottles, but it didn't help her sort out a conclusion. "I'm not a biologist, but how does someone synthesize a hybrid plant-animal antibody in a place like this?"

His upper lip twitched. "It's watered down tree sap."

She stared at him.

He smiled. "I don't know a lot about the details, sorry. But I'm sure you've seen some evidence for yourself. Plants not behaving like they should."

Heartbeat roots. Heliotropic trees. No, plants here didn't behave like she was used to. But hybrid antibodies in tree sap?

She picked up the bottle and swiveled in her chair, groaning in discomfort as she leaned toward the fire. The bottle's contents glowed a deep amber.

"You put this in my tea?" she asked.

"And on your side."

Her side. She hated thinking about her side, and the third-degree burn the size of her hand. It was numb now, but eventually she'd start feeling the pain.

She replaced the bottle on the table. "So, tree sap and fungal compounds to heal a fungal infection." She shook her head in amazement. "How do I know it's working?" When Ren didn't respond right away, she glanced at him, and panic fluttered in her stomach at his wary expression. "You know it works, right?" She lifted her cup to her lips.

He slowly nodded. "The infection isn't fungus. Mycelbacteria is the fancy word for it."

Siena almost spit out her tea. "*Mycelbacteria?* As in—a microorganism that's both fungus *and* bacteria?"

"Something like that." His eyes carried a cautious glint, like he was worried about what she'd do with this information.

"That's . . ." She trailed off. *Impossible.* Just like plant-animal antibodies. Maybe with the help of genetic engineering from some talented synthetic microbiologist, but not in the natural world.

Everything about this place was physically and biologically impossible. That was why Feyrer's team had drafted stacks on stacks of research notes.

Siena sat straight in her chair. "My stuff . . . the backpack I had on me—where is it?"

Ren frowned. "You didn't have a bag with you when I found you."

"I did! It was right next to me . . . It had to—"

Oh *god*.

She stood, almost collapsing at the sharp pain in her feet. "We need to go back and get it."

"Sit down. You're hurting yourself."

"I need my things!" She grimaced, leaning against the table to disperse her weight.

Ren eased to his feet. "You collapsed half a day's hike north from here. I'm not even sure I could find the place again."

Siena attempted to push herself from the table, but her legs trembled just to bear her weight. An onslaught of hopelessness crushed her as she sank to her chair. "There's no point in me getting out of here, then. No point in going back home if I don't have that bag."

He glared down at her, surely angry, given all the work he'd put into saving her. But she'd never asked for his help. She didn't even know who he was.

"Why not?" he finally asked.

Siena's nose burned, and she blinked the moisture from her eyes. *Stop feeling sorry for yourself.* She took a deep breath and composed herself. "Because of the research, and the photos. I have a record of mental illness. Delusional disorder. And I ran out of meds. If I don't come back with evidence, no one will believe what happened to me. They'll think I made it up, and then no one will help me rescue my—my research partner."

Ren didn't look at her with pity, which she appreciated. "Where's your research partner?"

"She . . . she left me. Went north."

"Does she *want* to be rescued?"

Siena wiped her nose with the back of her hand and looked out the window at the dark emerald infinity. She hadn't been able to bring herself to accept the glaring truth: Cam had forfeited rescue to go north—*deeper*.

"There's nothing waiting for me back home." She'd primed everything in her life for this study. She'd lost her research . . . her loved ones . . . "Everything. I've lost everything."

A strange weight lifted from her chest. Was escape something she'd ever really wanted? No . . . it was something she'd been told she needed to do to save herself. But what was the point in saving *only* herself when nothing waited for her? She'd have to start over. She couldn't . . .

Ren cleared the utensils and plates from the table, and took them to the sink with the mysteriously running water. "I want to show you something." From the end of the counter he picked up a cluttered tray and carefully brought it over, then set it on the table.

Not a tray. A *game*. A painted map of the forest covered a board. Siena's eyes traveled over its details—valleys, mountains, connected forests, zones of danger like open wounds on the land-scape—the whole fitting together like an organism.

"I know who painted this," she said, the work clearly Isaac's. He followed her everywhere. She looked at Ren, who kept his head lowered toward the board. "Do you?"

"I do."

Her chest warmed at the shared connection. Before she could ask Ren how he knew Isaac, he said, "You play chess?"

One corner of her mouth pulled into a crooked grin. "Enough to know this isn't chess." Siena studied the pieces. Dozens of small black and red cubes carved from hardwood scattered the board, the only other objects a piece of tooth-shaped obsidian and a quartz crystal, which sat on opposite ends.

"You're right." Ren tapped the top of the quartz piece. "But what if you expected it to be chess just because that was the only game you knew?"

Riddles. She may be a thinker, but she hated riddles. "I'm not following."

"Everyone who enters this forest expects it to be like a chess-board," Ren said. "They expect the same rules and logistics. If they identify as a bishop, they expect to move across the board like a bishop. Except they can't. They can't even learn a new way to move, because the rules keep changing and the board keeps evolving."

The board was the forest. Now the metaphor felt too obvious. "Alright."

He tapped a black cube. "Most of the individuals and small communities in the Briardark merely cope. They create religions, make alliances, fight for scraps until they die." Ren shifted his hand from the quartz to the obsidian. "There are no monarchies. No one is born into power here. The kings and queens are the ones who do more than cope. They figure out how things are changing and exploit whatever they learn."

"New money versus old money," she said.

He met her eyes. "The currency is knowledge."

That kind of wealth she understood. "Those who understand this place know how not to die from a mycelbacteria infection as they starve in the middle of a soaking-wet, pitch-black forest."

He smiled. "You made it far by yourself, you know. Deeper into the Edge than most. You know how to stay alive."

But in the end, she wouldn't have. Not without his intervention, which made her feel like a damsel. She wasn't; her real strengths simply lay elsewhere.

"There's social power," she said, veering their conversation back on course.

Ren nodded once, his eyes searching hers like he was waiting for her to string more together.

"Gods?" The word left her mouth as a question.

"Something's following you," he said.

"You," she replied.

"Something else," he said gently.

She swallowed, shifting her back against the chair in search of a more comfortable position. Some position that would make her less nauseous. "The Shadow." She met his finger with her own at the obsidian piece.

"So why would The Shadow want you?" Ren asked.

"I must have currency." She shook her head as she said it. "But I don't know how, especially now, with no data." She looked at him for answers, as if he could tell her what gold nugget of her knowledge this Shadow coveted.

*He will use you, and then he will kill you.*

"What if I don't have what he wants?" she asked.

"I don't think you want to find that out."

Siena sighed and pinched the bridge of her nose, a strong headache coming on. Ren swept up her mug and walked around the table to the fire, where he knelt and filled her cup from the kettle on the grate. He handed it to her, and remained kneeling at her feet, picking up the poker to stab at the coals.

She sipped her tea, then asked, "What is he? He looks like the absence of something. Not a person. He's figured something out about the forest, which changed him. Or made him able to change his appearance.”

“I think you’re right.” Ren set the poker down, then took a brush to the grate. “I think he was once a man.”

“A man who gained a lot of currency.” She shifted her eyes to the obsidian piece. In this metaphysical space, this Shadow treated physics like Play-Doh. “He always knows where I am. I’ve seen him. He’s . . . he’s spoken to me.”

Ren’s eyes darted to her. Despite his outward calm, she could tell this surprised him.

“He told me I wasn’t imagining things. It almost felt like he was trying to comfort me. Why would he do that? And why would he let me get closer to escaping?”

His shoulders softened in a defeated, tired way. “I don’t know.”

She could read him well. “He’s been unpredictable before. Done things you can’t follow.”

“Always,” Ren said. “It’s why we feel so beaten by him.”

*We.* Siena picked up the quartz piece. She lifted it for him to see. “*The Mother Reigns.*”

Shame flickered across his face. She knew what he’d done to that mule.

He may have saved her life, but she didn’t know Ren. Didn’t know the level of truth in what he told her, nor how violent he really was. Maybe those tinctures would cure her of this mycelbacteria, if that truly was what she suffered from. Or maybe they were poison.

Still, she liked something in the way he looked right now, kneeling at her feet and staring up at her.

Siena rolled the quartz between her fingers. “Who is she? The Mother.”

“A symbol,” he said, watching her face closely. *Waiting for a reaction.*

“A symbol,” she repeated.

“A symbol for the rest of us. The resistance against him, all who know how dangerous it is for one man to control an entire dimension."

*An entire dimension.* And if one man could use a dimension as a playground to be a god . . .

"He could get out," she whispered.

"Yes," Ren said.

She opened her eyes to the board full of black and red pieces, and picked up a red cube near the bottom, where a forest faded into darkness. "So this is you." She studied the cube, the simplicity of it. "And you've come to make sure I escape because The Shadow is following me, which means he wants something from me. Something that may give him more power."

"That's the plan."

"But what if whatever I know can help the side of The Mother?" Hope bloomed in her chest, so foreign that she pressed her free hand to her heart. "What if I'm supposed to stay?"

If what Ren said was true, then she had currency. Maybe she was supposed to remain here, in this horrifying, deadly, wondrous place. Make discoveries. Help the right people.

Something like anguish struck Ren's face. "I can't let you do that."

Siena clenched her hand into a fist atop her chest. "There's nothing for me back home."

"Listen to me." Ren rested both his hands on her knees. They were warm and heavy and carried the familiarity of a safety blanket, and she could feel her cortisol levels lowering by the second.

"There are hundreds of people here," he said.

She shook her head. "I would have seen them."

"They're north of us." He glanced at the board and back to her. "If you stay here, it's not just your life at risk. The Shadow will get what he wants."

"Won't he find a way, regardless? If he's letting me get away, then he must be doing it for a reason."

His hands fell from her knees, and he stood. "It isn't my decision to make. My job is to take you home."

Her eyes burned as he walked back to the counter, and she stared at the fire. "Is it The Mother's decision?"

He didn't answer.

That night, discomfort lingered in her trembling muscles and the wound on her back. Staying still was torture, as was tossing and turning. Her mind burning with a thousand questions didn't help the insomnia.

She watched Ren asleep on the floor. He trusted her not to slit his throat in the middle of the night and take over the cabin as her own. Trust felt inorganic in the Briardark, as if the forest itself bred only hostility.

He was so *strange*. To come out of nowhere in her most vulnerable moment with his perfectly divine timing, saving her from death. Coincidence, maybe, but there was something to him she hadn't figured out yet.

. . . Something he hid from her . . .

. . . Though he'd promised to tell her everything he knew . . .

*"Siena!"*

She startled awake. The fire had died down to a bed of glowing coals, the silhouette of a sleeping Ren in front of her.

*"They aren't here. Dr. Dupont!"*

She shook the sleep from her brain, eyes darting around the dark cabin. The voices—they sounded like they were coming from a television close by. Either that or her own head.

She'd been off her meds for at least two weeks, but it was impossible to tell withdrawal, starvation, and mycelbacteria infection apart. The festering deer she'd seen in the woods, eaten by some invisible predator—she still had no idea if that was real or in her head.

Maybe she was sick after all, and without her meds, the delusions were returning.

She listened for her name again, but sleep claimed her too quickly.

A week passed before her feet were healed enough to walk about the cabin. She spent most of the time sleeping, eating, and prying for answers about the north. Ren was often vague, giving away little about the other red cubes, only that small settlements and communities studded an otherwise desolate landscape. But he provided no details—his attempt to keep her focus on escape.

One morning, after Siena fit her feet into a pair of boots that didn't quite fit right from the chest, Ren showed her outside. Two gloomy structures stood behind the cabin and detached outhouse: the bathhouse, where Ren had nearly drowned Siena in a natural astringent to sterilize her body, and the storage shed, an airtight space that housed the meat, chests of supplies, and a pump house.

"There's so much here," she said as he resealed the storage shed. Her voice drowned in the ambience of the outdoors—the rain, the deep caws from the boughs, the amphibians soaking in the marsh between the trees. Her eyes adjusted to the darkness and the faint green light streaking through the canopy. The distant leaves reminded her of plant cells.

"It's not only for me," he said. "A few of us—those willing to brave the darkness for The Way Back—rebuilt the outpost together." He pointed toward the canopy. "This is the brightest point in the Edge. Whether you're coming north or south, you're bound to be in bad shape."

"A respite," she said.

"Something like that."

She looked south, as far as she could before the light faded, and wiped the rain from her forehead. "How much farther?"

"Twenty miles. We can clear it in one day, but there's no trail. It won't be easy for you."

"I can't imagine it's worse than what I've been through alone." Even with the lingering pain in her bones, the growing ache of the burn on her spine. Even with her torn-up feet and ill-fitting boots.

When she turned, he was watching her, shadows pooling beneath his cheekbones and in the hollows of his eyes.

"The heart of this place wants to be a forest," he said. "Wilderness. But south of us, the Briardark doesn't know what it wants to be. A playground, a dream. Rapid evolution. Paths to nowhere. Quantum entanglement. Lapses in time. Impossible life forms. The end keeps people stuck here. We need to be careful."

Siena nodded, though morbid excitement stirred inside her.

At the end of this world, reality cannibalized itself. And she would witness it with her own eyes.

# HOLDEN

"You moved right between my guys." Angel plucked Holden's piece from the board.

"No." Holden held his hand out for the piece. "I can move between yours and it's fine, but if you surround me, then you get my piece."

Angel wrapped her fingers around his piece and frowned. "That sounds like a made-up rule."

They sat at the small card table in the cabin by Glass Lake, autumn light filtering through the dirty window and creating a crescent across Angel's shoulder.

It was getting late, which meant they'd need to pack up and leave in an hour, and they definitely would not finish this game with Angel being as stubborn as she was.

"It isn't a made-up rule. Think of it as a stealth assassin sneaking past two guards."

She rolled her eyes. "Oh, please. You? A stealth assassin?"

"Trust me. I remember Zaid saying you could do this."

Angel sighed and replaced his peanut on the board, between her two cheddar Goldfish. "I'll ask Zaid when we get back, and if I'm right, then I get a free turn at the start of tomorrow's round."

"Deal." Holden scratched the scruff on his chin and glanced around Tiffany's cabin.

He'd been hiking to and from this cabin almost every day for the past two months. To his utter shock, Angel had faced her fear of the woods and started joining him in his daily trek three weeks ago. He knew a lot of it had to do with boredom; Clevenger had disappeared shortly after her arrival at the Fort, Maidei and Tiffany had gone home, and Frank was busy preparing the area for the first snow. Even after almost a month, Angel still complained about blisters and being out of shape, but Holden didn't care. His days had been getting lonely, and it was nice to pass the time with someone else.

On top of it, Glass Lake Trail bustled with couples and families alike, the eeriness that had once pervaded the woods masked by a return to normalcy. The fire was out, and instead of shutting down the entire wilderness area because of the disappearances and dry weather danger, additional rangers had been assigned to the lower trails.

The cabin was homier than two months ago, the cabinets fully stocked with a variety of canned food, extra gas tanks lined up near the stove on the narrow counter. A laptop and amplifier sat at the end of the counter, settings calibrated to pick up the frequency Dr. Clevenger claimed was a sign of the rift opening. So far, the amp remained silent, and a part of him wondered if a return to normalcy meant Deadswitch's metaphysical underbelly had gone to sleep.

*Two months.* It was a fool's errand, but he hadn't yet carved out the next chapter of his life, so what did he have to lose?

Time. He couldn't just sit here and play make-believe until a rift to another dimension magically opened. But he was too stubborn to give up. Both of them were.

Angel pushed her king off the board. "Your assassin may have been sneaky, but I still won." She gathered all the Goldfish and peanuts from the table and popped a few into her mouth. "I'm getting bored with this game."

Holden groaned. "We literally just learned it." They'd gone through every game at the Fort, which was more games than Holden had thought possible for one house to contain, even one with three floors and an attic. Checkers, chess, Uno, Chutes and Ladders, Risk (which lasted twenty-five minutes), Battleship, and Life. And Scrabble, too, but that one was a dud because most of the pieces were missing and all they could create were the eighteen words arranged from the letters in "Assign."

Angel had grown bored with all the games, so Holden had asked Zaid to teach them Tablut, the game he'd been playing with Maidei. Of course, he wouldn't let them take his precious board anywhere it could accidentally slip into a dimensional rift, so they made their own with a marker on the back of a Deadswitch map and used snacks for pieces.

"Don't know what to tell you," Angel said. "Predictability bores me, and the outcome to these things is always the same: either you win or I win."

"You're right." Holden leaned back in his chair. "That's usually how games work, which explains why you're bored with all of them."

Angel peered out the window and squinted. "What do you think we've got . . . an hour?"

"Give or take."

Her head whipped back to him. "Truth or dare?"

He raised his eyebrows. "Seriously? What is this, high school?"

"It's a creepy cabin in the middle of the woods where we've chosen to waste our lives until a dimensional rift pops open. So yes, basically high school. You gonna answer or what?"

Hell, if it entertained Angel, then what did he have to lose other than a bit of dignity? "Fine. Truth."

"Why don't you ever ask me about my divorce?"

He pressed his lips together to hide that she'd caught him off guard, immediately regretting agreeing to this.

"It's October," she continued. "We've been up here since the start of August. And you're not self-centered enough to not care."

"I *do* care," he said. "I just . . . From what I know of you, if you felt comfortable telling me, you would."

Mirroring his posture, Angel leaned back in her seat. "I guess I blab about a lot of things."

She did blab about a lot of things, and to be honest, Holden was surprised she hadn't shared more details about her divorce, but also didn't want to pry. Their friendship was strange, after all. They'd only started to like each other over the past few months, but that time had been intense, his revelations dreamlike, as if he would wake up any moment from a coma to discover he'd been hit by a bus and was still in Corvallis.

"Truth or dare?" he asked.

"I think I'm supposed to answer truth," Angel said.

"Why did you really get divorced?"

Despite her initial prompt and all this buildup, she hesitated, tracing greasy circles on their makeshift board with her finger.

"I didn't want to have sex."

Holden sensed she wasn't finished, so he waited.

"With anyone," she added.

"You're ace," he said.

"Sure, whatever you kids call it these days." She avoided his eyes and stared out the window. "Didn't want to get divorced, either. That's why I told nobody. And then when my ex finally confronted me about why I kept—you know—making excuses, his reaction was a lot worse than I imagined. He didn't even want to work something out."

She'd seemed so blasé about the whole thing that Holden had assumed they'd split over something petty.

"But I get it," she said. "I get why he was so angry."

"Are you serious?" Holden hadn't thought someone like Angel would so easily accept the behavior of a douchebag. "No. No way. He doesn't *get* to be understood."

"I wasn't honest with him."

"You were figuring out *how* to be honest."

"Holden," she chuckled sadly, and looked at him. "It's okay if I feel sympathy for him and think he's a shitbag at the same time. He was my husband."

Holden blew out a breath. He didn't have a right to tell her how to feel, but he was still angry on her behalf. Your significant other wasn't supposed to abandon you when you were dealing with something confusing.

Angel dragged her teeth across her bottom lip like she was nervous. "What are you thinking about?"

He was thinking about how he should have cared enough to ask her. "Thank you for telling me."

She narrowed her eyes at him, her lips perking up in a smirk. "Truth or dare?"

Holden rubbed his eyes. "Truth."

"Tell me why you and Becca broke up, but only if it's just as sad, because if it isn't, I'll feel like a loser."

After Angel's truth bomb, it was only fair. "Not as sad, but more pathetic." He drew a deep breath. He wasn't beholden to this dumb game, and yet he was tired of keeping such a large part of his past so close to his chest. "We kept getting into arguments about these dates and weekend getaways and conversations we had in the past."

"Okay," she said dubiously.

"The dates and weekend getaways and conversations never happened. My brain made up memories that never existed, and Becca thought I was seeing someone else."

Angel scowled as she listened and continued to scowl long after Holden stopped. "So you're fucked in the head?"

He shrugged. "I guess."

"Kind of weird to be dumped for something you can't control, huh?" She spoke more pensively than sarcastically.

"Yeah, weird," he said, slowly folding up their Tablut board. He was sitting here, right now, because of what had happened with him and Becca. Those false memories felt like divine intervention to get him to Deadswitch Wilderness, and yet, despite trying his goddamn best, he still couldn't reach Siena Dupont.

Holden stood, walked toward the counter, and shut the laptop lid, unplugging it from the amp. "Let's get out of here."

The first time Holden hiked to Glass Lake after learning about the rift had tested his resolve. He spent the whole time in a cold sweat, wondering whether he would fall prey to Tiffany's and Dr. Clevenger's experience. Wondering if he deserved it for his sheer stupidity.

Then he reached the cabin, set up the laptop and amp, and waited.

Sometimes he brought Francis when the loneliness was too much, and he even stayed overnight twice to test if sleep was a factor in getting the rift to open. After a few weeks, Angel joined him, claiming she felt sorry for his *pathetic ass*.

It had taken Dr. Clevenger and Dr. Feyrer four weeks to pass through the rift the second time, and return to the unfamiliar forest. For Holden, four weeks would have been four weeks ago. And yet he still attempted, because Zaid hadn't kicked him and Angel out of the Fort yet.

They reached the trailhead at sunset, and Holden drove them to the ranger station. They walked the rest of the way to the Fort. Dead silence and stale air greeted them as they entered, until Francis's collar jangled and he ran down the stairs. After distributing ear scratches, Holden set his bag near the door, walked into the kitchen, and washed his hands.

He opened the fridge and took stock of the groceries. Zaid promised to keep the fridge full if Holden cooked most nights.

He chopped vegetables for pasta with chicken, focusing on the knife and the bell peppers instead of the whole clusterfuck of his life choices.

He'd tried to save Dr. Dupont. He'd done his best long after the fire swept across the sister peaks, and the mission to find the research team switched from rescue to recovery. And he kept trying, long after the bodiless memorial put together by the Yarrows, which he hadn't attended. But now, the first snow was right around the corner, and after that, Glass Lake would no longer be a quick hike away.

It was over. He felt it in his bones, though he didn't let himself grieve. He didn't deserve to, because Siena Dupont was nothing to him. Just another person who'd gone missing in the woods, one of hundreds every year.

He'd started looking for jobs, applying to a new one every time the satellite internet worked for over five minutes. His meager savings could get him to Portland and cover a few months' rent before he landed a position.

As long as he remained detached, moving to the next chapter of his life would be as easy as turning the page.

He finished up the pasta sauce just as the front door opened and shut, and Frank moseyed into the kitchen. "Zaid invited me. Hope that isn't a problem."

"Never is." Holden nodded toward the stack of plates. "Just help me set the table, will you?"

Frank did, and eventually the four of them were seated around the end of the table that wasn't covered in Zaid's crap.

"You cook better than my mother did," Zaid mumbled as he chewed.

"You say that every night." Holden did his best to mimic Zaid's voice. "*Terrible cook. She always wondered why the dog got so fat, too.*"

Frank chuckled.

"How are you doing, Frank?" Angel asked sincerely. "Haven't seen a lot of you."

As Frank released a sigh, Holden plucked a piece of chicken from his plate and fed it to Francis beneath the table.

"Been rough," he said. "We're in the postmortem stage of the fire, which is tougher than fighting the damn thing. Gotta deal with a bunch of bureaucratic nonsense." He grabbed a paper napkin and wiped his mouth. "Getting word that winter's coming early this year, so luckily that'll slow things down. You still hiking up to Glass Lake every day?"

Zaid had told Frank about Dr. Clevenger's story not long after the scientist left. Even though Frank brushed it off as utter nonsense, he was at least polite about it. The ranger knew about Maidei's experience when she disappeared, as well as Siena's audio files from the future that Holden had found. Remaining skeptical was probably how Frank kept showing up to his job.

"Every day," Holden responded. "Until the snow stops me. So I guess I have a couple weeks left."

Frank clapped his shoulder in a way that reminded Holden of Clyde. "You did everything you could. Those researchers were lucky to have you fighting for them. Don't think we'd even know they were missing if you hadn't shown up. Would have just assumed they burned up."

*Didn't really matter.* The ending was the same, regardless.

He twirled noodles around his fork. "Maybe we should take tomorrow off."

"Nah," Angel said. "We have a couple weeks until the snow starts and we have to throw in the towel for good. Might as well give it our all. Plus, Francis needs to stretch his legs." She peeked beneath the table. "Dontcha, buddy?"

"Sure," Holden relented. A couple more weeks of this wouldn't kill him. The snow was a deadline, one he could work with.

Plus, it gave him some time to apply to more jobs.

Thick clouds coated the sky as Francis led Holden and Angel

around the shore of Glass Lake. It was the first time he'd seen the lake vacant of guests since starting the daily hikes.

A gust of wind blew over them, and Holden tugged his sweatshirt tighter around his body.

"Okay, maybe we won't keep doing this until it snows," Angel said as she fought her wind-blasted hair. "This sucks."

"You go ahead," Holden said. "Set up the amp. I gotta take a leak."

Angel left for the cabin, and Holden ventured into the bushes, Francis bounding into the brush ahead to find a sniffable tree.

As Holden peed, the wind died, and his surroundings went quiet. A ringing erupted in his ears.

Francis poked his head out from behind a tree, listening.

"Come on." Holden waved Francis ahead of him and climbed out of the brush.

As they neared the cabin, Francis released a growl.

"Angel?" Holden yelled, jogging to the cabin door. He yanked it open, the stench of plant rot hitting him in the face, and stumbled back.

The whole of the cabin floor had fallen into a sinkhole. Nothing but soil, roots, and the mouth of the darkest tunnel Holden had ever seen.

From the darkness, Angel screamed his name.

# CAMERON

The Tooth stank like shit from where she stood on the road, just out of sight. Shit and death. Only the desperate would dare stay in such a place, and here she was. God, she was so fucking desperate. She'd never hated herself more than in this moment. An embarrassing wretch of a person. An obsessed person. Journal Siena was right—she'd hyperfixated on Avery for seven years, and would go so far as killing herself to find her. In a lovely addition, she'd now also go so far as killing herself to prove Tammy wrong.

There was no Mother, and she was no imaginary bitch's sacrifice.

Cam continued toward The Tooth, mud squelching beneath her boots. She didn't bother sneaking around back. It was midday, and she hadn't shown up for her morning scraping shift. Tammy knew she was gone.

But the catwalk was empty. Had the guards gone looking for her?

The gate creaked open long before she neared The Tooth's walls. When she stepped through to the village, only Tammy, in a pair of dirty overalls, stood in front of the smoldering bonfire pit.

The *Elder* leaned against the shovel she held and simpered at Cam. "The Mother's will is stronger than yours after all."

Cam fought to keep her expression neutral. "Where is everyone?"

"Getting ready for the feast, of course," Tammy said. "And you should, too. Tonight, join us by the gate when you hear the bell."

Cam glanced around. Not a single pork-addled villager roamed the streets. Her fingers tingled with anxiety, and she clenched her hands.

She turned back to Tammy, whose eyes flickered like she was waiting for a retort, or anger at the very least. The only card Cam had left was her anger, and she wasn't ready to give it up. So she left for her cabin without a word.

Upon entering, she noticed her table was missing, but nothing else, not even the bag beneath her bed. Odd—though it wasn't like she would need it any longer. Her stomach twisted with unease, and the last thing she wanted to do was eat, but she had to. She couldn't imagine this feast being anything more than butchered pig, and once she was in the woods, she'd need enough energy to figure out where to go.

Ruby's jerky was salted, and it was the best goddamn thing Cam had ever put in her mouth. As protein and electrolytes flooded her system, the world around her sharpened like she'd just chugged a vat of coffee. Sustenance.

She chuckled to herself; even after a lifetime backpacking through the wilderness, starvation was a new worry. Perks of being an overfed American. She rolled up the remainder of her jerky in the cloth bag and tucked it into the oversized pocket of her cargo pants. Her dated and dorky hiking ensemble was finally proving useful. She fit her water filter, knife, flashlight, extra underwear, and Avery's map into the pockets she'd sewn into her clothes, then patted around her body, as though the act would provide her some comfort. It didn't.

Cam tried sleeping a bit and failed, her stomach knotting around the jerky too tightly. Every time she heard a noise outside, her adrenaline spiked. She cracked her shutter and watched the sunset as voices finally filtered into the streets.

She could check if her hole in the fence was fixed. Still make a run for it.

"I have nowhere to go," she whispered to herself.

At dusk, a bell chimed at the gate, and Cam stepped from her cabin into the muck of the village. It wasn't raining. Of course it wasn't raining, praise the blessed-fucking-Mother. At least she wouldn't be soaking wet when they cast her out of the village tonight.

Mist clung to the air, the night a soft haze, like the backdrop of a portrait. Unsettlingly beautiful. She used to be perfectly content walking on her own in the eastern California mountains on a night like this, eyes adjusting to the dark, her mind finally quieting as leaves crunched beneath her boots.

Instead, acid fear burned through her stomach, and she refused to show that fear to anyone tonight. Not even steel could withstand acid. She needed to be stronger than any alloy. Impossible, but she had no choice.

The mist carried laughter and banter, but the air was suspiciously empty of the smell of meat. The torches around the perimeter were extinguished. She followed the only source of light to the front of the village. Her eyes flitted left and right as she peered down alleys and into corners, but saw no one. Tammy had told her to wait for the bell, but everyone else must have been given instructions to arrive earlier.

She approached the bonfire and a long line of tables and mismatched chairs. So this was why her table was missing. They were even chronologically ordered by the numbers carved into them.

Everyone in the village was here, the conversation like a roar of flame. Some sat while others stood at the bonfire. A few even carried cigarettes and cigars. They must have had them from their lives before and saved them for the special occasion.

Everything felt too happy. Too bright. And where the hell was the food?

Bert approached her with a thin smile. She hadn't seen him in weeks, and that same uncanny familiarity about him triggered her amygdala, her mind screaming at her to run. But the only way to go was out the open gate. Why was the gate open? Was it a symbol of something? Her exit?

His mouth split open. "Everyone, sit!" he boomed. "The Mother's Chosen has arrived."

Some idiot cheered, and as the villagers of The Tooth scrambled for a seat, Bert touched her arm. "You're with me."

She stepped out of reach, but then followed him to his seat at the head of the table that faced the gate. Candles adorned all the tabletops, melted wax dripping through the cracks in the wood. Their table was unnumbered, unlike the others. She sat to Bert's left while Tammy sat to his right, bonfire light glittering on her sweat-slick forehead. She looked at Cam like she wanted to eat her.

Was firsthand cannibalism better than secondhand cannibalism to these people?

The table quieted as Bert took a breath.

"We begin tonight as we do every year, with an account of our faith, and why ritual and dedication is the only way we survive." Bert set something on the table and pushed it into Cam's view.

The deck of cards.

"It started with a search for the truth, as it always does. Humanity likes to tease apart the elements of the universe, decipher what makes things tick and hum and call it science. I was a man of science, until this world swallowed me whole and reminded me why faith is the crux of our species."

"Amen," someone shouted from the foot of the table. They all were riveted, even those with the shakes so bad that they could hardly hold their head up.

A bead of sweat rolled down Cam's temple. She didn't want

to wipe it away for fear of someone noticing her nervous anticipation.

Bert placed his hand on the card deck. "The first time I drew the cards, I became obsessed with the image of our Mother. I spent weeks, months in the woods in search of her, and find her I did.

"She is a thing of beauty. Tender, albeit omnipotent. Critical but fair. A beacon of life, for she wants us to survive in this vibrant place. She believes we can. And while we must do much on our own, we are guided by her hand of mercy. A gift, once a year, so we may flourish.

"Upon our first harvest sacrifice, we found the cabins and the crag. The next year, the hogs arrived, the gift of long-lasting nourishment. Every year but the Year of Doubt has brought supplies or aid to our village."

Cam had no idea what the Year of Doubt was, but so much of this religion was literal, so she assumed it was a year where this community forwent the sacrifice.

Down the length of the table, a few of the silhouettes shifted. A nod here and there, but most everyone had fallen still. Cam spotted Thia, the woman she'd patched up in the clinic yesterday. Her skin was pale and glittering with sweat. Feverish from infection. Cam hadn't done enough to clean her wound, then again no one could have. Death came too quickly out here, but Bert had survived years. She couldn't imagine there was anyone left who'd lived through this history alongside him.

What were the more recent boons? What had some of these folks actually witnessed?

She scoured the table for Dee, but couldn't find her face.

"It is once again time for us to sacrifice, to show our merciful Mother we are still here, and still thriving. That we are growing stronger, but still require her blessings to thrive."

Bert bowed his head. As did Tammy. Heads bowed in a wave down the table, and the newborns followed the leads of the others. Cam's eyes darted around wildly for any sign of what the next several minutes would bring. Beyond the strip of candle-light, there were only still bodies, bowed heads, and darkness past the open gates. Even the bonfire had dwindled to smoldering coals.

And it remained that way. Bert didn't pray out loud. No one did. Seconds ticked by, and then minutes. Cam bounced her knee, faster, faster, faster, the wood squeak of the chair the only sound in the entire goddamn forest. There were no birds, no crickets. Nothing beyond the fence. No one else at the table so much as shifted in their seat or lifted an eyelid.

If hell was a place, it was right here, right now. This silence, this wait, this ambiguity was almost as bad as when she was dragged underwater to the bottom of the tarn, and into the Briardark.

Fuck this place. Fuck these people.

She counted the bounces of her leg. One, two, three, four . . . one-nineteen, one-twenty, one-twenty-one . . . eight-ninety-nine, nine hundred . . .

She made it to almost three thousand before a twig snapped somewhere beyond the gate. A couple of heads swiveled toward the opening.

"Be still." Bert nodded at Tammy, who bent, disappearing beneath the table. She reappeared holding a rifle, which she rested on the wood in front of her.

Cam pressed her palms to the tabletop, ready to jump and run. "What the hell is going on?"

Everyone's eyes darted to her, the Toothers taken aback by her sudden interruption. Cam's heart thudded in her throat.

Bert lifted the hand in his lap and put it on top of hers so quickly, she hardly had time to register the glove before she felt the cold, rigid metal encasing his hand. It looked not like armor, but a medieval torture device, each finger adorned with a three-inch steel claw sharp enough to gouge the table. The claws were so close to her flesh that if she moved her hand at all, one would cut right into her wrist.

"Still," he ordered. Cam froze, forcing her hand still until it was all she could think about.

"It's here," Tammy said, her eyes trained on the open gate. Hushed whispers rolled across the table.

Deep in the pit of Cam's belly, the real repercussions of her choices manifested. She buried them with all the false optimism she could muster up. Every sad, trembling villager was in on the performance, one they'd clearly rehearsed together. Bert was a profoundly terrible writer who wouldn't know subtlety if it socked him in the jaw. And the spectacle to come, the one that waited to take center stage, Cam would laugh at it, because the terror that lived in her now was too pure to withstand much longer.

Once the usher hit the house lights, everything would be *fucking fine*.

"*Still*," Burt said.

Screams shattered the night. A silhouette emerged beyond the open gate and jumped, thundering across the far end of the tables, so heavy it splintered the wood. Antlers darker than night rose above all of them. A stag? A buck? It was so dark, she could see nothing but its obfuscated shape, like it didn't know whether it wanted to *be* a stag. It was an ink stain. An idea. It meandered forward along the table length, *clop, clop, clop,* its footsteps vibrating through the tables as it crossed them. Candles toppled and rolled to their demise.

A man fell back in his chair. Once he hit the ground, his limbs quaked too violently for him to crawl away. No one helped him. The only ones who jumped from their seats did so with ease. Newborns, all of them. The sick—the ones who'd been here longer—stayed put. They'd seen this before.

Cam jerked her arm to get away, forgetting about Bert's glove, and cried out when the claw dug into her flesh, blood gliding along her skin. "Let me go!"

As the stag neared the head of the table, a sharp ringing pierced the air, high-pitched and insufferable.

Tammy stood and grabbed her rifle, stepping onto her chair and then the table. She aimed the gun at the stag, and Cam clapped her free hand over one ear as she pulled the trigger.

*Boom.*

The dark animal staggered, its inkstain legs collapsing. Some of the veteran villagers finally dove from their chairs, screaming as tables skidded apart or crushed beneath the stag's weight. The beast slid and fell, its head lolling to the side, one of its massive antlers skimming the shoulder of a young woman who hadn't yet jumped back. She crumpled alongside the animal.

"Penn!" the man beside her shrieked.

Cam pushed herself up to see, but Bert's claws still wrapped around her stinging wrist. Who knew what kind of infection lay dormant on the metal? God, she was fucking done for, and she hadn't even been sacrificed yet.

The commotion didn't dissipate; the man who knelt by the fallen woman sobbed uncontrollably, and Cam wanted to throw up in panic just watching him. The woman on the ground hadn't so much as twitched.

Cam forced her body to relax, and Bert removed the metal glove from her hand. She shoved her wrist toward the candlelight, examining the wound. Bloody, but shallow.

At some point, Tammy had stepped off the table, but Cam couldn't remember when. The Elder crouched near the crying man, and pressed a hand to the shoulder of the unmoving woman.

"Dead," she announced.

The man wailed and punched the earth with his fist. Dead, how? The antler of this strange animal had merely grazed her.

Tammy stood. "The death is proof enough. We should move on without the roll."

"We have to go through with it," Bert said. Cam could hardly hear him over the commotion of the villagers, some crying, others muttering like they were speaking in tongues. A few groups huddled together, trying to soothe one another or hold each other up. Many were too feeble to stand, watching idly and apathetically from their seats.

Cam took the opportunity to leap away from Bert and run toward the body. She shoved Tammy out of the way.

"I said she was dead!" Tammy said.

"Like fuck I trust you," Cam said, but it was obvious the collapsed villager was beyond revival. Her eyes were orbs of dull obsidian, scream frozen in death. The man had flung his body over her torso and continued to weep. Cam almost knelt to check for a pulse and then clenched her fist.

Bad idea to touch a body.

She glanced at the dead stag, expecting some definition, now that she was closer, but her brain revolted against making sense of the dark mass. Eyes watering, she blinked and looked back at Bert, who withdrew a spherical gem from his pocket. He held it up within his gloved hand for all to see and then threw it across the table.

The gem knocked over one of the remaining candles, molten wax flinging through the night, before rolling to a stop. Not a gem, but a die, the candlelight illuminating its dozens of faces, each etched with a number.

"The Lover reads," Bert said, and motioned for Cam to approach the die.

Though Cam stood motionless, her insides sped forward, taking flight, breaking the sound barrier. *Run run run runrunrunrun.*

The crowd quieted. She glanced around at them staring at her, meager, swollen-eyed, sniveling. Menaced, she pulled back her upper lip in a snarl. She hated them. Hated how, in this moment, she was one of them.

Sloppy footsteps pattered as a man raced toward the gate. A shot rang out. Cam clapped her hands over her ears as he rag-dolled face-first in the mud. The woman closest to him jumped and cowered, covering her head with her arms. She didn't drop to help him, but it didn't matter. The man lay still in the mud.

Tammy lowered her rifle. "We stay until the feast is over." She nodded at Cam. "Go on."

Despair clawed at Cam's throat. There was nothing left to do but listen to Bert before anyone else got shot. Leaning closer to the die, she read the metallic numbers etched into—was it quartz? "Forty-seven."

A young woman standing at the edge of the crowd released a desperate howl, the way one sounded when their greatest fear inevitably came to fruition. Cam had made the same noise the day Grandma June died. Denial. It was the sound of denial. The woman's wail shot through Cam's body, chilling the tips of her fingers. She took a step back, and then another, hoping to blend into the darkness enough to run, but Tammy's eyes were on her. Holding her rifle, she stared at Cam like she was the next piece of wild game. She wouldn't dare shoot Cam, would she? Mother knew best, after all.

The woman spun from the table and ran right past Tammy, who whipped around, caught her by the hair, and dragged her down to her knees.

Light erupted as one of Bert's hulking goons lit a torch with a melting candle. Cam didn't know his name. Another of his men had taken over for Tammy and scuffled with the woman. The torchlight illuminated her heart-shaped face and bright skin.

The new catwalk guard. A newborn. Cam carefully approached the table close to where the woman had been standing before she'd read the die. The number 47 was carved into the wooden surface.

Bert lit a torch off a candle and walked the length of the mess of tables, toward the fallen stag. The flame passed over the animal, and it was like someone had taken a knife to the fabric of reality and cut from it the shape of this deer. No smoke and mirrors. No trick was this good.

With his gloved hand, Bert grabbed one of its legs and rolled the tangible creature onto its back. The stag lay sprawled out like it was about to be field dressed. Bert's clawed hand hovered over its chest, and then he inched it lower, beneath the sternum. His hand sank into the deer's upper abdomen to the rip of skin and snap of tendons, as though the animal were a real warm-blooded mammal. He reached up and beneath the rib cage, grimacing, now elbow deep in inky matter, though Bert didn't drop dead like the others.

He reached higher, clawing through what had to be the diaphragm and lung tissue. With another wet rip, he tore from the void a black lump almost too big for him to grip within his glove.

More torches erupted behind Cam, but she only faintly registered the light, unable to tear her eyes away.

Bert knelt next to Forty-Seven—the catwalk guard—as Tammy wrenched open her mouth. But it was all for show. The woman couldn't eat the heart, because the moment Bert placed it against her lips, her body seized. Her eyes rolled to the back of her head and then lost their white sheen, the color bleeding from her skin and leaving a rubbery, translucent sac for her insides. Dark veins spidered across wiry muscle and pockets of fat.

Cam released her breath in a long hiss, too horrified to scream.

"We know the cards speak truth because we see that truth with our very eyes." Bert stood straight. "And I ask, does this mean our devotion to our Mother is no longer faith, but the science of survival?"

The moment Bert turned toward her, Cam stumbled back, arms swiftly restrained by two large men.

Sacrifice. He'd always meant to kill her with this poisoned beast. Was she supposed to ascend to whatever afterlife these lunatics believed in and be The Lover to The Mother there?

Bert approached her with the heart raised, and she thrashed to no avail.

She deserved this. Her punishment for avoiding Avery after college, then failing to find her. Her punishment for leaving Siena. Her punishment for being selfish. And now this motherfucker would be the last thing she ever saw.

She clamped her mouth shut. He could push the deadly heart into her face all he wanted, but she wouldn't give him the satisfaction of pretending she would eat it.

He gripped her face with his unadorned hand the second he was close enough, fingers jamming into the hinge of her jaw.

"Open up, Cameron."

*Cameron.*

She'd never told him her full name.

The torchlight flashed across Bert's face, and she saw him for the first time up close—really, truly saw him. His beard mostly masked his facial features, an uncanny face she'd mostly dismissed. Because he was so young. But now it was unmistakable: the high cheekbones, the heavy brow ridge over icy eyes. She never looked at men so intently, but she knew these features because she'd been forced to exist around this man for years, just to get credit for this nightmare of a study. Features she'd once considered kind, harmless, and sometimes obnoxious, his journal entries always far, far too spiritual to be from a scientist.

"Feyrer," she said.

He seized the opportunity and jammed the heart into Cam's mouth.

**Type: Artifact, Variable #11**
**Item Description: Single page torn from Field Journal
branded notebook. Medicinal recipe written in BIC Cristal
black ballpoint pen.**

**Text:**
*Metabolic Tincture*
*Usage: Topical use on open wounds only. Apply IMMEDIATELY
after injury. May not work on large wounds.*
*Ingredients:*
*18–24 hook vine leaves*
*2–3 blacknight fern roots (not to be confused with bracken),
trimmed*
*Filtered water*
*Preparation: Crush leaves into paste. Boil roots with leaves for thirty
minutes. Remove roots. Strain into a bottle.*
*Notes: Hook vine contains enzymes that speed up metabolic reac-
tions. DO NOT OVERBOIL.*

# SIENA

She wasn't healed. Not even close.

Not like she would have known that, lounging about Outpost 5, but now she was on the narrow trail, treading behind Ren in the gloom. She could see more of the Edge with Ren's lantern than she could with either her headlamp or flashlight, and she wished she couldn't. In hindsight, she missed her ignorance to the forest's innards. The lamp cast too many willowy shadows, illuminated too much rot and death. Off the trail, a ribcage clamped around a slimy trunk like teeth, as though the tree had grown from a nutrient-rich body.

"Human?" she asked Ren.

"Looks like."

How many bodies had she unknowingly passed since entering the Edge? Ren had told her she made it deeper than most, though "most" was an ambiguous number of people. She didn't ask for fear of the answer.

Once the two of them fell silent, the pain in her side and her feet swallowed her every thought, scabs itching, burning, and stinging, muscles trembling just to bear the ache. Blood soaked her socks, warmer and stickier than mud.

Twenty miles. Twenty miles had felt so easily accomplishable, and now she wasn't sure if she could make two.

What would Ren do if she sat right now and refused to move forward? He'd told her it was his job to get her home, some duty to his Mother faction, guilting her with the claim that staying would risk more than her own life. The Shadow wanted something from her, some nugget of knowledge buried within the folds of her brain, which made her so dangerous that Ren had followed her from the research cabin to ensure she'd make it out.

As she trailed him and his lantern, the mud sucking her boots every time she stepped, she understood why he hadn't wanted to interfere. Her time at the outpost had provided some answers, but many more questions. Hundreds of people lived in this Briardark, this dimension, something she couldn't grasp to save her life. She wanted to see it for herself so much that she'd conjured dozens of ways to escape Outpost 5 while Ren slept, all of them ending with her dying in the Edge. This goddamn biome. This *hell*.

Ren glanced back at her, the flickering light of his lantern reflecting in the plastic eyes of his mask. He'd outfitted her with an oversized waterproofed coat that fell past her hips, and a balaclava that covered most of her face. She flexed her sweaty fingers in a borrowed pair of ski gloves, only now realizing how hard she'd been clenching her hands.

He slowed, which she took as permission to stop, pressing a hand to her burnt side. Her heart pounded violently enough to make her nauseous. The journey so far hadn't even been strenuous with his guidance. She was just a wreck.

"What is it?" he asked.

"The scabs on my feet and side are ripping. It hurts to breathe." Her chest heaved as she tried to drag in enough oxygen. Somehow that only sharpened the pain.

His irritated grunt was hardly audible beneath the patter of rain.

"It isn't my fault." She hated not seeing his face or communicating via expression. Was he worried? Angry?

Suddenly Ren's head shot toward the rumble of thunder.

No . . . not thunder.

Again came the rumble, ground trembling beneath her feet. A steady beat, each *boom* drawn out. She held her breath and listened. *Boom.* The rain picked up. *Boom.* It drew near enough for her to pick apart distinct noises within the boom. A crackle like snapping branches. A rush like fire. The scream of an animal.

"We need to move," he barked, and she jumped in alarm. "I'll carry you."

"No." She couldn't slow them down. Pain was temporary—she had to push through it. "Go."

Ren took off into the dark, and she remained at his heels, watching his feet as they moved over root and rock. She gritted her teeth hard enough to break a molar, lightning strikes of pain shooting from her feet to her knees.

The boom rumbled once more behind her, followed by a crack and a shriek like a mountain lion. Or woman.

*Keep moving.*

*Boom, boom, boom.*

The booms weren't thunder, the cadence too consistent. They were *footsteps.* Footsteps heavy enough to shake the earth, each one groaning like a creaking tree. Snarling like a wolf. Weeping like an injured old man. The sound kept morphing, shifting. Terror ricocheted throughout her rib cage, Siena suddenly compelled to scream loudly enough to meet the volume of the steps.

Ren turned, grabbed her arm, and dragged her along with him.

He'd led them into a trap. Maybe this was the plan all along, for the shrieking behemoth gaining on them to tear her apart. Then Ren wouldn't have to worry about whatever valuable knowledge she held in her brain.

But if that were true, he would have let her die north of the outpost instead of coaxing her back to life.

Her legs shook horribly as he pushed her past her limits.

The sky flashed, and the entire forest lit up at once. A scream lodged in her throat; she could see everything. Every set of eyes in the boughs, on the ground. Lumpy concoctions of fungus and moss, growing in bulbous sacks from trees, dripping something like oxygenated blood.

"Shit," Ren hissed.

The light died, and she was blinded. Disoriented, she stumbled about until her toe snagged on a root and she fell. Ren tripped over her.

*Boom. Boom. Boom.*

Siena blinked until shapes reformed in front of her eyes. She growled through her pain and stood, grabbing Ren's hand and helping him up.

"Watch my lamp," he said. "Don't look anywhere else."

She wanted to ask why, but they were off again, the ground slickening with moss and mud. A few times Ren stopped and redirected them toward the thinner edges of the briar, the garbled, screaming thunder crawling ever closer.

Another flash. It startled Siena so much that Ren's warning slipped from her brain, and she glanced up at a synchronized pulsing in the knots of the lichen-drenched trees, like they had beating hearts.

"Focus on the light!" Ren yelled above the booming.

What the hell was happening?

"Focus on the—"

Another flash, though this time it didn't die, and Siena shielded her eyes as the forest fell silent.

"Ren!"

Tears streamed down her cheeks from the light's intensity, and she covered her face with her forearms. Green burst across the backs of her eyelids. The temperature shift alone knocked the wind from her, the air so intensely warm that her soaked clothing hissed as water evaporated.

Vertigo washed over Siena as she fought to breathe. She lost balance, and braced herself for a fall that never came.

When she finally coaxed air into her lungs, it tasted like honeysuckle. She dropped her arms, blinking away tears until blurry, earth-colored shapes took form and slowly sharpened. The impenetrable canopy was gone, daylight streaking through the surrounding verdure. A bird tittered somewhere behind tufts of the greenest pine needles she'd ever seen. She followed the arrow-straight path beneath her feet, southward, the trees so perfectly geometric, evergreens spaced evenly between lush, red-crowned maples. Wallpaper perfect. She was the protagonist in a cheap cartoon retelling of a fairy tale, her surroundings benign.

Horrifyingly benign.

She must have fallen. Hit her head on a rock.

A shadow darted through her peripheral vision, and she whipped around. Nothing—nothing but a waver in the air, a distortion of heat. When she blinked, it was gone.

"*Ren!*" she screamed.

Fear clotted her throat as she scanned the trees. He'd told her to focus on his lantern, but she'd been too disoriented, and now . . .

She burst into a jog, but the agony was too intense, like the nerve endings in her feet were grating directly against the hard dirt. Slowing to a limp, she screamed Ren's name again. The dense, pristine foliage ate up her voice in this cheery panoramic toy, the woodland path repeating over and over again.

Her abdomen cramped in panic. Not even the sun or the heat could comfort her, though she did stare up, confounded by the sun's brightness and how the light shifted rapidly across the sky. Before long, stretching shadows covered her path, and the day deepened to a burnt orange.

All she had on her was a canteen, a meager stash of jerky, and a lighter. Ren carried his own supplies, but they were supposed to have reached The Way Back without camping.

Siena kept her eyes peeled to catch any movement other than the squirrels chasing each other up tree trunks. She yelled Ren's name.

Behind her, the booming rumbled to life again, now even closer, and it dawned on her that this noise wasn't new, but one she'd only heard before at a distance, when she'd described it as a visceral hunger. But it was an amalgamation of noises. The chaos of the universe, the rush of undiluted atmosphere, the shriek of fear. Creation and destruction at once, as though the Edge was the gestation grounds for the entire forest.

Dusk fell with unnatural quickness, the cookie-cutter world suddenly drowning in blue twilight. Her heart leapt at a small trail slithering from the path, the differentiation hopefully signaling an end to this nightmare. Siena dipped into the forest, the atmosphere sharper and earthier. Up ahead, a glow pierced the dusk. She ran her hands over imperfect bark patterns as she crept deeper, limping over rotten trees in her path. The moisture returned, the fetid air teeming with mist. A few meters away, the soil undulated like it was made of water, and Siena slowed.

A cloud of illuminated haze lit up the clearing before her. The rumble dissipated as a chittering took over.

She waited beyond the clearing, cloaked in shadow as her eyes adjusted to the new light. The ground continued to roil and chitter, though it sparkled beautifully, like iridescent seafoam across the ocean's surface.

An insect flew past Siena's ear, its wings beating briefly in her hair before zipping forward and diving into the sparkling ground, which hissed and buzzed at the interruption. She slapped a hand over her mouth as a swarm of beetles shot from the ground and into the night.

Not water. Not foam. An infestation.

The beetles' nacre shells shimmered in waves as they crawled and tumbled over each other synchronously, their iridescence both hypnotic and vile. Siena kicked out, shaking off the beetles skittering beneath the hem of her pants and up her legs. Her eyes traveled from the ground to the glow beyond the mist, and the soft gossamer tendrils of the beetles' web.

She lifted her boot and stepped forward, scratching the deep itch to feel them crush beneath her foot. But as she did so, ringing pierced her ears, and she stumbled as her vision blurred. The beetle lair spun around her until pressure forced her eyelids down.

She was going to pass out.

Her head snapped back, and she peeled her eyelids open. She lost purchase with gravity, and floated.

Before her, in a stunning display of impossible geometry, Webs crisscrossed in shapes she'd never seen, at angles she couldn't comprehend. The bugs fluttered upward and beat her body with their wings. They weren't suspended, not like her, and scattered out of alarm, out of fear, out of survival instinct. But she couldn't. The lack of gravity trapped her, even when she flailed her arms and legs.

*Why?*

Why was she entangled when they could go free? Why was her matter somehow different from theirs?

*They aren't beetles.*

*thump THUMP. thump THUMP. thump THUMP.*

The dark space beyond the web stretched infinitely, but the heart thumped somewhere beneath her.

*thump. THUMP.*

*thump. THUMP.*

*thump. THUMP.*

The web's light pulsed to the beat.

*thump.*

*THUMP.*

*thump.*

*THUMP.*

The light gathered into beads and shot outward, zipping through synapses and down nerve cells, filling the void with the silhouette of a root system.

A nervous system.

She'd been here before, after The Shadow bled from Isaac. Back when she'd been naïve about the strength she would need to get out of this place.

*I am everywhere.*

Except it didn't speak to her now, nothing in the beyond but the thud of a molten heart, miles and miles beneath her. Her head was quieter than it had been in a long time.

Her insides teetered on the edge of a drop. Gravity flirted with her, sentient, as it toyed with the idea of pulling her organs from her body.

*"Check the bed!"*

Her own voice echoed from above. Siena lifted her head to a cathedral-like dome of celestial sky, Emmett an angry man in the moon.

*"I'm losing my patience."*

She was projecting a memory from the night of their engagement party, when she'd woken up screaming. The first time she'd experienced her *delusions.*

*"You're right."* Her voice echoed. *"I'm losing it."*

No. That was wrong. She hadn't said that.

She'd argued with him. Told him to stop patronizing her. That night was burned into her brain along with every time she'd had delusions, because she'd thought back to those moments so often, trying to tease apart hallucination from reality. Insects desperate to lay their eggs inside her body, tangling in her hair, prying open her nostrils, skittering across her abdomen, burrowing into her belly button.

She'd been combative that night because she'd been so certain.

Emmett's face softened. *"You're not losing it. Stressful days lead to stressful dreams for you. You okay? Need some water?"*

This wasn't a memory. It was a lie.

Thump. *THUMP.*

Back on Mount Agnes, when she passed through the tree tunnel from one world to another, the beetles had been there. Again, when the passage to the Briardark collapsed, and she, Emmett, and Isaac were stuck in a microverse, she'd pinched one between her fingers, then released it, trying to follow where it flew.

The bugs weren't an omen—a harbinger of panic. They shifted reality.

Emmett's face vanished.

She raced through a tunnel of wet forest sounds until darkness swallowed her. Her feet gained purchase with a slosh of mud. Rain splashed against her clothes in its slow and suffocating drip. The cloying stench of plant and animal rot overwhelmed her senses.

Siena was back in the Edge. She exhaled in relief, happy to return to this festering, unending hell. In the abyss, her stomach unclenched, her heart returning to its resting rhythm.

Footsteps sloshed around in front of her. The muscles in her legs tensed. "Ren?" she called out. A splash, another squelch. Closer this time. Siena jammed her hand into her coat pocket and found her lighter.

"Ren," she repeated. Silence answered her. Something was wrong.

She extended her lighter. A tall figure loomed ten or so paces in front of her, motionless.

Not Ren. Ren would have said something.

They stepped closer and kept their hands at their sides, but the flame wasn't bright enough to see much else. Her fingers trembled so badly, she almost dropped the lighter. She took a hesitant step back, though retreating wouldn't solve anything, because she was directionless. Trapped.

"Sen . . ."

A nickname she knew too well. A voice, gruffer than it should be. Her blood ran ice cold as he closed in on her, one slick footstep after another.

Weak light flickered over the black stone filling his right eye socket, then the scars spidering from his forehead to his cheekbones. Everything else about him was just as she remembered. Just as she knew him.

Emmett.

# CAMERON

There was no death for Cam when her mouth touched the meat of the stag, only the hot iron tang of blood drizzling down her throat, and the tough chew of heart.

She could only mull this over for half a breath before gagging. Bert—no, Wilder Feyrer—clapped a hand over her mouth before she could spit it out.

"*Swallow.*"

Cam thrashed against the arms of the men constraining her. Feyrer grabbed her neck and dug the heel of his other palm against her mouth, then pinched her nose shut.

She swallowed the heart out of panic, and Feyrer released his hold on her. Cam drank in air. She coughed hard in an attempt to throw the meat back up, trying to rip her arms free so she could stick a finger down her throat.

"This is your sacrifice," Feyrer announced. "Your divine intervention."

She could see the whites of the eyes of those standing around the table, every fucking person awestruck into silence. Rage filled the face of the man who knelt near the first dead body. A touch from the void animal had killed his . . . friend? Partner? But not Cam. Because Cam was the . . .

*Horseshit.*

This was a trick, just like the cards.

*Then explain Isaac. Explain Feyrer standing right in front of you.*

Feyrer turned back to Cam, a gleam in his eye. It wasn't a wicked gleam, even though she wished it were. She hated that his eyes were full of wonder.

"Goddess, protect us from Shadow."

"Wilder . . ." she whispered.

Feyrer smiled at her. "Took you a while this time, Dr. Yarrow."

He knew who she was, even though he was so much younger than when they'd worked together.

"Gather 'round," Tammy said. "Our Lover is about to enter her new world the way she was born into her old one."

Her skin felt like it was stretched too taut over her bones. She couldn't breathe, stretch, move her joints. Misery trickled into her abdomen, filling up her hollow, hopeless body. The men who held her took advantage of her sudden stillness, adjusting their grip on her arms.

Hesitant, the villagers slowly gathered around her. She recognized most of them, like Spice, whom she shared a scraping duty shift with. She looked remorseful.

No, not remorseful. *Embarrassed.*

She still couldn't find Dee among the faces.

Bert stepped away from Cam, and Tammy approached, holding a dirty cloth grocery bag in one hand, rifle in the other.

Cam's paralyzed throat held her scream hostage. Tammy pulled the bag over her head. It smelled like shit and mildew, and Tammy held the excess bunched beneath her chin. Then the Elder kneecapped her with the butt of her rifle.

In a burst of pain, Cam fell to the ground.

"A shame," Tammy said. "I'm sure you spent so much time sewing those pockets, trying to decide what to take with you."

The zipper on Cam's coat was dragged down so forcefully, it

ground against the track and snapped. *Broken.* Cam's only jacket. Tammy yanked her head up. Hands and the sharp edge of a blade tore the shirt from her body, her flesh puckering with the cold.

Her will to fight returned, and Cam thrashed as hard as she could, but it didn't matter. The clothes they couldn't wrangle from her, they cut from her body. Everything. Even her shoes. Every time she took another breath and screamed "STOP," she heard nothing in response. Was the entire village still watching her, stark naked and fighting for her life? Her dignity?

"Please," Cam whispered. She never begged. Not for anything in her whole goddamned life, but now . . .

Above her, metal clanged against metal.

"Go forth into the new world as you came into this one."

Viscous liquid splattered against the bag and the top of her head. She smelled the vile, bloody filth immediately as it cascaded down her shoulders, her breasts. It saturated the bag, and she dipped her head to keep the fabric out of her mouth. Her efforts helped little; she tasted iron and death, and spat it out against the bag. Once dragged to her feet, Cam was forced forward, mud squelching between her bare toes.

She slipped over the slick ground until ferns and foliage whipped at her bare legs. They'd taken her beyond the gate.

"Tell me where I'm going," she begged. "Tell me what's happening."

The men dragging her said nothing.

Cold mist lapped her bare flesh, thorns and twigs tearing into her legs and feet. They shoved her forward so quickly, she could hardly catch her breath, but she screamed at the top of her lungs anyway.

They didn't gag her. They didn't care. And she thrashed the entire way. By the time she was forced to her knees again, her body was numb and flayed by the forest.

All the work she'd done to stay clean. All the confidence she'd had, thinking she could best these lunatics from inside their trap.

One man bound her wrists behind her back with rope, then

they lifted their hands from her, and their footsteps faded into the dark.

"*Hey!*" she screamed. They couldn't do this to her. Not like this.

Her hands shook as she cried. Freeing herself took as long as the journey to get wherever she was. She split her nail below the quick as she worked the knot. Mist clung to her body, the moisture loosening dried blood and snaking down her skin in rivulets. Soon she was soaked.

When the rope finally unraveled from her wrists, she tore the bag from her head and shivered in the unforgivably cold night.

Fog muted the light from the moon. Only black deciduous skeletons pierced the still, gray veil. Pebbles and detritus dug into her knees. She wrapped her arms around her wet body, and released a string of uncontrollable whimpers.

Cameron Yarrow was alone in the raw, festering wilderness, naked and covered in blood.

No Mother came to fetch her.

# SIENA

"Emmett." Her voice quietly shook.

"Sen." His expression was calculating and detached, her pet name monotone. Not that he was emotionless. Excitement flickered in his one eye, the scars on his cheeks and chin quivering as he forced a smile back.

He was trying to *suppress* his emotions.

She reached out, daring to touch his face with a gloved hand. Tangible. Not a figment of her imagination.

The moment he shot up to grab her wrist, a branch snapped to the right. Emmett's head whipped toward the sound, and Siena slammed her fist with the lit lighter against his temple.

He released her and staggered back, the gleaming white of his eye rolling around before the lighter went out.

Darkness suffocated her. Emmett stumbled about as she fell against a tree and slipped behind it.

"*Sen.*"

One step forward, and then another. Her shin slammed into a log, and she almost tumbled over it. Orange light erupted behind her. He wielded a torch.

"*Sen!*"

She pressed her back against a tree, away from the light. Her whole body shook with both fear and pain, her feet so numb and limp that she could hardly control where she stepped. She couldn't outrun him, but she could hide.

Foliage rustled, and the glow of the flame dimmed. He was looking for her in the other direction. She risked creeping toward the next tree, and pressed herself against the trunk. Where had he come from? It was like he'd been waiting for her, sitting in this spot in the dark for an ungodly amount of time. What did he want, to seek revenge on her for leaving his body to rot? She'd had no other choice, and he'd come back to haunt her.

"I just want to talk to you," he said, his voice far too calm. "I have a lot to tell you, and I think you'll want to hear it."

The flame of the torch brightened as it swung in her direction, light catching on the plastic eyes of a gas mask.

Ren.

He lifted a finger. *Quiet.*

Dammit, she wished she could see his face, but with the dark and the mask, she didn't know what was about to happen.

Slowly he stepped forward, raising his unlit lantern and pushing it toward her. She took it, and cradled it against her so it wouldn't squeak.

In Emmett's torchlight, the knife in Ren's right hand gleamed.

Who did he think Emmett was? Did Ren recognize him as Siena's partner? Without the ability to see his face, she had no clue to his level of confidence. Whether ghosts were a common occurrence in the Edge, or if Ren was as shocked and afraid as she was, she didn't know.

Regardless, she shook her head rapidly, a silent plea. Whatever he was planning, it couldn't be to protect her. Confronting Emmett was too dangerous; she felt this truth in her bones.

"Run," he whispered, and then sprang forward, toward Emmett.

At the thud of bodies colliding, Siena stumbled forward until she could no longer see. Behind her, one of them cried out, but she was too far away to tell who.

*Go back. Help him.*

She hesitated. With no weapon, turning back now would only get herself hurt or killed. She had no other choice but to trust Ren, and follow his instructions.

*Run.*

Siena fumbled with the lamp until she found the knob and turned it, light bursting forth and illuminating a tangle of sopping briar. She had to push forward to stay hidden, even though no one ran to catch up with her, and all she heard were the nickel-sized drops of rain pelting the earth.

Her ear rang the way it did at the start of a panic attack, though she didn't feel at the brink of one. Her mind was sharp, and she wasn't about to squander the clean break from Emmett. *This* Emmett.

Siena focused on the ringing, which wasn't coming from her own head but somewhere out in the dark, like a siren. With the noise as her north star, she slid from trunk to trunk, the lantern guiding her further into the unknown. She was too loud, moving too slowly, especially if the doppelgänger overtook Ren and sniffed out her trail.

*I have a lot to tell you, and I think you'll want to hear it.* He'd spoken it so casually, as though teasing her with a bit of academic gossip that he'd overheard in the lab. Either he didn't plan on hurting her, or his words were bait, because he knew her, didn't he? How utterly drawn she was to secrets, knowledge, and missing puzzle pieces.

But none of it would matter if he tried to hurt her, or worse.

The ringing drove her in one direction, her way of walking in a straight line instead of in circles. She needed to put some distance between her and Emmett, concentrating on her quiet breath and her feet slopping through the wet leaves. The ringing grew louder and more refined as the trees thinned, and she stalled at the edge of a clearing. A hulking, beaten-down structure stood before her.

Siena stepped forward and lifted the lantern, light illuminating the run-down husk of a cabin. Outpost 6. One more to go. Ren knew where they were, and the landmarks. She would wait here until he shook Emmett and caught up with her.

She approached, her light rolling over the sign above the door.

*Outpost 7.*

*What?*

They hadn't passed Outpost 6. She would have remembered. Unless . . .

*Paths to nowhere. Quantum entanglement. Lapses in time.* Ren had recalled how the Briardark acted in the southern Edge. Her little waltz through the fairytale forest had been more than just a psychotic break. And now she was here, faster than predicted. The end.

She'd made it.

Her body reacted with a shudder, panicked and unsure, but she needed to seize the opportunity of shelter at the very least. She ducked under the eaves and felt around the door with her hands, before turning the rusted knob.

As expected, the hinges screeched, in tune with the ringing scream.

Siena slipped inside and quickly shut the door behind her. Even with the balaclava covering her face, the stench of mold and rot overpowered her.

The lantern shone bright in the enclosure, casting a glow over flaky, soggy planks. Some had rotted away, leaving black gaps between. The farthest corner had crumbled to almost nothing.

The outpost was empty. Not even an old shelf lined the walls. No bottles or wrappers on the ground. No stove or fireplace. No clothes spread out to dry. No history.

Siena spun and examined the back of the door with the lantern. Two large rusted hooks were screwed into the wood on either side of the door, a bar propped against the wall. Better than nothing, though the door would crumble with a large enough shove.

She picked up the bar and rested it between the hooks. Panic fluttered inside her. *Think.* There was nothing to think about. She was here. She'd made it to the outpost on the map with the circle with two lines slashed into it. The passage. The Way Back. Isaac had known it would take her home, and so had Ren.

Looking around, she caught sight of herself in the cabin's only window, and peeled her balaclava from her head. She recognized nothing. The fat in her cheeks were gone. Her skin hung from her skull, grayer than a corpse. Strands of hair had escaped her tie and now hung limply around her face, patches of her scalp peeking through the top of her head. Her lips were split in many places along the line of her mouth, like someone had sewn them shut with dark thread.

Her massive eyes blinked astonishedly, the only part of her unshrunken. A husk, like this outpost, so little left that she didn't know if she could ever grow the rest of herself back.

The orb of the lantern reflected brightly in the window. Beyond, the blackness was absolute, Siena a beacon within a sea of dark matter.

A beacon. *Shit.*

The handle on the lantern squeaked as she turned the knob and snuffed out the light.

She stood still in the pitch black, trying to calculate the likelihood that she'd given away her position with the lantern. Did she *want* to give away her position? Did Ren know the Edge well enough to find her without a light of his own? No—he was merely human. He needed his eyesight.

Tap.

Tap.

Tap.

The gentle sound came from the glass, less than two feet in front of her nose. Her insides liquified.

Tap.

Tap.

Tap.

She couldn't step back. She couldn't move at all. Siena jammed the key into the ignition of her brain, and the starter turned over and over. Every spark of thought refused to form.

Holding her breath, she waited for the noise to break the steady ringing once more. It didn't come, but she felt the presence of someone else right in front of her, just on the other side of the glass, intense and unwavering. The lantern squeaked as her hand trembled. She knew they could hear it, whoever they were.

Not Ren. Ren wouldn't play these games.

If she did nothing, she would be here forever, waiting in the dark. No sunrise approached. No dawn raced to save her. She breathed in deeply, breath faintly rattling in her lungs, and then reached up to turn on the lantern. A hiss, then unrelenting brightness, and Siena was met not with the face of Emmett, but Ren. Blood filled his eyes and dribbled from his nose. His slack mouth hung limply open, tongue lolling out to the side. His neck ended in a violent mess of torn flesh and muscle.

Emmett stepped forward, and pressed his forehead to the glass. Siena stumbled backward and screamed until her throat was raw meat.

A monster wearing the skin of her dead ex gripped the head of the person who had spent his last months making sure she escaped. Ren was dead. This thing had killed him.

Something strange happened then. With a rush of warmth, anger flushed away her fear. She wanted to rush the window. Burst through the glass and grab this thing that wore Emmett's skin by the throat, squeeze his neck so tightly that his eye popped from its socket. Yank on the eyeball until the optic nerve snapped, and eat it. Jam her fingers into the hollow above his collarbone with enough force to break the skin and tear through muscle. Saw through his neck with her hands until every one of her fingernails broke, until she could see his spinal cord, until she could wrap her fist around it and shake him until his head snapped off.

"*What are you?*" she roared. She could taste his blood in her mouth.

Emmett dropped Ren's head. It thudded against the ground.

"Don't be silly," he said.

"You're *dead*."

His hand slipped behind him. She expected him to pull a weapon from beneath his clothing. Instead, he pressed something small and flat against the glass. A card. A wizened man peering at her between the bars.

**THE WARDEN.**

"I have you cornered," he said.

She'd been foolish enough to believe a map painted on the wall, but if the passage at the research cabin had collapsed, what was to say that this one hadn't?

"Why are *you* here?" she choked out with a sob, hating herself for crying. Her tears quenched her molten rage when she wanted to rally. Wanted revenge.

She stepped back, staggering when the wood beneath her groaned and gave under her weight. She took her eyes off Emmett to glance at the broken planks on this side of the outpost, where the floor yawned open to darkness. Except this cabin had been built atop solid ground. She remembered from when she'd first entered.

Siena stared down into the hole. Far below her, a web of light strung across the gaping maw.

The Way Back wasn't in this house. It was beneath her.

Siena glanced up as this Emmett flashed her a wide-toothed smile. Through the grimy window, she spotted a missing molar.

"I know what The Shadow wants from you," he said.

The shrill ringing crescendoed, though it couldn't mask the thrill bolting through her. She couldn't trust this *thing*, but how did it know the one question she kept asking herself? How could it see inside her?

"I don't believe you," she said. Even with the murky glass

separating them, she loathed the way he smiled at her like he could see her hesitation.

She dropped her chin to the light in the depths, and stomped on one of the rotting boards until it broke and fell. The web of light exploded in ethereal tendrils as the plank burst through it. She listened for it to hit the bottom of the sinkhole. Nothing.

She glanced up, but she'd had her eyes off him for too long. Emmett no longer held the card, but a rock the size of a brick. She shielded her face as he threw it at the window. Glass shattered everywhere. The rock landed next to her, cracking more floorboards.

"Siena." Her name was more animal growl than spoken word, but she caught the waver in his voice. He was afraid—maybe of the hole beneath her.

"I know what The Shadow wants from you, and I know you don't want to leave." The doppelgänger swatted away broken glass, hopped over the windowsill, and landed with a splintering of wood. "I won't let you kill yourself."

"You know what's beneath us," she whispered.

"And I know what you're about to do." He slid right against the wall, planning on circling all the way around the room to reach her. He was broader and bigger than the Emmett she knew. Her Emmett. There would be no escaping him once he caught her.

"Why should I believe you?" Her eyes darted to another plank less than a meter away, farther from Emmett and about as rotten as the one she stood on now. If she jumped, her weight could break it, and then she'd fall through the beetles that shifted reality.

The Way Back.

*Unproven.*

There was no proving this. Nothing but intuition.

"You feel like you belong here," Emmett said. "Somewhere deep down, you're fighting against the idea of going home."

She stalled, searching for a counterargument. Anything to convincingly refute him. She couldn't. He was right. He was so right that she felt the edges of her will collapse. She wanted to believe this murderous fiend because she hungered for the real reason why she had to endure this torturous escape from the Briardark.

She wanted to believe he knew what The Shadow really wanted from her.

But this Emmett had killed Ren. And if he really knew her—if he really wanted to coax her from the outpost—he wouldn't have committed such an atrocity against the one person who'd kept her alive.

"You're lying," she said.

Siena jumped the moment his face fell. As her weight hit the plank, it snapped. She thought of her mother, the way her papery skin had felt as Siena gripped her hand for dear life on amusement park rides.

This wasn't like that at all.

At first there was resistance, like a cord wrapped around her feet, dragging her through an atmosphere thicker than water. She burst through what remained of the web of light.

Then, the pressure bore down, and with it she felt guilt. Grief. And the end of everything she'd ever wanted.

She couldn't scream, couldn't breathe, couldn't move. Felt nothing against her, not even her clothing, until her mother's papery hand slipped into her own and Siena's sob remained trapped in her chest. Days. Weeks. Months. Until her body hit the ground.

# SIENA

She perceived someone hovering over her before the catastrophic agony. It knocked the breath from her lungs as she lay upon the hard ground, broken and dying.

Memories trickled back into her head like sludge down a creek bed. She'd fallen and crashed into the next circle of hell. Her lungs denied her new reality, and continued to expand and deflate, ushering oxygen into her bloodstream. The air was different—dry. Her lips parted, and she tasted ash and mineral.

Above her, a pretty woman with tawny skin and big eyes looked as frightened as she felt. Then suddenly—almost violently —the woman threw her head back and laughed.

"Dr. Dupont," she said. "You're here."

Her face crumpled like Siena was more beautiful than God, then she wept tears as big as her eyes. How . . . *strange.*

Dr. Dupont. That was her name, right? When was the last time she'd been called that?

Her lungs expanded again, and Siena smelled iron, calcium, and magnesium silicate. She'd grown up near this dirt, studied this dirt, spent her whole life breathing this dirt.

She smelled the Sierras.

She wanted to relay this to the woman above her, but the only thing that left her mouth was a guttural groan that shook the pieces of her skull.

"Holden!" the woman screamed. "*Holden!*"

Siena's ears rang. The *ringing*. She squeezed her eyes shut. Tears trickled over her temples. The pain. That was all it was. Nothing else other than a hollowness inside, her rib cage a dusty, aching cavity.

"She's here," said the woman. "She's fucking *here*."

Footsteps. Someone else getting closer. "Is . . . is she alright?"

Siena's eyes fluttered open. Her heart thrummed hotly in her throat.

That voice.

He knelt next to her. She lingered on his dark eyes and the slope of his jaw. His kind face. A *young* face, with smooth olive skin free of scars and trauma. Another doppelgänger, but he stared at her with so much vulnerability and shock, reaching out to touch her arm as if to remind her he wasn't here to hurt her.

He'd come all this way to make sure she got home.

Ren.

rOVE7r2p$6

# BROODMOTHER

Briardark Book Three
Coming Soon

S.A. Harian grew up near Yosemite and now lives in Portland, Oregon with her partner and dog. She's been writing for most of her life and spends her free time hiking, cooking, and playing video games. The Briardark series is her passion project and a culmination of her curiosities and fears.

Read the special author's note and join the Discord at briardark.com

9 781959 500056